Praise for
A More Perfect Union

"Amidst hunger, deprivation and the whimsical cruelties of slavery, two people dare to steal happiness. This graceful, assured debut novel creates an unusual slave narrative that starts in potato-famine Ireland and deftly weaves a touching American love story. The deceptively easy prose bristles with danger and possibility and I loved the at once thrilling and gentle pace of the novel. Tammye Huf is a wonderful storyteller."   —Marina Salandy-Brown

"A riveting love story across the challenges of race and poverty...Huf's delicate blend of passion and compassion is compelling, impressive and never sentimental."

—Andrea Stuart

"A gripping and moving tale of romance. Tammye Huf shows meticulous care for details of setting and nuances of character and motive that make remarkable events deeply plausible."

—Barbara Lalla

"A resonant and topical love story, intricately plotted and compellingly told, and a visceral exploration of what it means to be deprived of one's freedom. The stories of Henry, an Irish immigrant escaping the Great Famine, and Sarah, who is sold into slavery on a southern plantation, poignantly illustrate the dehumanizing experience of being deprived of choice, in small ways as well as large, on a daily basis."

—Umi Sinha

A
MORE
PERFECT
UNION

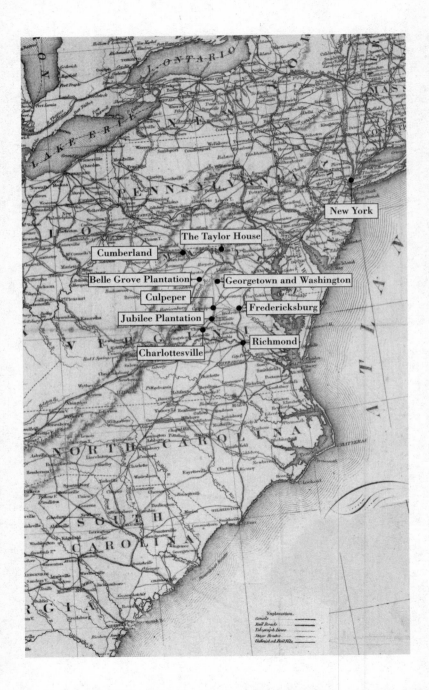

New York

The Taylor House

Cumberland

Belle Grove Plantation

Georgetown and Washington

Culpeper

Fredericksburg

Jubilee Plantation

Charlottesville

Richmond

A MORE PERFECT UNION

TAMMYE HUF

FOREVER

New York Boston

Forever
Hachette Book Group
1290 Avenue of the Americas, New York, NY 10104
read-forever.com
twitter.com/readforeverpub

Originally published in 2020 by Myriad Editions in Oxford, England
First U.S. Trade Paperback Edition: January 2022

Forever is an imprint of Grand Central Publishing. The Forever name and logo are trademarks of Hachette Book Group, Inc.

The publisher is not responsible for websites (or their content) that are not owned by the publisher.

Library of Congress Cataloging-in-Publication Data
Names: Huf, Tammye, author.
Title: A more perfect union / Tammye Huf.
Description: First U.S. Trade Paperback Edition. | New York : Forever, 2022.
Identifiers: LCCN 2021032994 | ISBN 9781538720851 (trade paperback) |
    ISBN 9781538720844 (ebook)
Subjects: LCSH: Virginia—History—19th century—Fiction. | LCGFT:
    Novels. | Historical fiction.
Classification: LCC PS3608.U34965 M67 2022 | DDC 813/.6—dc23
LC record available at https://lccn.loc.gov/2021032994

ISBN: 978-1-5387-2085-1 (trade paperback), 978-1-5387-2084-4 (ebook)

Printed in the United States of America

LSC-C

Printing 1, 2021

For my family

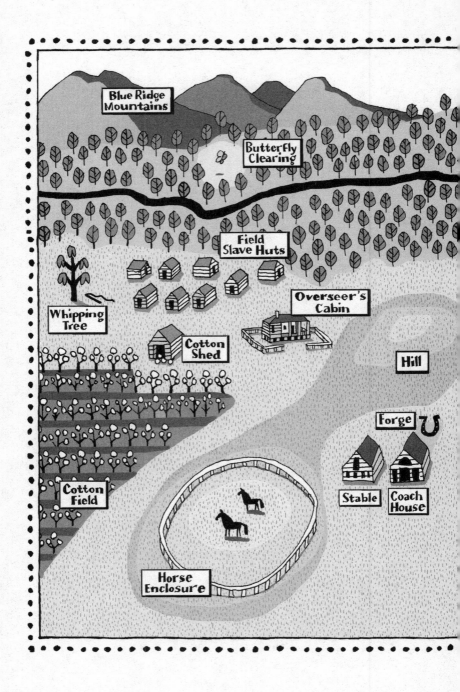

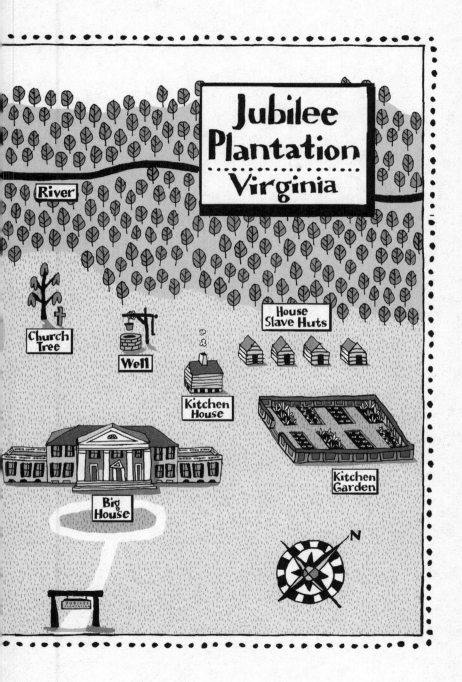

July 1848

Chapter 1

Henry

Two dead men walking up the road. That's what we look like, Da and me trudging out to the work gang in rags and tatters. Da hitches his threadbare trousers up. With nothing left to cling to, they've taken to sliding down every few steps. The string I use to tie mine still holds.

The deep pit we pass is one of ours. We dig ditches one week that we fill in the next, or build roads to nowhere, earning just enough to keep us alive. The English answer to the Irish starving.

Da and me walk three miles over dirt roads running through green hills, but when we get to the relief works station there's a grumbling crowd of surly men.

The relief works man, over from England, holds out his hands for quiet, but no one settles down, so he shouts over the noise, "In light of the fact that your harvest will be ready in a matter of weeks, the decision has been taken to suspend the relief works program. You should all go home and wait for the harvest."

"Those bastards don't know what they're doing," Da says.

"You can't cut off the work gangs before the harvest comes in," a man behind me says. "People've still got to eat."

I grunt in agreement.

"That's the English for you," Paddy Murphy says, from beside Da. "They're sending us home to watch plants grow."

The grumbles turn into shouts as the landlord's bailiff comes riding up.

He trots his horse right into the middle of the group and the men quiet down. "I need five men for a job."

He's barely got the words out before I say, "I'll do it."

It takes less than five seconds for him to get workers together. From the fifty men clamoring to do whatever it is he needs done, he picks Paddy, Killian, Liam, Seamus and me.

Da tugs at my arm. "Let me go for you, Henry. You don't know what he wants you to do." A heavy tiredness pulls at him, bending his back and pitching his body to the right where he struggles to hold his shovel. Five years ago, when he broke his arm, I watched him split kindling one-handed with a single swing.

"No, Da," I tell him. "You go on home."

"Aye," says Paddy beside us. "You'll want to make a start with your waiting for the harvest."

The five of us follow the bailiff to the Doyles' place, and I get a prickling in my gut. John Doyle died in the spring leaving Mary to struggle alone with her four little ones.

From a burlap sack tied to the back of his saddle, the bailiff takes out poles and clubs and hands them to us.

"You can't mean for us to be tumbling Mary's home," I say.

"She's not paid her rent," he says. "She's been warned."

"Don't the landlords have enough?" Paddy says. "They have to go after widows and orphans now too?" He throws his club in the dirt, his flaming red hair matching his fiery temperament.

"They're not orphans, they have their mother," the bailiff says. "Now, either you tumble it, or I'll get five others."

Tumbling is what the landlords do to us when we can't pay the rent. Our houses are knocked together into a tumbled heap, stone on stone, so that the tenants can't sneak back in again once they're out. It's happening more and more, so that now there're hundreds of tumbled homes sprinkled around the countryside.

All five of us are shuffling our feet and feeling wrong about it. But if we don't do it, it won't save her. He'll have another eviction gang here in the time it takes to ride out and come back again. This hut is coming down today, no mistake. We might as well get the money for it.

"Are they still in there?" I ask.

"Of course they're in there, Henry. Where else are they going to be?" says Paddy. He turns to the bailiff. "The Devil take you," he says, but he picks up his club. "We'll not knock it down on their heads."

"So, get them out," the bailiff says.

None of us moves to do it.

He scowls down at the five of us from on top of his horse's back. "The troublemaker can do it," he says.

"Me?" Paddy blusters, gesticulating with his arms. "What do I tell her then? That even though she's a poor, starving widow with four children to look after, her landlord isn't rich enough yet and he needs to boot her out of her little hut here so he can sleep at night? Is that what you want me to go in there and say?" Paddy throws his club back into the dirt.

The bailiff runs his hand over his face. We can all see he's regretting having chosen Paddy to come along. "The black-haired troublemaker can do it. And if you don't stop throwing your club about, you're off this gang and they'll do the job without you."

Killian, Liam and Seamus all have black hair too, but I'm the only other one who spoke out, which would make me the black-haired troublemaker.

"Off you go then, Henry," Paddy says to me. "You'll think of something to say."

Mary's hut is rocks and dirt walls. There're no windows and I have to duck to get through the door. Inside it's dark and damp and there's a lingering scent of piss and shit from poor John who couldn't get up in the end to relieve himself. I guess there's only so much you can scrub out of a dirt floor.

Huddled in a pile of rags on the ground, Mary sits with her four children. The hunger's hit her bad. Her arms are bone-thin and her skin hangs about her face with no padding to fill it out.

"There's an eviction gang here, Mary."

She doesn't move or even look at me. She just stares at the wall of her hut.

"You have to go now."

She doesn't seem to recognize me or hear what I'm saying.

"The bailiff's here and everything."

She blinks a few times and lays her hand on her wee one's head. "No," she says to the wall.

"I'm sorry," I say. "But you haven't paid your rent. They won't let you stay."

She sighs and settles further into the cluster of rags that serves as their bed. "No."

The bailiff yells into the squat doorway, "Get them out, or we'll tumble it on their heads."

I hold out my hand to her. "Come on, Mary. You don't want your children getting hurt."

"What difference does it make if we die in here today, or out there in two weeks?" she says. "You know we won't survive with John gone and no place to live."

"We look after each other here," I say. "You know that. You'll be all right."

I'm lying to a widow so I can tumble her home. This is what Da wanted to spare me. There was a time when we used to help each other. Now we just survive.

"You can stay with us," I say, surprising myself.

We don't have room for them, or food for them, and ever since Dermot and Emily died Ma's been in a bad way. I've no idea how she'll react when I show up with these five. I hold out my hand to her again, and she takes it.

We all come out and I breathe in deeply, clearing my nose of the stench of her hut. The air has a pre-harvest crispness to it that tastes cool and sweet against my tongue.

The bailiff's off his horse, standing back to one side of the hut, and Mary and her children stand a ways off to the other side and watch us hack at her home. We wedge poles in the crevices between the stones, shifting and pushing until the walls crumble and the roof falls in.

Then the five of us pocket our wages. When the paying's done, I wave Mary and her children over to me.

"Let's go then," I say.

"What are you doing with them?" the bailiff asks.

"I'm taking them home with me." My stomach gives a little flip worrying about Ma.

"You can't do that," he says. "They've been evicted."

Liam, Seamus and Killian slip away, but Paddy steps up to the bailiff waving his freckled arms. "Well, it's nought to do with you, is it?" he says. "You've already knocked their home to bits. Your work here is done."

"The law says you can't take them in," the bailiff says. "If you do, you'll get evicted too. They have to get clear off Lord Edwards's land."

"All of it?" exclaims Paddy. "That greedy English bastard owns the whole damn hill. And the next."

"It's the law."

"English law."

"You watch your mouth there, laddie."

"You watch my arse." Paddy pulls his breeches down and we all get a good look at his scrawny white backside as he dashes away.

I tell Mary and her children to come on and we trudge off.

"It's not worth it," the bailiff calls after me. "It'll be your place next."

I can't take them home. Instead, I take them to Father Michael. I don't know what he'll do with them, but at least they can stay in the church while he thinks it through. Nobody'll tumble a church.

Father Michael used to be round and jolly. Now he's saggy and solemn. He comes out to meet us in the churchyard like he's walking in a funeral procession. I guess the last few years have put him in the habit.

"The bailiff says I can't take them to mine, so I brought them to you," I tell him.

He nods. He knows what I've been a part of, but I don't think he judges me for it. He just looks sad and broken. "I'll try to find a place for them at the poor house," he says.

Mary looks stricken. "They'll take my children."

The poor house separates the men and the women and the children. I'm ashamed to look at her. For the thousandth time, I curse the English landlords for taking our healthy crops, our barley, wheat and rye, and shipping them away to sell. Lining their pockets while we starve. And I curse the rot that's come like a plague out of the Old Testament to blacken our potatoes and famine us. I stop just short of cursing God for letting it happen.

Father Michael says our blessings are coming, and that it's easier for a camel to get through a needle than for a rich man to get to Heaven. But no matter how much Bible he throws at us, I want to be rich. I want a warm house with glass in the windows, and a door with a knocker on it. And I want to eat my fill every day and never again feel this gnawing in my belly. People say it's the disease and the hunger that's killing us, but I say it's the being poor.

Father Michael leads Mary and her children into the church.

"I'm sorry," I say to her retreating back.

When I walk home through the valley where whirling fog clings to the land, I pass eight more tumbled homes scattered among the grasses and the heather. I knew every single tenant. If this keeps up, none of us will be left.

Coming up the path to our hut, I pass our potato patch, mercifully full of green stalks and leaves. Beth's perched on the gray rock wall waiting for me.

"What's for supper?" I ask.

"Roast lamb," she says with a smile.

It's a game we play. The Indian corn they shipped in for us to buy with our work-gang wages is bland and hard as rocks, no matter how long you boil it. Beth and I pretend we're eating lamb or beef or some other impossible food. We tell each other our stomachs ache from overstuffing. It's childish, for sure, but somehow it helps.

We eat our gruel around the rough plank table Da made years ago. Then we push the table aside and Ma, Da, me, Maggie and Beth all stretch out on the dirt floor waiting for sleep and morning.

We smell it when we wake. The stench of rot has climbed up out of the ground overnight and shoved its unwelcome way into our hut. Da looks at me. There's a panic in his eyes that shoots right through me. We hurry outside, already knowing. The smell in the air is worse as we rush, panting, to the rim of our plot, sucking in stinking lungfuls.

Every leaf that was lush and green yesterday is spotted brown. Every stalk, wilting and blackening.

I sink to the ground and dig. Scratching at the dark soil, my thumb plunges into a potato, easily breaking through the skin to the sludge inside, so rotten it's liquid. The foul stench catches in my nose, making me gag. I pull my thumb back, wiping it clean in the dirt. Da is gray as the fog. The pain clenching my gut is more than hunger. It's fear for the days and months to come. It's knowing we have to leave, or we'll all be starved dead by winter's end.

October 1848

Chapter 2

Sarah

Most of the afternoon, the slaver's got us in the yard for showing. Singing, dancing, playing cards. Mister Maddox is as sly as they come. He's got the white folks thinking we're the cheerfullest bunch of slaves money can buy. Even shaved a man bald to hide his gray hair and sell him for younger.

When it's time for the auction, he chains us up again and shuts us in a room behind the Planter's Hotel, pulling us out one by one. The woman with the missing tooth. The tall man with the wide chest. The man with the notch in his ear. The man that tried to run. The woman with the long neck. Isaac.

The chain round my ankles digs at where my copper skin's been rubbed clean away, but that ain't nothing to the fear snaking in the pit of my belly. When the slaver tells me to get up, I don't want to move, but I do. I seen him do things on the march from Charlottesville to Fredericksburg, chained to the man in front of me and the woman behind, so I jump up soon as he calls my name. A jet-black boy won't look me in the face as he unhooks me from an iron ring in the floor. I take small shuffling steps 'cause of the ankle shackles, but I take them quick 'cause I see the look the slaver's giving me.

Mister Maddox is a lizard of a man, all waxy skin and beady eyes. The few greasy hairs he's got growing out the top of his head look like pig whiskers. I flinch when he reaches for me. He unfastens my chains and the shackles slip from my wrists and my bleeding ankles.

He sets me beside the hotel wall, and I grab on to the wood siding. The white paint flakes off as I worry the slats with my fingers. It's almost my turn on the block. The sticky heat of summer's eased off and it'll be a spell before the biting cold of winter comes. There's not one speck of white in the whole blue sky. From behind yellow-green leaves I can hear a dove coo.

I shut my eyes and breathe out long and slow.

Above the noise of the crowd, the voice of the auctioneer calls out. "I have seven hundred. Do I hear seven-fifty for this fine specimen? Strong as an ox and docile as a lamb."

It's Isaac he's talking about, up there on the block. My brother. The auctioneer tells him to take off his shirt and show the people his muscles. I hate the auction man. I hate Mister Maddox. I hate them all. The bidding gets up to nine hundred dollars.

I don't notice how I'm humming till Mister Maddox says, "Sing something cheerful or shut the hell up."

It's a Jesus-help-me church song I'm humming that Momma sometimes sings. I sink down to the ground, pull my legs up to my chest and lay my head on my knees. Momma. She's got to be crawling out of her skin with worrying about us. Before this happened, she'd have sworn up and down that Master'd never sell us. Guess you never know.

The auctioneer shouts out, "Sold!" and I look up.

Mister Maddox's got hold of Isaac by the arm. He pulls him down from the auction block and hands him over to a red-faced fat man with three chins. Isaac hangs his head as the fat man slips a rope round his neck.

"Isaac," I call out. His eyes snap over to me. I touch the wooden carving I wear on a string round my neck and Isaac nods at me. He says my name and something else I can't make out.

"Come on, boy. Don't dawdle. I didn't buy you to dawdle." The fat man tugs on the rope and Isaac stumbles after, led away like an old cow.

My whole chest squeezes in tight. I want to scream out, but I know better than that. The tears creep down my cheeks and I rock back and forth, my arms hugging at my knees. Mister Maddox reaches down and jerks me to my feet.

"Wipe your face and perk up, girl. I won't have you driving down your price looking like that."

My stomach knots and my hands tremble, but I do like he says. The tears come back again.

"Look here," he says, quiet in my ear. "If you want to stay a house slave, you better cut out all that crying. No one wants to hear you blubbering all day long."

I nod and he waits for me to stop, but I can't.

Nostrils flaring, he says, "You're going to cost me money, girl. I'll be damned if I let you get yourself sold as a field slave."

I cringe from him, but I also wipe my face and stretch my mouth to a smile, trying to look like I won't be no trouble to nobody. I don't know what he paid for me, but I know Master George wouldn't let me go for no field slave price. And I know field slave work would break me in two.

I can tell my smile don't sit right 'cause Mister Maddox looks me up and down, scratching his chin-stubble and frowning. He pulls at my clothes and pushes at my breasts till he's got me just about popping out of the top of my dress. I want to slap his hands away. Instead, I blink back my tears before they spill out and he sees them. He looks me over again and nods, and then he pulls me to the block and orders me up.

The auction block is as high as a table with just one step for climbing up. I grip the rough edges with both hands to keep me steady as I struggle on.

Beside me, the auctioneer points with his cane, calling me a prime house girl. He makes me turn in a circle while he boasts about how quick I clean, and how I never been a day sick, which is a bold-faced lie. He don't say a thing about knowing the healing herbs. Guess white folks don't care about that. Guess quick-cleaning-slave-who-don't-get-sick is about all they need to hear.

Then they start in with the money.

There's near on twenty men crowded round, but only four of them that's bidding. Right in front of me stands a raggedy man with caterpillar eyebrows who looks like the liquor got hold of him. He's staring at what Mister Maddox done to my breasts. He don't put his eyes nowhere but there, and I'm some kind of glad he ain't bidding. It gets up to seven hundred and they start to slowing down. Then the raggedy man says seven hundred and ten and my heart takes a panic jump right up to my throat. I start praying, not him, Lord, not him. Someone else bids and it all starts up again, but this time that man is hollering out prices with the rest of them. Ain't no secret what he's after me for.

A dark-haired woman in a fancy blue dress comes out of a dry goods store across the street and walks right on over to the crowd of men. She links arms with a man in a brown suit who's bidding off to the right of the auction block I'm perched on.

"A man like that shouldn't be allowed to keep slaves," she mutters when the raggedy man outbids him again. "It's shameful." She wrinkles up her high forehead and stares at me with small, close eyes.

The auction's up to seven hundred and ninety.

"I have seven-ninety. Do I hear eight hundred?" The auctioneer looks round the crowd of men, but not a one speaks up. "Going once to the man in the red vest."

I look over, and it's the raggedy man he means. My whole body goes to ice. I've seen his kind. No-account men who can barely afford to feed their slaves, working them half to death in the day and never letting them alone in the night.

"Going twice," the auctioneer shouts. "Last chance, gentlemen."

Some of the men shake their heads. The auctioneer takes off his hat and fans himself with it.

I clasp my hands and get to praying something fierce, just begging God not to let that man take me.

"Sold."

I can't hardly breathe.

Mister Maddox pulls me down and I trip over my own feet, smashing my knees and elbows on the ground. Behind me, the men laugh. I bite the inside of my mouth to keep from howling and pick myself up. As Mister Maddox leads me off to the side, I tremble so hard I have to fist my hands in my skirts.

The raggedy man comes up to take me, but Mister Maddox keeps hold of my arm.

"She's yours when you've paid for her."

My new master looks me over and licks his lips. He will own my days and my nights, and every drop of blood and every bead of sweat. The eagerness I see in him to explore what all that could mean for the two of us terrifies me.

An official man with a money pouch steps up to take the payment.

"I got six hundred and fifty with me now," my new master says to the money pouch man. "I'll get you the rest next week."

"Hell and tarnation, Jeb, you know that's not how this works," the man says. "This is the third time you've bid for a slave you can't afford to buy."

Jeb looks at my breasts and sets his jaw. "I can afford her," he says. "You let me take her back home tonight and I'll have the money to you tomorrow."

The official man spits on the ground between them. "I'm not fool enough to let you take a slave you haven't paid for." Tucking the money pouch into his vest, he steps back through the auction crowd to the brown-suit man, whose arm's still linked with the blue-dress woman. They talk a spell and then he leads them to where Mister Maddox has me by the arm.

"This gentleman had the last bid at seven hundred and eighty," the official tells the slaver. "Since Jeb can't pay, that's the price you get."

Mister Maddox nods, throwing evil looks at Jeb.

The woman lowers her eyebrows, making her forehead even higher and her eyes even smaller. "You should be ashamed of yourself," she says.

Jeb's red face turns redder. He hunches his shoulders and strikes off for the tavern.

The woman's husband counts out seven hundred and eighty dollars, and I am his.

Chapter 3

Henry

My first look at America stabs me with homesickness. There're no craggy cliffs, no green hills. New York is a gray, dirty city, crowded and noisy. But it's full of busy industry. Of loading and unloading ships. Of flush-faced and well-fed people.

The captain of the ship is the first down the gangplank. His shoes make a hollow echo as he walks, like knocking on a door. We're a sorry-looking lot, filthy and flea-bitten, spilling into the city like rats out of a hole.

When I step onto the street, the ground feels wrong after six weeks at sea. My legs want to fold up under me like a new foal's. I don't trust them to move, so I stand there on the dock with the crowd jostling around me, blinking in the light. I fill my lungs with air that reeks of dead fish, but it's a damn sight better than the stale rot I've been breathing for over a month down in the hold.

New York is the busiest place I've ever seen, but, even with all these people around me, I feel alone for the first time in my life. When the harvest failed, Ma lay down and never got up again, which took the fight right out of Da. They were both gone within days of each other. Maggie, Beth and me were left to keep starving or get out while we were still breathing. We took our chance on a coffin ship, which lived up to its name in the weeks we spent cramped and miserable in the airless hold. The typhus took Maggie a week after we set sail from County Cork, and Beth passed only days ago from God knows what. Take your pick. The shitting sickness, the coughing sickness, or the killing fever. A good third of the passengers wasted away during the crossing. Maggie and Beth were tossed overboard like the rest, with not even a priest to bless them.

I thrust my hand in my pocket and wrap my fingers around a small rock I keep there. The piece of home I took with me the day we set sail. I rub the rock, flicking it between my fingers as I follow the heaving mass of immigrants up South Street.

The herd is headed to the Five Points, the Irish quarters, as they called it on the ship. We pass grand homes and squat shops and horse-drawn carriages near about as big as our hut back home, but what I notice most as we walk are the signs. *Irish Need Not Apply.* They hang next to every posting for a job.

After a while, the cobbled road gives way to dirt, and the dirt to mud. With every step the mud gets thicker until the sludge squelches over my bare feet. It's up to my ankles by the time we reach a five-way crossing. The Five Points. There's a tavern and a butcher and a brothel, it looks like. This place smells of unwashed bodies and of waste and decay. There're Irishmen here all right. Huddled in doorways and standing in the streets. But not just Irishmen. A man as dark as coal sits on a stoop, his bright white eyes track us as we walk. Another man stands behind him, the color of peat. I can't help but stare.

Someone puts his hand on my arm and calls my name. I'm wound so tight I spin round with my fist back ready for whoever it is. But I hesitate, as my brain catches up with my body, realizing he knows my name. Then I see who's got my arm. Ennis Flanagan. He left Cork a year before I did with his wife and their two little ones.

He hugs me like we're brothers. "Henry O'Toole. Jesus, Mary and Holy Saint Joseph, it's Henry bloody O'Toole."

I hug him back, happier than I can say to see a familiar face. "Ennis Flanagan."

"Wait till the Missus sees you. And you won't recognize the boys. Growing like weeds and tough as teeth."

"All of you made it, then?" I ask. "All four?"

"Aye. Luck of the Irish, we had. And Saint Christopher protecting us besides."

I mean to hide my bitter jealousy, but he notices my silence and possibly the clenching in my jaw. He understands what I'm not saying and claps me on my back.

"Where're you staying?" he asks.

I shrug. "Nowhere yet."

He pulls me around and leads me toward a shabby alley. "You can come back with us then."

"Have you got room for a fifth?"

"Fifth? We're ten to a room, you daft bastard. You'll be lucky eleven."

Ennis works at a window factory. He got the job when an accident killed two men and injured ten more. The Swedes and Poles and Germans threw up a fuss, so they let the Irish and the Negros in, paying half of what the other men got. But it's a job.

I can't find any work at all.

After the first week, the Dead Rabbits approach me offering a spot on their fire brigade. "What you do," they tell me, "is you set the fire yourself, see. So, when you're the first gang on the scene putting it out, you get the fire brigade money."

I tell them setting fires to put them out is even more daft than digging ditches to fill them in again. And anyways, what kind of man makes his living by burning people's houses down?

By the second week, I see how things are with the gangs here, and I realize it might have been a mistake to turn the Dead Rabbits down. I avoid them as best I can, because, although I don't think they see me as an enemy, it's clear I'm not a friend. And I still can't get a job. Folks hiring take one look at me and know I'm Irish. I don't stand a chance. It's not my black hair or blue eyes that give me away. It's the hungry, half-starved look of me, and the rags I wear and no shoes on my feet. It's only the Irish fresh off the ships who walk around like that.

By my third week, I'm sick to death of having doors slammed in my face. And when a rival gang, the Plug Uglies, recruits two of the men sleeping in our eleven-person room, the Dead Rabbits decide I've offended them by association. When I go to look for work, I get hostile stares from men holding clubs and flashing butcher knives. I take to sneaking out before sunrise and slipping back in cloaked by the dark, avoiding all the gangs, which is pretty hard to do in the Five Points.

Every day it's the same. No Irish.

I get up early, picking my way through the bodies still sleeping, and I traipse through New York determined that this will be the day that I find something. When I come up empty again, I've no stomach for going back. I walk downtown and sit at the harbor feeling in my pocket for my Ireland stone.

I stay there hunched on a barrel, sitting right through the evening and into the night. When I get up to go it's a ways past midnight.

I've only walked a few blocks when I hear a scuffle in an ally. I peek in to see two ruffians beating and kicking a man on the ground.

"Stop, you!" I call out.

One of the two digs in the man's pockets and they take off running. The gentleman on the ground is in a bad way. They took a boot to his face and who knows where else. When he breathes, I hear liquid in his lungs and when he tries to talk there's blood. I can't be here. There's no helping him. If I stay, I could be blamed.

I stand to go, but I hold off from leaving. I think how easy a man could find a job with that white cotton shirt and those leather shoes.

Before I know what I'm doing, I take off his shoes and I go for his trousers. He stops breathing while I'm pulling at his jacket. When I have it all, I bundle the clothes in my arms and run.

Huddled by the Hudson River, I scrub the blood from his shirt with river water and change into his clothes. I kick my old things into the water, watching as they float and then sink.

At first light, I walk up and down the city looking for anyone hiring. There's a blacksmith with a sign warning: *No Irish Need Apply*. I march right into the shop and, flattening my vowels in the American way, I ask for the job.

He looks me up and down and asks my name.

I say a silent apology to every O'Toole who came before me and hope they understand.

"Henry Taylor," I tell him without a flinch.

"You have any blacksmithing experience?"

"Some," I lie.

He tells me to put on an apron and stoke the fire, and by God I do.

Later that night, lying in my new quarters above the shop, my hand goes for the rock in my right pocket, but it's not there. Then I remember. I left it in my old trousers. My piece of home is lost somewhere in the Hudson River.

Chapter 4

Sarah

Sitting on the back lip of the carriage, my chest squeezes tight. I never did have much, but I always had Momma and Isaac beside me. I watch the ground move under my dangling feet. The road stretches out as we keep clip-clopping on, taking me farther and farther from everything I know. The knot in my belly's so big, it's like I swallowed a stone. I pray for Momma back at Summerville and for Isaac wherever he's headed. I finger the carved wood hanging at my neck that my brother made me and think how, from here on out, I'm on my own.

A burly, mahogany man sits hunched up next to me. Every time the carriage jolts, our chains jingle. The noise has got my nerves on edge, and I'm as jumpy as an alley cat. But the mahogany man, he sits rock still, breathing hard and blinking back tears. Mine slide down my dusty face.

Up in the carriage, I hear our new master and missus talking and laughing. Sitting to the front, a clay-red slave drives the horses trotting us on.

When the sun's tucked down low on the horizon and the shadows stretch out long, we turn in under a wooden gateway and ride up a wide drive. I sit calm as I can, but inside I feel like a hive of bees, 'cause I know whatever's coming is just about here.

The driver stops the horses in front of a white house, smaller than the Big House at the Summerville Plantation, but more cared for. Even the porch steps've got fresh paint. Up front, the driver hops out of his seat and lowers the carriage steps. Our new master climbs down and holds out a hand to steady his wife.

"Red, go get the overseer," he says to the driver. He pulls his wife's hand through his elbow and leads her up the steps to the wide front porch, past the thick columns propping up the portico, and then on into the house.

When the overseer comes, pink-faced and puffing from the walk, he takes off our chains and tells us to get down from the back of the buggy. We rub our wrists while he looks us over, inspecting us.

The driver, Red, tips me a sympathetic nod before he leads off the horses and carriage.

"You pick cotton before?" the overseer asks the man beside me.

"Yes, sir."

He nods, like he was expecting that. "Good."

I look down at my feet as he turns to me. I never picked a day in my life and I don't care to start now. The master paid a house slave price for me and I hope he don't like to be wasting his money, but I don't know how things work here and I ain't fixing to find out the wrong way.

The overseer looks back at the field slave beside me. "Now, if you work hard and get them fields picked, you'll be fine. You hear?" He lays his hand over the whip coiled at his right hip. "But if you go breaking the rules and acting up, you'll get to know me." He takes up his whip and tap, tap, taps at the man's chest. "And I'll tell you right now, boy, you do not want to get to know me."

"No, sir."

The overseer nods and puts his whip back on his hip. "Now, you can call me sir, or you can call me Master Mulch. You hear me?"

"Yes, sir, Master Mulch."

"That's fine, boy, that's just fine." He takes a step back and looks him up and down. "What name did they give you?"

"I's called Jim, Master Mulch, sir."

The overseer tips his chin up and shouts out, "Red!" When the coach driver comes jogging on back, he tells him, "Show Jim where he'll sleep and eat, and make sure he finds his way to the fields on time in the morning."

"Yes, sir," Red says, but he hesitates, looking between me and Master Mulch. "You want me to go get Maple for this one?" he asks.

The overseer slits his eyes at him. "I want you to go do like I said."

Red looks back at me and then up at the house.

"Go on, now, get," Master Mulch barks, and Red leads Jim away.

Master Mulch runs his eyes over me from head to toe and every part in between till my skin starts to crawling. "Well," he says, at last. "You don't have the look of a field slave." He takes my hands and rubs his thumbs all over my palms.

I know I can't pull them away, so I look up to the house instead.

"Don't have the hands neither," he says. He grips my arms and starts feeling at them like he's feeling on a horse for the muscle. He squeezes on my shoulders and down my back, but he pulls away when the master comes out with a stout woman behind him.

She has the same high forehead and close-set, small eyes as the missus. Her dark hair's pulled into the same tight bun, but her lips are fuller, and they pinch when she looks at me.

"Ah, Ralph. There you are," my new master says, peering down at us. "I take it you've already sent the new field hand down."

"Yes, sir, Mister Johnson. You want this one for the cotton?"

"No, no. She's not right for picking. Anyone can see she's for the house."

"Well, then." Master Mulch taps twice on my backside, and pushes me toward the steps. "You best get on in there."

I scoot away from him up the front porch, as fast as I can get.

"Maple, see what you can do with Sarah here," Master says to the woman behind him. "My dear wife wants her for Thomas, but I'm sure you can get more use out of her than that."

Master strolls down the steps whistling while Maple motions me over with a flick of her finger and leads me inside. The entrance is long and wide with paintings hung all along the walls. When I follow her to the stairway, one of the dark wood floorboards squeaks under my foot. The woman glares back at me.

"Sorry, ma'am," I say, and I hop quick off the noisy board.

She pinches her lips and raises her eyebrows. I can see the nastiness and the hardness in her and I hope she ain't fixing to aim it at me.

"Miss Martha wants you sleeping on the floor in Master Thomas's room," she says. "He's been waking up the whole house with his night frights and it's going to be your job to keep him quiet. In the morning you come on down and find me in the kitchen house, and I'll get you to work helping with breakfast and give you your chores for the day."

I blink at her, piecing together the meaning behind her words. She said Miss Martha and Master Thomas, not your missus and your young master. She said in the morning I'll find her in the kitchen house making breakfast. Here I am thinking she's a cousin or a spinster aunt, but she's a slave.

I swallow the "yes, ma'am" sitting ready on my tongue, and instead ask, "What's wrong with Master Thomas?"

"Thrown from a horse," she says. "Don't know why anyone would put a six-year-old boy on a horse in the first place, but they did, and now he screams the house down almost every night thinking about it."

"What's Miss Martha want me to do with him?"

"Get him back to sleep. And you'll be calling her Missus. It's Master and Missus here. I call her Miss Martha because I've been calling her that since she was little."

I look again at her high forehead and small, close-set eyes. "She grew up with you?"

She nods. "I was twelve when she was born. I been taking care of her all her life. Couldn't do without me when she got married, so her daddy gave me as a wedding gift." She spits out the word "daddy" in a puff of bitterness and I know why she looks like the missus. And I know why she looks so angry. Their daddy gave his older daughter to his white daughter as her slave.

Maple must have come from a long line of slave mothers and slave-owner fathers to wind up so light she could pass for white. Looking like she does, it would be so much easier to run. I wonder if she's tried.

"I guess they don't got the railroad up here," I say, trying to ask without asking. It's not enough to know about the underground railroad helping runaway slaves, you've got to find them too.

Maple squints at me with her daddy's eyes and purses her momma's lips tight. "You best get that thought right out of your head before someone comes along and beats it out. Everything you do gets paid for one way or the other. If you ain't the one paying, you can sure bet someone else is."

November 1848

Chapter 5

Sarah

In the weeks that pass, I learn I was right about Maple. She's a hard and bitter woman. I reckon it's a sour thing for her to be "yes ma'am-ing" and "no ma'am-ing" her half-sister all day long, and I hear she left a daughter back at Missus's daddy's plantation, but we all got a story.

I'm the only slave sleeping in the Big House. The other house slaves stay in cabins out back, behind the walled garden by the kitchen house, where they can get a few hours break from being under some master's eye. The field slaves sleep in shacks down by the cotton fields, close to the overseer's cabin. I got to curl up every night on Master Thomas's floor waiting for him to wake me up with his bawling.

But it could be worse. Master's ideas about the Christian way to treat slaves keeps the overseer's whip on his hip, and we get Sundays to ourselves after Master churches us. But I don't want to settle in here. If I get sold on again, I want to slip out easy and not be clinging to nothing I can't stand to lose.

In the first house slave cabin, a blind old woman lives with her gray and feeble husband. She has two sons who work the fields, and four grandchildren. Even without her sight, she walks the plantation sure-footed. Like she's rooted here. Like the belonging goes both ways.

Back when she could see, blind old Bessie cooked for Master, and for his father before him too. Now, she likes to spend her days at the kitchen house, getting up under Maple's feet and on her very last nerve.

"I don't know how you can serve this bland food tasting like nothing," Bessie says, taking a spoonful from Maple's pots.

"Your mouth is as blind as your eyeballs," Maple hisses back. She tells her to leave off messing with her pots and goes stomping out to find Annie and Willa, who she calls "two of the laziest souls God put on this Earth."

When she's gone, blind Bessie shuffles over to the spice shelf. Feeling three jars over, she takes a big pinch of a red powder and drops it into the pot, gives it a good stir and shuffles on out of the kitchen house.

Maple gets Annie and Willa to take the food up for serving. After a month on Jubilee Plantation, she still only has me pouring the drinks. In the dining room, with Master and Missus at opposite ends of the table, and little Master Thomas in the middle, I pour the wine and the water—scurrying from one side to the other, and then back to the sideboard to get the lemonade for Master Thomas.

"This food is spicy as the devil," Master cries out, making me jump and nearly spill the pitcher of lemonade. He drinks down his whole water glass and then takes up the wine.

Little Master Thomas spits his first bite out, thrashing in his seat and howling.

I dash back to the sideboard and take up the cream I set there for the tea. He needs milk to cut the spice.

"Drink this," I tell him, giving it to him right from the pouring cup.

He just sticks his tongue out, wiping at it with his fingers.

"Go get Maple!" Master shouts to Willa and Annie.

I kneel down and put the cream to Master Thomas's mouth. "This will help," I say. "Roll it round your tongue."

Master Thomas does like I say. I can see when it takes hold by the way he stops squirming. I leave him with the pouring cup of cream to sip on and go refill Master's wineglass.

He drains it down and I hurry over to get the water pitcher. As I'm pouring the water, Master Thomas picks up his plate and throws it on to the floor.

"I don't want that," he cries. The plate breaks in two and food splatters the rug.

"No," his father says, pushing his own plate away. "Neither do I."

As I set down the water jug, Maple comes in wringing her hands. "Miss Martha, I don't know what happened," she says. "It weren't like that when I made it."

"Even when Bessie was going blind, she never cooked this badly," Master says. "If you don't know what you're doing we'll get in someone else who does."

"No, Master. This weren't my fault."

"You nearly poisoned my son," Master shouts.

I crouch down to clean the mess on the floor. I could say it was Bessie who added the chili powder, but I don't want to get in the middle of it. And I especially don't want to wind up on Bessie's wrong side, so I hold my tongue and pick up the pieces of broken plate.

"Matthew, sugar," Missus says smoothly, "let's not be dramatic. No laws were broken. I'm sure she meant no harm trying out a new dish. And now she knows never to make anything that spicy again."

On Jubilee Plantation whippings are reserved for slaves who break the law. Man's law or God's law, is how Master talks about it. I don't move in the silence that grips us all waiting to hear what he'll say.

"No laws were broken." He nods at his wife, biting down his temper. Then he turns to Maple with that controlled kind of anger, so cold it's hotter than a prodding iron. "But you're mighty fortunate Sarah was here to help my son."

A tremor goes through Maple and she lowers her eyes.

"Yes," Missus says, relieved. "We are all glad of Sarah's quick thinking. I never would have thought to give the boy cream."

She smiles down at me where I'm crouched on the floor picking up the food Master Thomas threw. By the door, Maple has stilled like a snake before it strikes. When she looks over at me, I can feel the venom in her stare.

Chapter 6

Maple

I pull the brush through Miss Martha's dark hair, careful to hold it tight before I work through the snags. I got Sarah down in the kitchen house washing dishes by herself, and she deserve it too. I don't care if it was Bessie who ruined my cooking like she says, she let me serve it without saying a word and stayed quiet while Master tongue-lashed me into next week, and nearly lashed me for real. She'll be washing dishes by herself for a long time.

"I'm going to want my blue dress washed this week," Miss Martha tells me, looking at herself in the mirror. "And the hem needs mending. Do you think Bessie can still do it?"

I purse my lips and work through a tangle. "Don't know," I say. "She makes a lot of mistakes these days. If you ask me, she uses being blind as an excuse to be spiteful." Can't nobody tell me she thought she was just adding salt tonight. She knows what she did.

"Then give it to Annie to mend, I suppose," Miss Martha says.

She's watching me in the reflecting glass, so I keep my face quiet, but I want to roll my eyes at her and shake my head. Annie's likely to steal half the pearls from the dress and say they fell off in the grass.

"Don't you worry," I say. "I'll give it to Willa. She's better with the needle."

I move round her head dragging the brush down her back. I let the bristles scrape lightly across her scalp the way she likes it. She closes her eyes and her pulled-up-tight posture softens as she leans back into the chair. I give her a few minutes to relax into me fussing with her hair, and, when I speak, I use the bedtime voice that used to ease her right off to sleep when she was little.

"I been thinking," I say, low and gentle.

"Yes." The muscles in her face relax.

"You got Sarah here working at the house now. And you still got Annie and Willa. And Bessie's been trying to get Clover and Samson and Callie May brought up from the fields."

"You know your Master won't let bucks work in the house. Not even Bessie's own boys. Clover and Samson will stay in the fields." She sighs. "And as for Callie May, we don't need her in the house. She's more use in the field."

I bite my lip and gather my words, while I run the brush across her head. "Seems to me," I go on, "if I weren't around, there's enough folks here to keep the house running just fine."

"But you are around." She pins me with her eyes and raises her eyebrows. As well as I know her, she knows me too. "What's on your mind, Maple?"

"I been thinking about my momma, and about my husband, Freddy, and especially about my Rose."

"I'm sure they're all fine," she says. "We would have heard if they weren't."

"I been thinking, now that you're set up here at Jubilee, I could go back home. To your daddy's place."

She settles back in the chair. "I suppose you could visit for a spell."

The sound of the scrape of the brush against her hair fills the room.

I gather my nerves and I say what I need to say, "I was thinking I might live there again."

"Live there?"

"Well, I was thinking of how Master never does like to break up a family, and, well, we're a family. I thought he might let me go back and be with them."

She knocks my hand away from her head and twists herself around to see me straight on instead of through the reflecting glass. "He won't separate a family if it can be helped, but he's not fool enough to give away his slaves, willy nilly, to whatever plantation they might have family on." She turns herself back around and speaks to my reflection. "And anyway, I'm surprised at you, Maple. I would have thought you preferred being under my husband's eye than under my father's whip."

She closes her eyes, so I'll start up with her hair again.

I brush slowly and try a different way. "Seems like you settled in here real good. Master Thomas is already six years old, and doing just fine with Sarah looking out for him. That's the same age my Rose was when I left her to come out here with you, going on seven years ago." She don't even open her eyes to that, stubborn as she is. "Sure would be nice to be back with my girl."

Miss Martha sighs like I'm some child she got to explain why cake and pie ain't fit for supper. "Maple, my father would not buy you back. He has enough slaves without you, and he wouldn't spend the money on a slave he doesn't need. And besides," she reaches up to take my hand clutching the brush and holds it in both of hers. "I cannot manage here without you. You are indispensable to me. You always have been." She gives my hand a squeeze and a pat and releases it.

I pull the brush through her hair and down her back. Again, and again. I keep a mask on my face, stiff and expressionless, so she don't see that if I could I would smack her across her mouth. I would pull at her fine straight hair till it came out in dark clumps in my fists. I would scream in her selfish face. I have cared for her since the day she was born, when her father, my father, charged me to look after her.

If I don't get back with my family I will break.

I pull air deep into my lungs. I time my breathing with the brushing of her hair to settle me. When I trust my voice to speak, I say, "It's a hard thing to be separated from family, year on year."

"But you have me," she says, her eyes flying open, digging into me, hinting at the thing we never talk about. "At least we're together. We can be a comfort to each other."

I keep my eyes trained on the back of her head and on my hands gliding up and down her hair. I take deep, long breaths. This woman ain't never been a comfort to me.

"My father won't live forever. One day the whole of Belle Grove Plantation will be passed on to me, and Matthew will surely bring over your daughter and your husband, and even your mother, should she still be living. Be patient, Maple. They will be here with you when the time is right."

I feel like I'm a bee in a jar, shook up and poked at till all my insides are buzzing.

January 1849

Chapter 7

Henry

Mister Reardon, the blacksmith, takes me in and makes me his assistant, and I don't go back to the Five Points. I sleep above the shop and spend every waking hour pounding iron. I like it more than I thought I would. It's a good job to have as the days get colder, working by the forge. The rhythm of the pounding does me good, and at the end of the workday I look over what I've done and know that I've created something. I catch on quickly, and after a month Mister Reardon is pleased enough with my skills to take to heading over to the tavern across the way in the afternoon, letting me finish up by myself.

It's gradual, at first, when business starts to die down, but as the weeks drag through the winter it becomes the thing we don't talk about. Shortly after Christmas, a traveling blacksmith came to town and stopped traveling.

There's less work coming in and, before I know it, I'm doing all the jobs we get and Mister Reardon's spending his days tongue wagging with the barkeep.

It's a Tuesday when he eats his breakfast and goes on across the icy road to the tavern, leaving me to the few orders we've got. Some nails and ax heads and a window grill. Pretty soon, I hear a commotion across the way and walk over to see what the problem is. A wagon's hitched up outside of the tavern and in its bed there's freshly made plows and scythes and hoes and all sorts.

Inside the tavern, Mister Reardon is being pulled off a man whose nose is smashed and bleeding.

"I go where I get the best price, you crazy bastard." The man on the plank wood floor spits out bloody mucus.

"That's enough of that," the barkeep says to Mister Reardon, laying a rifle on the counter, his finger snug on the trigger. "If you've got problems, you're not settling them in my place." He sees me hovering in the doorway. "Get him out of here, Henry. Give him some strong coffee and a hot bath."

I lead Mister Reardon back to his shop, his breath puffing white in the winter air. He goes to the nails I've made, fingering through the pile, grumbling that they're too long and too thick.

"You can't go picking fights with folks who don't hire us," I say.

He scowls at me. "I won't be driven out of business." He pronounces his words in the deliberate way people have when they've had too much to drink and they're trying not to slur.

"Have you considered matching his prices, or offering a deal?" I ask. "Maybe you could do discounts for repeat customers. A traveling blacksmith can't offer anything for the future."

He sways on his feet and I grab his arm to steady him. He jerks it away.

"No," he says staring past me, to the walls of the shop where we hang the tools.

I sigh. A drunk man is a terrible thing to reason with.

"As you wish, Mister Reardon. But it seems to me you'll have to do something. The problem's not likely to fix itself."

He nods. "You're right," he says. "I have to deal with this."

I pull up a chair for him, so he'll sit before he falls. "Why don't you have a seat there? I'll make us some coffee, and we can think of a plan."

When I come out with the coffee he's not in the shop. I hear the neigh of his horse and rush outside, hot coffee sloshing over my hand. He mounts the horse and I throw the cups in the yard, the steam rising in great billows, as I run toward him. I'm less than halfway to him when he gallops off clutching his blacksmith's hammer in his hand.

I know where he's going and I know this can't end well.

I sprint after him as fast as I can. By the time I get to the clearing where the traveling blacksmith has set up camp, I'm hunched over with a cramp in my side, dragging myself on, wheezing in the cold air.

Ahead of me, the left arm of the traveling blacksmith is bloody and bludgeoned, but with his right arm he's pounding at Mister Reardon's face. He's got him pinned to the floor with his knee, beating him in rhythmic strikes, like he's hammering out lead. Off by the horse's feet, Mister Reardon's hammer lies in the dirt.

I lunge myself at the traveling blacksmith and wrestle him off, rolling with him on the frozen ground as each of us tries to get the upper hand and the top position. Somewhere in all the tussling and grappling, his hands find their way to my neck. He plants himself on top of me and I can't fling him off. I pry at his fingers but they stay locked around my throat. I hit him twice in the gut, but since I can't get my hand back for the momentum, the blows don't shift him. Black spots cloud my vision.

Off to my side, I see Mister Reardon stand up. I've got to hold on till he gets to me. I strike again at the traveling blacksmith but the power's gone out of me. Mister Reardon drags himself over to us. I need air. I need him to hurry. He stands behind the traveling blacksmith and raises his hands. I can just see that he's holding the hammer. It comes down as a shattering blow with a sound like cracking rock, and the traveling blacksmith goes limp on top of me.

I push him off and roll out from under him, gasping and coughing. The hammer's torn through the side of his head and the wound is gushing blood. I kneel over him and press my hands to the wide gash to stop the bleeding, but the blood flows through my fingers, pooling on the ground, soaking the frosted grass. My whole body shakes like teeth rattling in a cold winter.

"Is he dead?" Mister Reardon still holds the hammer.

The man's glass eyes stare up at the sun. A fool can see he's dead, but still I kneel there with my hands pressed to his head.

"The son of a bitch did that to himself," Mister Reardon says.

I can't catch my breath. I don't want to be here. I don't want anything to do with this, but I can't even make myself get up. I've seen plenty of men have the life squeezed out of them back home, but it was never like this. Bloody, brutal, murderous.

"He shouldn't have come here, is all," he says. "This would never have happened if he hadn't of come here."

I take my hands from the man's mutilated head. The bright red blood has gone dark and sticky between my fingers. I wipe my palms against the stiff grass, but the blood still sits in the folds and creases of my skin.

Mister Reardon prowls around the dead man. "I'm not getting strung up for the likes of him."

You killed a man, I want to say, but I can't make the words come. The shakes have grabbed hold of me something fierce.

He drops the hammer and grabs the dead man by his armpits, dragging him back toward the leafless bushes. I watch as he stashes the body under some shrubs and covers it with rotting leaves. When he's done, he steps up close to me and leans in, his whiskey breath making me wince.

"You take his forge and horses and get out of here. It's the only way."

I shake my head. He's drunk. And crazy. Somebody'll find that body, for sure, and it'll look like I'm the one who killed him if I take his things and go. I've already stuck my neck out too far. I should have stayed back in the shop and let them punch it out between the two of them.

Mister Reardon gathers what supplies lie around the traveling forge, tossing them into the wagon. Cooking pans, a stool, even his own blood-smeared hammer.

"You..." My tongue is thick in my mouth. "You've got to turn yourself in."

He pins me with iron eyes. There's no emotion in them, only survival. "It's your hands covered in his blood." His temples pulse with his heartbeat.

My lungs squeeze like I'm choking all over again. "I didn't kill him," I say.

He clamps his hand on my shoulder and squeezes his meaty fingers until they dig into me and he sees me flinch. "There's no telling who the law might find guilty."

I ball my fists at my sides. They still stick with blood. I must be the biggest eejit that ever lived. I glare at the blacksmith, wanting nothing to do with riding off with a murdered man's forge and horses.

"Come nightfall, I'll dump the body in the river," he says. "And I'll tell people the bastard's moved on."

When I don't move to hitch up the horses, he does it himself and then hands me the reins. "You want something in life, you got to take it, Henry," he says, like he's giving me his kindly, fatherly advice.

He says I should go west, so I go south because I don't trust him. He could easily turn me in as the murderer and get the law after me.

Fast, but not so fast that I look suspicious, I ride out of New York thinking of the dead man whose clothes I still wear, and this new dead man whose forge and horses I now own. I shudder. Seems I'm climbing out of poverty, but I pray to Christ I'm not losing my soul as I go.

Chapter 8

Maple

If there's one job I can't stand it's clothes scrubbing. I hate the hot water full of lye soap that makes my hands red and rough for days. I hate that Miss Martha wants every dress washed after she done worn it only two times. I hate that nobody makes that child wear clothes for play and clothes for good, like we got nothing better to do all day than wash and mend for a six-year-old. And I hate washing the drawers of the master who never learned to clean his backside right. Soon as I got put in charge here, I gave that job to Annie and Willa 'cause it wasn't gonna be me doing it.

They wash, but they only do it right if I check on them. Otherwise they'll rinse everything in cold water and call it clean, no matter what it comes out looking like. Or smelling like.

When I get in from hollering at Miss Lazy and Miss Slow-and-Lazy, I come in the kitchen house to get some black-eyed peas simmering for supper and looky here who's poking around my kitchen. Miss Spicy-pot.

"Oh, no you ain't," I say. "You get yourself away from my pots. I ain't gonna let you get me again."

Sarah jumps when I speak up, but she don't step back from what she's doing. Instead, she tosses some dried-up green something into the pot and stirs.

"This ain't no game," I say.

"I'm making something to help Ben," she says. "He can't get a breath in good."

I sniff at the pot and the smell goes straight up my nose. I snort and straighten. "Your stinky soup ain't gonna help that man. Let him pass on in peace."

"Bessie asked me to make something to ease him." She stirs in the pot and tosses in some more shriveled plants.

"Well, I don't want none of your witch's brew in my kitchen house, you hear?" I wave at her like swatting gnats. "Go bother someone else. I'm not gonna be looking over my shoulder while I'm fixing supper, trying to keep you from slipping something in again."

"You know that was Bessie."

"I don't want you in here," I say.

She act like she don't even hear me talking, just stands there stirring her weed-water.

My blood boils and I reach over and pop her upside her head.

"Ouch." She ducks and whirls around.

"Don't make me march up to the Big House and tell Miss Martha I got a problem with you," I say.

She rubs her head and hangs her mouth open like she can't believe I hit her. I know she's scared of me. She should be scared of me.

She swallows and her brown eyes go small. "You keep on and I'll tell Bessie you're stopping me from helping Ben." Ain't no force behind her quiet voice.

I spit air through my lips to show her what I think of that. "Bessie ain't got nothing to say over Miss Martha," I say, and snatch up a rag to take her pot of weeds off my fire and out of my kitchen.

"No," she says, standing between me and her pot like she thinks she's gonna block my way. "But if Bessie tells Master, he's gonna take her side in it. Bessie raised him up from a babe."

I make a warning face and plant my hands on both hips. Miss Sassy-thing needs to learn her place. I got half a mind to tell Miss Martha to stick this one in the fields.

"Cooked for him till she went blind," she says. "And he still talks about how he misses her cornbread."

I squeeze on the rag in one hand and slap her across her head again with the other. Ain't no way this uppity thing is coming into my kitchen and talking about my cooking after what she and Bessie done.

She jerks away from me and flings her arms up around her head in case I come back again for another blow.

"Miss Martha gonna take your side," she says, "but Master got the say around here. Ain't no way he's gonna side with you over Bessie. And maybe not even over me." She brings her arms down and juts out her chin. A challenge.

She's been getting uppity ever since that night she stood by watching me nearly get whipped for something she and Bessie did, with Master's words making her bold: *You're mighty fortunate Sarah was here.* I swipe at a bundle of her dried herbs on the table beside us, knocking them to the floor. "You better clean your mess up out of my kitchen. I don't want to see it. I don't want to smell it. And if you got so much extra time to be brewing up potions, then you need more work." I step toward her, crowding her till she steps back. "You scrub that porch, front and back. Them pillars too. And you best get it done before dinner 'cause you gonna be serving. And washing up after." I throw the rag into her simmering pot and leave her to it.

April 1849

Chapter 9

Sarah

I walk along a dirt road running through an open stretch of scrub sprinkled sparse with trees. I been five days at the Welleby plantation, rented out to Edith Welleby on account of she's expecting her fourth child and wants just about her whole house redone before that baby comes. I been sewing curtains till I can't see straight no more. Don't know how much she's paying Master for my work, but that woman was hell-bent on getting her money's worth.

After five long days I'm bone tired, but I got a lightness to my step too. It's being alone on the road that does it. Walking half the afternoon without a soul to answer to. The spring's finally knocked the chill out of the air and the critters seem just about as eager as me to be out and about. I seen squirrels and field mice and even a snake. A rabbit darts in front of me and disappears under a huckleberry bush. I strain, looking for its burrow and watching to see if it'll come out again. And I stay as long as I like waiting on it.

When I'm good and ready, I make my way on, batting away a cluster of midge flies hovering just above the road. I breathe in deep, letting the sweet air slide down my throat and fill my lungs. I swing my arms and tip my head back, eyes closed, listening to the leaves rubbing against each other and the tall grass swishing beside me.

The wind picks up as the clouds push in. An April storm's on its way, rolling in quick and coming on strong. But I don't hurry. No telling when I'll be out like this again. A little snatch of no one watching me is a precious thing.

Two horses pulling a wagon come clip-clopping up behind me. I step off the road into the long grass and the scrub that scratches my shins. You never know who's going to drive round you and who's going to run at you for sport. A dark-haired white man sits up top his cart, clicking his tongue at his horses to keep them moving. One of them is nervous, ears twitching every which way. The man nods to me as they pass, and I drop my eyes and pull back further into the short brush.

Back on the road, I've only gone a few steps when the rain breaks loose, sudden and coming down in sheets. I run toward an oak tree up ahead for shelter, but when I'm almost there, the man pulls off the road and hurries his horses back round to the tree, getting there first.

I hold back in the rain, looking for another tree, but there's only skinny, scrawny nothings nearby. No good for sheltering. The next decent tree is an elm a long way off.

"Don't you want to come out of the rain?" There's a tune to his way of speaking that don't sound like Virginia. He climbs down from his trap and strokes his skittish gray horse.

My dress clings to me and I wrap my arms round my chest. I expect his eyes to dip down to the curves of my hips under the thin, wet cloth. Instead, he looks square at my face.

"There's plenty of room," he says. He steps back a stretch making space for me.

I glance over to the elm in the distance.

The wind picks up and the air cools. I'm nearly soaked through. Shivering, I step in under the branches.

"Where're you headed?" he asks over the noise of the rain beating down around us. His voice dips and falls like it's dancing to its own music.

"I been hired out," I tell him. "I'm headed back to the Johnson plantation." I reach into my pocket for my pass to prove I ain't a runway. He don't look like a slave catcher, but then he don't need to be one to check me. The pass is damp and the ink is blurring. I don't know if the words are too watered over to read, but I hold it out to him anyway.

"What's that?"

"My pass, sir."

He looks at me like he don't know I got to show him a pass if he asks for it. As I hold it, heavy drops of rain hit the paper, smearing it worse.

"I don't need to see that," he says. He turns to his skittish horse and scratches its neck.

I fold the pass and tuck it back into my pocket. The rain is coming down harder and I press in a little closer to the trunk and wring out the hem of my dress.

"I'm looking to see what blacksmithing I can find on the estates around here," he says, crossing over to his chestnut horse and stroking the wet from its mane. "I just worked a stretch at a tobacco farm a few miles past the last town." He tips his head the way we came. "The Parson's plantation."

I ain't been off Jubilee since I got here, except for the last few days at the Wellebys. Never heard of a Parson plantation. I bite my lip and keep quiet.

He steps away from his horses and faces me. "So, do you know any plantations nearby that could use a blacksmith?" His eyes are soft and he smells of wood-fire smoke.

I shake my head, and look down at the scuffed leather of his shoes.

A boom of thunder cracks across the sky startling him, me and his horses. The gray one bucks and he grabs its reins, talking to it soft and calm. The next crack of thunder is even louder and the horse thrashes against his harness and tries to rear. Soon enough, the chestnut one starts to bucking every which way too. They're going to hurt themselves tied up to the wagon like that. The man reaches over, unhooking the large gray as thunder cracks a third time. The horse jerks back as he's releasing it, driving the coupling into his hand.

"Ahh, damn it! Bloody hell!" he roars. The man cradles his hand under his arm as the gray horse shoots off up the road. "Begging your pardon," he says to me.

My face pulls up in surprise for him to be begging my anything. I want to tell him to show me his hand. If he's cut himself, I can help, but I don't say it. Instinctively, though, my eyes search the scrub grass for feathery clumps of yarrow plants while he frees the second horse.

Lightning strikes just up the road where the gray horse bolted off to. The storm's right on top of us, and we got to get out from under this tree. We hurry into the open, picking our way over the brush, with him tugging at the chestnut horse who's straining to keep out of the pouring rain. I slip on the wet grass and he catches my arm and tugs me upright and further out into the clear. Up the road, the gray horse comes thundering back our way, eyes wild.

"Hold her," he shouts over the storm, thrusting the chestnut's reins into my hands. Then he charges on to the road toward his frightened horse.

It rears up when he gets close to it, waving his arms, blocking the road. I gasp, thinking it's going to trample him for sure, but he dives to the side as the horse comes down. He jumps up quick and snatches the reins, pulling the animal back down when it tries to rear again. He digs his injured hand into its mane, keeping a tight hold of the reins with the other hand, and settles it down to where it can walk. A few minutes later he leads it over to me and the chestnut where we stand in the rain.

Blood drips from his injured hand that hangs at his side.

"Your hand," I say.

He lifts it and turns it over. There's a long gash running clear across his palm.

"It needs yarrow leaf," I say.

His eyes soften as he watches me curiously. "Have you got some, then?"

Dropping the reins of his horse, I hurry over to a patch of scraggly plants growing in a clump, and pick a few spindly leaves, wiping them clean on my wet dress. I put them in my mouth, chew quickly and run back over to him. Taking the chewed leaves from my mouth, I lay them over his palm. He lets me do it. Then I tear a strip off the bottom of my dress and wrap it around his hand, tying it tight. If Momma could see me now, ripping up my dress to fix some strange white man's hand, she'd have a fit.

After I've tied the cloth, I look up and he's staring down at me. More than that, he's staring into me. His blue eyes trap my brown ones and pull me right out of myself.

The noise of the rain pounding down around us fills my ears, so I don't know how I hear his whispered "thank you" as clear as I do. A ghost of a smile plays at his mouth, climbing up his face until it lights up his eyes.

I'm still holding on to his hand. His pale skin in my dark fingers brings me back to my senses. I let him go and run through the downpour, pretending I don't hear when he calls out for me to wait.

Chapter 10

Henry

I stay under the oak tree for the night and let the storm pass. In the morning the sun is already bright as it climbs up the east and my hand feels a good sight better. But I linger, finding myself looking up the road she disappeared down.

When I get my pair of Morgans hitched, I trot them up the muddy road I've been looking at all morning. After a stretch, it swings me around a bend that hugs the side of the next plantation.

A split-rail fence stretches around a field where Negro men and women hack deep furrows in tidy rows. The sound of hoes striking the ground, and the smell of wet earth turning over after the rains reminds me of home. I stamp down the longing rising in my gut.

Behind the workers, a white man in a broad hat sits astride a Quarter Horse with a rifle slung over his shoulder and a whip on his belt. I keep moving, skirting around the edge of the property along the mud-slick road, until I come to the entrance: an elaborate wooden archway that seems to serve no purpose but to impress.

The painted sign fixed at the top tells me I've come to Jubilee Plantation, and the wide circular drive that loops in front of a deep porch with four pillars tells me there's money here. As I ride up, I count eight chimneys and twenty-two windows, and that's just on the front side of the house.

Pulling my horses to a halt, I clamber down and give each one a rub before thumping the dirt from my clothes and wiping my leather shoes on the back of each leg. Then I climb up the wide steps to the front door, and knock.

There's a moment before the door opens when my nerves get the better of me and I worry that someone'll come and chase me off the porch. The son of a tenant farmer doesn't march up to the front door of a grand house, bold as you please, without some knee quivering.

I remind myself that I'm Henry Taylor now. The further south I go, the less likely they'll know me for Irish. With fewer immigrants down this way, our accents don't count so much as Irish, Scottish or Swedish. We're just foreign, which suits me fine. But I keep the Taylor. O'Toole is asking for trouble.

When the door eases open, she's standing there. Her soft brown eyes look back at me, round as moons. Her mouth drops, gaping in surprise.

I pull myself straighter, trying to think of what to say. Glancing down at the hem of her dress, I see the frayed edge where she tore off a strip. When I look up, she's staring at my bandaged hand.

"You look drier," I say.

"I…" She glances behind her into the house.

I remove my hat. "I never introduced myself," I say. "I'm called Henry." I take her hand and bow. Her ripped dress and chewed leaves press between our palms. Although she tries to hide it, surprise is plain to see on her face. I like that she doesn't know what to make of me. "I've come looking for work," I say. I've still got hold of her hand.

In this moment, I feel the promise of America. I could be anything.

"Blacksmithing work?" she asks.

I smile, pleased she's remembered. "Yes, miss." I release her hand because I really ought to.

A small boy runs up to her, pulling on her skirts. "Sarah, come on, Mother says you can take me to hunt for crickets on top of the hill." He tugs at her with eager energy.

"Now, hold on. This man needs to talk to your daddy," she tells the boy. "He's a blacksmith, so he can fix that fireplace grate in your room." Her voice has the gentle pace of an unhurried mare. "I reckon he could even mend your pail and shovel." She glances at me as the corners of her mouth lift and stretch. "For making mud pies." Her smile is like the sun.

"Can you, mister?"

"I can." I answer the boy, but I look at her. Sarah. I take in the curve of her cheek. The slope of her jaw. "With my eyes closed, I can."

She pulls the door wide and steps aside to let me in. I want to touch her as I walk by. Instead, I squeeze my hat in both my hands.

She leads me to a bench along a wide hallway and disappears to speak to the plantation owner. The child sits beside me, telling me he'd like me to make him a poker for his fireplace—he and Sarah use a stick. When she comes back, she walks three steps behind the plantation owner. The boy hops up to take her hand and they slip out through a back door.

Matthew Johnson is a tall, soft-spoken man who's more than willing to have me fix his son's fireplace, and few dozen other things besides. He takes me down a narrow rear staircase to a hallway-like section of the cellar that he calls the "carry-through." His slaves use it to carry his meals through from the kitchen house to the dining room. He shows me some iron-ringed barrels that need re-hooping and some hooks and buckets that need repair. We exit to a wide lawn behind his house that runs into a wood. Nearly in the center of the lawn, but not quite, is a grand old walnut tree, all twisted arms and gnarled bark. To our right is a walled garden.

"My wife had an idea for an iron door to this garden," he tells me. "Something elaborate and decorative."

I tell him I can make one, though I've never made anything like that before.

"That's the kitchen house," he says, pointing to a hut just behind the garden. Beside it I see more roofs over the garden wall.

"There'll be a fair few things to mend and make in there. Pots and the like. Speak to Bessie and Maple about it, but get my approval before you start any work."

"Understood, sir."

The left side of the lawn carries on to the coach house and stables and the fields beyond. He tells me I can stable my horses with his and sleep above the coach house.

"When you've set up your forge, you should start with re-shoeing the horses," he says.

I walk around the side of the house to the front drive where my forge and horses stand, and find Sarah struggling with the child. She's pulling him in the direction of the house and he's trying to break free from her, straining to go back toward the stables and the fields, the way they've come.

"You can't go there right now, Master Thomas," she says. She's got him by his arm, looking worried but determined as he shouts and flails.

Hearing the noise, his father comes flying around the corner behind me.

He charges up to them. "What do you think you're doing?" he yells into Sarah's face.

She cringes away from him, releasing the boy. "Please, Master. He's too young to see a whipping."

"I want to see," the boy howls.

"What whipping?"

"He ain't but six," she says.

"Tell me what you're talking about," Mister Johnson thunders down at both of them.

"We were over on the hill and heard the lash, down by the quarters at the sycamore tree. But a whipping ain't for a child."

Mister Johnson straightens. A quiet anger tightens his mouth, straining the skin around his eyes. "Someone is being whipped on my plantation?"

"Yes, sir," she says.

"Red!" he bellows in the direction of the stables. "Red!"

A lanky Negro comes loping out at a clip. "Master?"

"Go down to the whipping tree and tell Mulch I'd like a word."

Red's eyes go flat and he takes off in a dead run past the coach house and the stables.

Mister Johnson bends down to his son and ruffles his hair. "Sarah was right. There are things you're not yet ready to see." He straightens up and speaks to me as if we've been in the middle of this very conversation. "Obedience at Jubilee is a firm requirement. I'm a reasonable man. If you have another opinion you can speak to me about it, but if I say a thing will be done, then it will be. I am Master here, and no one else."

His son pulls at his clothes, hopping about for attention.

Mister Johnson turns to Sarah. "Bring him inside," he orders.

Sarah takes the boy's hand and tugs him to the porch.

"But I don't want to go," he wails.

She guides him up the porch steps, but when they reach the top the child lurches back, dragging Sarah, making her trip and lose her footing. Flailing her arms, she pitches backward down the steps.

I scramble over, catching her before she crashes to the ground. We're both panting. Her eyes are wild until they lock on to mine.

"I've got you," I say. She smells of honeysuckle and pine. Like the first warm day of spring. She's in my arms and I can't move.

Behind me, I hear Mister Johnson clear his throat, breaking my paralysis. I set her back on her feet, slowly, keeping my hand on her elbow to make sure she's steady.

"Thank you," she says.

The boy takes her hand again, and this time, as they climb the steps, he leaves off from yanking at her.

Mister Johnson is staring at me and I feel myself go red. If he couldn't see my interest in her before, he sees it now in the flush of my face.

"I believe in rules, Mister Taylor. Rules allow for the clear running of a business. I have a rule that punishment or mercy is doled out at my discretion, which is something Ralph Mulch seems to have forgotten." He glances toward the fields where a short man strides past the stables toward us, followed by the Negro man Mister Johnson sent to fetch him. "To you, I would say, I do not allow bed warmers on my plantation." He takes a step closer. "It is an ungodly practice, and here we honor God."

I haven't got an idea in heaven how to respond to that. I can guess what he means by a bed warmer, but as I try to corral my thoughts to give an answer, he turns his attention to the overseer who's come up beside us. We both notice the whip in the man's hand.

Mister Johnson is bristling with anger. "What is this I hear about a whipping, Mulch?"

"It's that Jim you picked up in the fall. He's getting lazy. Covering less ground than he should."

"Didn't he break his arm felling trees on the new land I'm cultivating?"

The man shrugs. "Cotton don't care about that, Mister Johnson. The ground ain't going to hoe itself."

Mister Johnson draws himself up to his full height, a head taller than his overseer. Stepping close, he looks down his nose at his hired help. "Before you damage another man's property, you should check to see that he wants it damaged." The overseer starts to say something, but Mister Johnson speaks over him, silencing him. "Suppose I'd wanted to loan him out tomorrow. Are you prepared to reimburse me the lost revenue?"

"He wasn't hardly working, Mister Johnson, and if he gets away with it—"

"I decide who gets whipped and when and how many lashes. If you want a future at Jubilee you will abide by my rules. Now get him off the tree and get everyone back to work."

Chapter 11

Sarah

Maple's got me cleaning up after her in the kitchen house instead of in there serving dinner. I don't mind. It gives me a chance to make up a numbing tonic and sneak down to the field slave huts.

Jim's stretched out on his stomach across a pallet, moaning. His shirt's off and red stripes cross his back, oozing pus and blood. One of the water boys sits beside him shooing flies away from his wounds.

"I cooked you up something," I say

Jim turns his head slow, like rolling a boulder, to see who's talking. Since that day we came in here on the back of a wagon we hardly said two words to each other. "I ain't hungry," he says.

I kneel down next to him. "It's not for eating." When I dip a rag and dab it on his back, he winces and grunts. "It'll take some of the pain and keep it from infecting," I say.

Copper, another field slave, comes in with a bowl of gruel for Jim. "You bring him laudanum from the Big House?"

I shake my head. "This will do him fine." Already Jim don't grunt when I dab his back and his breathing's easier. "You sleep here with him?" In the corner there's a heap of pallets and it's likely one of them is his.

Copper nods.

"Put this on his back again if he wakes up in the night." I set the bowl down and leave the rag floating in it. "And don't let him eat till tomorrow." I pull leaves out of my basket. "Boil water and put this in it and let him sip on it as much as he can take."

Copper looks over at the big man drifting off to sleep. "How you know about all that?"

I get to my feet. "I got to get back before they finish eating supper."

Leaving the slave huts, I keep my head down and walk fast as I pass the overseer's cabin. I ease up my step as I walk by the empty paddock where they let the horses out during the day. When I get by the coach house where the blacksmith's got himself set up, I slow my step. He's set hammer, tongs, bellows, leather gloves and all kinds of metal working pieces on a tidy bench against the coach house wall, while his forge and anvil sit out in the open. I reach out and run a finger along the smooth metal of the anvil as I go by. It's warm, like he ain't been finished long.

"You know how it works?"

I jump, pulling my hand away. When I turn, he's standing behind me, soot dusting his clothes and a leather apron draped round his neck.

"I didn't mean no harm," I say.

His eyes dance and his mouth pulls crooked across his face. "If it takes me hammering on it all day long, I guess it won't fall apart if you touch it." He unties his leather apron and, lifting it over his head, hangs it on a peg on the coach house wall. His hand is wrapped with the same bandage I made for him out in the storm.

"Your hand any better yet?" I say.

"I've never had an eye for doctoring. Maybe you could take a peek."

I pull off his bandage. His gash is closed, but it's red and raw. I run my fingers over the line to feel how the wound's healing. There's a bulge where the skin's weaving itself back together. He pulls his hand flat, making the skin stretch, showing it clear.

"Well, look at that. That's quite some healing touch you've got."

"Best to keep the air on it now." From my basket, I pull out a flask with the water of boiled walnut husks, and I pour it over his palm.

"How did you know you could use that plant?"

I use my thumb to rinse his palm as I pour. "Just something my momma showed me."

"You saved me days of trouble. And probably an infection besides."

When I pull out a cloth and start to dry his hand, his little finger hooks around my thumb. I pull away.

"Looks like you're just about fine now, Mister Taylor," I say.

"That'll be thanks to you," he says. "And it's Henry."

I pick up my basket and hold it between us like a shield. "You'll want to keep it clean as you can."

"Maybe you can check on it again tomorrow."

I don't answer. Just turn and strike out across the yard for the kitchen house.

When I get there, Maple's waiting for me. She throws me a hard look that don't need much interpreting.

"I been to see Jim," I say. "Give him something for his stripes."

"Humph," she says putting her back to me. "All I know is this mess won't clean itself."

I tuck my basket in the corner and get to work.

May 1849

Chapter 12

Maple

I'm making corn cakes when I hear heavy boots stomping up
to the kitchen house. Ain't no way it's Master or Miss Martha
walking up here like a bear in heat, so I don't turn around
when I hear the boots stomp right up inside.

"Where is he, Maple?"

I about jump out of my skin when I hear that voice. I whip
around and see my ears ain't lying. My old master stands there,
dusty from the road and scowling. His close-set eyes draw in
tight and his big forehead reaches right over his bald head.

"You tell me what you know, girl."

I ain't seen this man in seven years and here he comes out
of the clear blue talking about *what I know.*

"Hello, sir," I say.

"You hiding him?"

Jeremiah Keeler looks around the room, behind baskets
and in food sacks. Even looks in the fireplace. "Freddy ran," he
says, when it's clear there's only me and him in the kitchen
house. "Now, you tell me if you've seen him."

"My Freddy?" I say, like some other Freddy might run to me
if he got the chance. He can't be right. Freddy wouldn't leave
our daughter. But could he have run with her? My heart steps
up its beating and I pinch my thigh to keep the excitement
out of my voice. "And Rose?"

"No. Just Freddy."

I slump a little where I stand, surprised at myself that I can still hope. "He wouldn't leave Rose," I say. "If he's gone, slave stealers must've snatched him meaning to make money out of selling him on."

"Off my land in the middle of the night? No, Maple. He ran all right. And God help you if you're hiding him."

"I ain't seen him in seven years," I say. "Or Rose, or Momma. Not since you sent me here."

That gentles him some and he comes around the wood table to stand closer. He reaches out and runs his fingers along the side of my face and cups my cheek. "You look exactly the same," he says.

I don't. I'm heavier and I droop, but I still look just like him.

"You haven't changed either," I say, because even though he's fatter and redder and balder, with wrinkles spreading like lice, he still forgets and remembers and forgets who I am to him.

Miss Martha comes in and he jerks his hand away from my face like touching hot coals.

"Well?" she says. "Are you satisfied enough now to be civil and take tea with your daughter?" He turns to her and she blushes when she reads the uneasy surprise in his face. She clears her throat. "Maple, make my father and me some tea please and bring it to the sitting room."

He lets her take his arm and she leads him out. At the door he pauses. "If you hear something," he says, "I trust you'll tell me."

I watch the two of them walk on, arm in arm, and hardly notice the knot in my chest.

I take two stout breaths to clear my head. Master Jeremiah's here at Jubilee, which means Momma must be here too. That man never went nowhere without dragging her along, even when his wife was alive and gave him hell for it.

I make the tea, but instead of bringing it straight in to them, I first dart upstairs to where I figure Momma'll be unpacking his trunk.

When I hurry into the room, Kitty's there from the old plantation, a slave girl grown into a woman. She's wearing a deep blue dress of raw silk with a high ruffled collar, a dress as fine as anything Miss Martha owns. Playing at being the missus in her fancy clothes. And there's me, carrying tea, looking like I've come to serve her.

"Where's my momma?" I say. She's already got me feeling prickly.

She goes clear across the room and says, "Hello, Maple," right out the window, like she got a pet bird out there with my name.

Me and Kitty weren't never friends, but we wasn't enemies. And now here she go, acting like she's too good for me.

"You trying not to talk to me?" I ask.

She don't answer. Don't turn around. Don't nothing.

"I done something to you?"

She shakes her head at her make-believe bird. She must know something about Freddy, but what I want to know right now is why she's here and not Momma. I have a feeling like ice under my skin.

"Did something happen to my momma?" I hold my breath waiting to hear.

She looks at me finally and its pity in her eyes.

I set down the tea on the dresser and now it's me facing the wall, not looking at her. My throat closes up and my eyes sting. "Did she pass away?" I ask. I blink hard three times before I can look at her.

She stands in front of the window with the sun shining in all around her, worrying her hands. "She didn't pass," she says with a heaviness in her voice.

"Best tell me," I say, sitting myself on the bed.

She flicks her eyes to the door, the dresser, then to me on the bed. "She got sent to the fields," she says.

I want to laugh. It just would never happen. "Momma ain't no field hand," I say. She's been in charge of the house since before I was born. And she's been Master Jeremiah's favorite all that time. "He'd never put her in the field." Lord knows his wife was screaming for it every week. That, or sell her. If he wouldn't do it while she lived, why would he do it now she's dead and gone?

"Times've changed, Maple."

The skirt of Kitty's dress sways as she walks to the bed. When she sits beside me, her feet poke out from under the hem, showing matching blue silk slippers. He never dressed Momma up like that.

I don't know how to feel. Momma hated being in his bed, but if getting out means picking cotton with a whip singing overhead from sunup to sundown, then it's a hard price. And I don't know what to think about him dressing Kitty up like a doll.

"You look real pretty," I say.

She smooths her hands down the front of her dress. "I got three more just like this." She flashes me a smile that dies on her face before it reaches her eyes.

When I climb back downstairs carrying the tea tray to the parlor, Miss Martha's sitting rod-straight across from Master Jeremiah's slug-slouch. Both of them look ready for this visit to be over.

I set the tray on the table between them and pour the tea.

Master Jeremiah hands his cup back to me saying, "Maple, sugar, get me some fire for this, would you?" He means a shot of whiskey.

I look over at Miss Martha, who clears her throat. "We don't serve spirits until after supper at Jubilee."

He looks at me like he's waiting for me to fetch his whiskey anyhow.

"Maple's got to follow our rules now," she says. "Matthew's and mine."

He bristles at that, and so do I. I hold his tea, not sure what to do with it.

"If I'd known he'd turn out to be no better than a Puritan Yankee, I'd never have let you marry Matthew Johnson."

In the strained silence I set his cup back down on the table.

"Might as well take that away," he says, shoving the cup. "Without fire it tastes like piss-water." Tea sloshes over the tray and spills on the wooden table, and I take off my apron to sop it up.

"Welcome, Jeremiah," Master says, entering the room with Master Thomas scurrying beside him. "This is certainly a surprise." He offers his hand to his father-in-law, who doesn't stand to shake it. Master shoots Miss Martha a look.

"Good afternoon, Grandfather," Master Thomas says with a face fit for a funeral. His daddy must have warned him not to go bouncing around like a cricket on hot coals.

"Well, there he is," Master Jeremiah says, beaming. "My only grandson. Come here and let me look at you." When the boy comes close, Master Jeremiah takes hold of his chin and turns it left and right. "You've got too much of your father in you, but I think you got my nose." He winks at his grandson.

I go to carry his tea away when Master Jeremiah calls me back. "Maple, come over here and help me take these off," he says to me, lifting his booted foot. I lay the cup back on the little table and crouch in front of him, pulling at his boot.

"Father, we are having tea," says Miss Martha.

"Jeremiah, if you'd like to get comfortable, perhaps you'd prefer to rest in your room before supper," Master says.

The first boot comes off and I topple over from pulling at it.

"That's not a bad idea, Matthew. Maybe I will."

Miss Martha's voice has the crisp snap of dried sticks. "I was just explaining to Father that we'd find a suitable place for Kitty to sleep."

"And I was explaining to you," her father says, "that she'll stay in the room with me."

Master looks from his wife to his father-in-law, his expression pulling into a deep frown. He hooks his thumbs into his waistcoat and says, "It's nothing against you, Jeremiah. We simply do not permit slaves to sleep in the house. Not here."

Miss Martha puts her teacup down and sits more at ease with Master here to handle her daddy.

Master Jeremiah holds out his other leg and I grip the second boot.

"Now, what kind of hospitality is that?" Master Jeremiah says. "After I took the trouble to bring my own girl, so I wouldn't have to borrow one of yours?"

Miss Martha gasps and red blotches climb up Master's neck. They's all clear on what borrowing a slave girl would look like. If Master Jeremiah weren't his father-in-law, I believe Master would throw him right out.

"Sarah sleeps in the house," Master Thomas says helpfully into the silence.

The second boot slips free and I tumble backward with it.

"Is that right?" his grandfather says, a cat grin sliding up his face. He waves the boy closer. "Tell me, Thomas, where exactly does Sarah sleep?"

"In my room."

"Well, now." He smiles his victory at Master and Miss Martha. "If Sarah can stay in your room, I guess Kitty can stay in mine," he says to the boy, counting on nobody wanting to explain the difference to a six-year-old.

The smell of his un-booted feet taints the parlor air as he props them on a footrest and wiggles his toes.

"Your manners have grown crude without Mother to temper you," Miss Martha says.

He leans back into the armchair. "My manners are just fine."

Master grits his teeth. "I will not have shenanigans under my roof."

"What's shenanigans?" Thomas asks.

Master looks fit to burst.

"Playing around," Miss Martha says. "Like when you want to run in the house."

"Oh," Master Thomas says. "Don't worry, Grandfather. We can play shenanigans outside."

Master Jeremiah throws his head back and laughs. "I will look forward to that."

Chapter 13

Henry

At night when the kitchen woman gives me a plate of food, I take a portion and wrap it in an oil cloth. I can't get out of the habit of saving something back. After years of hungering, I have a great need to keep vittles at the ready.

I eat my meal propped against the coach house, looking at the pillars and windows and balconies of the Johnson home. I don't know if Father Michael would call this coveting. I don't want *this* house. Just a house like this. With a room for sitting down and a room for eating and a room for writing letters, all with glass in the windows and a fire in every hearth.

Through the noise of the cicadas, I hear music behind me, rhythmic and swinging. I know it must be the slaves, though something about it sounds like home. Not the tune or the voices. Something deeper than that.

It nudges at a longing in me. I miss my family. I miss Ireland. The hills and the crag rocks, sure, but also gathering like this, with a fiddle and a fire, turning a hard-worked day into something to sing about. I miss the spirit of the place and the people who make it so. I came here for a better life, and I'm eating, that's true. But I'm eating alone.

When my plate's empty, I go to the edge of the trees and stand unnoticed in the shadows, watching. The man who drove Mister Keeler's coach stands by an open fire, a fiddle to his chin, fingers flying over the strings. There're men and women jigging around him, mostly house slaves, but a few from the field, or so I guess from the condition of their clothes. I recognize Red, the horseman. Blind Bessie and old Ben. The two children who bring buckets of water for my work. And Sarah.

The tune the man plays has a jaunty bounce that whips everyone into clapping and hopping.

I pick my way closer, but as I come near and they notice me, they quit their dancing, one by one, and then the music stops as well. All of them stare. Silent.

"A fine evening," I say.

They look at their feet. A few mumble, "Yes, sir."

"I heard you playing," I say. "I thought I might come over and listen."

They don't respond. They're waiting for me to go, pulling back from me like I'm a viper slithered into their gathering.

My eyes are drawn to Sarah. In the moonlight she seems to glow with a yellow-brown gloss, like polished wood.

Red, the large man who cares for the horses, steps in front of her, blocking my view.

"Something we can do for you?" he says in a deep, cautious voice. Then he adds, "Sir." The pause is long enough to turn it from a term of respect into something that borders on threatening.

My knees give a little wobble, though I know I'm not in any real danger. I'm a white man in Virginia, and a black man can't lay a hand on me, provoked or not, without going to the gallows. And I guess that's the problem. And I can understand it, sure enough. We wouldn't take kindly to an English landlord coming into an Irish wedding because he liked the music.

"It was a lovely tune," I say, backing away.

When I'm a good ways off and can't be seen, I hear the fiddling start up again. Quieter. Restrained. But with an anguished longing. Every tired, lonely, homesick thing I'm feeling is woven into that tune, and I stop, hidden beyond the brow of the hill, to listen.

Chapter 14

Sarah

I'm digging in the kitchen garden in the afternoon heat, pacing my hoe to the rhythmic strike of the blacksmith's hammer, steady like a heartbeat, when Missus comes out. She's hardly said two words to me since I been here, except through Maple.

"Well, look at this, Sarah. The garden is positively flourishing under your tutelage."

I don't know what she's trying to say, but she's smiling, so I say, "Yes, ma'am."

"And I'm very pleased that Thomas is so fond of you."

After sleeping on his floor and tending to every squeak he makes in the night, he's taken to following me around half the day. "Yes, ma'am," I say.

It's too hot for what early May should be, and she pulls out a fan and flaps it in short, jerky spurts. "Your master and I think it's time for him to get back on a horse."

I brush the dirt from my hands as she talks. Even I know it's her daddy whose got them bothered about it. At the supper table last night, he wouldn't stop talking about how a boy can't be allowed to be scared of a horse, and how if he don't get back on he'll spend his life fearing everything he should be mastering.

"And we've decided," says Missus, "that since he enjoys spending time with you, you're exactly the right one to help with that."

"Me, ma'am? I can't ride no horse."

She waves her fan at me to hush me up. "For now, just take him up to the paddock and get him comfortable with them again."

These fool people never stop coming up with fool ideas. How am I supposed to get him comfortable with horses when I don't know the first thing about it? I'm liable to get the boy kicked in the head. "Maybe Red would be—"

"No, no. Not Red. You." They don't want him fearing what he should be mastering, and he's afraid of Red. "I'll send him out to you. You can finish that later," she says, nodding at my hoe. Turning her back, she marches herself up to the house, and a minute later Master Thomas comes out. He takes my hand and off we go.

Up at the paddock, Master Thomas has a mind to stay right on back from the fence. While he works up the nerve to get closer, the three horses in there don't bother to even look up at us from their grazing. As we inch nearer, Master Thomas pulls at my skirts and tangles up in my legs.

"You want your cobbler, you better go on up there," I tell him. His momma promised him peach cobbler if he strokes one. "They ain't gonna hurt you," I say. "Look how they's minding their own business."

I nudge him forward, but he scurries behind me, clutching at my thighs and peeking around my hips.

"Come on, let's you and me go pet one," I say.

"You first," he says.

I don't take but a couple steps before I feel him tugging at my skirt behind me.

"Let's go back," he says.

"Now, don't be silly," I say. "They's just horses, as gentle as you like. Don't you want to pet it?"

He shakes his head.

"If you pet one, you can tell your momma and your daddy what you did. Lord have mercy, will they be proud of you."

He don't move closer.

"And, on top of that, you'll get your cobbler," I say.

We both hear the brush of long grass at the same time and turn. The blacksmith is leading a large brown and black horse up the hill. It's got its head near about on the man's shoulder. He reaches up and scratches its muzzle.

"Afternoon," he says to us.

I nod at him and Master Thomas takes a step back, keeping his distance. The blacksmith opens the gate and leads the horse in. He slips the rope over the animal's head, strokes its neck, talking soft in its ear like he did to his own horses that day in the storm.

Thomas steps out from behind my skirt.

The blacksmith comes up to a gray horse, pats its back, circles around and pats its neck and slips the rope around its head.

"What are you doing?" Thomas calls out.

"Shoeing horses," he says. "And what might the two of you be doing?"

Thomas looks around, not sure of his answer. "I'm fixing to pet one," he finally says.

"Fixing to? If it's petting a horse you're wanting, then why not just go on and pet it?" He turns to look at me. "And what about you, miss? Do you fancy stroking a horse?"

I shake my head. "I'm just here for Master Thomas. He ain't too sure about the horses since his fall a while back. He's working up to it."

The man nods. "I see." He clicks his tongue and leads the horse a few steps toward us. "Well, this one's pretty friendly. Why don't you come say hello?"

Thomas takes my hand and creeps toward the blacksmith, tugging me along. When we're standing right up beside the horse, the blacksmith reaches out and takes Thomas's hand, and guides him in stroking the side of the horse. The grin on that boy's mouth is near about wide enough to reach his ears.

"You try, Sarah," Master Thomas says.

"I don't need to try," I say, but the blacksmith takes hold of my hand and leads it to the horse like he did with Master Thomas.

I feel the smoothness of the horse hair, rose-petal soft, and I feel the warmth of the blacksmith's touch as he drapes his pale hand over mine, his healing wound pressed against me, guiding me along the horse's side. His hand is slick with sweat. Mine too. In fact, my whole body is dripping in the heat. I got sweat rolling down between my shoulder blades and under my arms and between my legs. The sun is beating down so hard today, like it wants to burn our clothes away.

I pull my hand from under his and shake at my skirt, trying to get some air circulating.

The blacksmith clears this throat. "Would you like to sit on him?" he asks Master Thomas.

The boy nods, but backs away. "Will he throw me off?"

"Not a chance."

The horse neighs, tossing his head, and Master Thomas backs further away.

"Would you like me to sit on him with you?" the blacksmith says.

Master Thomas nods. "But he hasn't got a saddle."

"Aye, but we don't need it. There's a mounting block just there that we can use," he says pointing to a wooden stoop by the fencing. "And we won't go thundering across the countryside on him, bareback like an Indian brave. We'll just stay here with him. We don't need a saddle for that."

He leads the horse over to the block, but Master Thomas doesn't follow. "Sarah should go first," he says.

There's some things a slave ain't supposed to do, and riding the master's horse is one of them. "I can't be riding no horse, Master Thomas."

"It'll give the boy courage," the blacksmith says. He ties the horse to the fence by the mounting block and steps over to me, taking my elbow. "You're doing him a favor," he says, leading me to the horse.

Standing in front of it, my stomach does a little flip at the idea of getting on. All of a sudden, it looks bigger and stronger and like something you can't control.

"Don't worry," the blacksmith says, leaning into my ear. "I won't let anything happen to you."

I know better than believing in promises, but hang it if those jitters don't quiet right down. I step with him on to the mounting block and let him settle me atop the horse. He climbs on behind me and adjusts my legs forward, nesting his right up behind them. Reaching around me, he pats the horse, calming it.

"Lord, have mercy, I'm sitting on a horse." I grab hold of its mane in both my fists.

"Let's walk him over to Thomas."

"What do you mean?" I stammer.

He leans down to unleash the rope from around the fence with one hand, and hooks his other arm around my waist. Then he drives his heels into the animal's flank and clicks his tongue and we move, swaying side to side over to where Master Thomas is standing.

The child jumps up and claps his hands. "You're riding. You're riding. Now me."

"You'd make a fine horse woman," the blacksmith says, quiet in my ear.

Between the moving horse between my legs and the blacksmith against my back, and the sweltering heat, I'm starting to feel light-headed.

He swings his leg over and hops down from behind me.

"Place your hands atop my shoulders," he says.

When I do, he reaches up to my hips and pulls me off, landing me just in front of him. I wobble a little, winded and breathless, and he rights me.

"Thank you, Mister Taylor," I say.

He shakes his head. "Please, call me Henry."

"My turn," Master Thomas shouts. He runs over to the mounting block and can't stand still for waiting.

The blacksmith lets go of my waist and leads the horse back over to the block. When they're both settled on its gray back, the blacksmith takes the young master twice around the paddock before saying he's got to get back to work. They dismount and he leads the horse out of the gate and down the hill for shoeing.

It don't take Master Thomas but a minute to remember the peach cobbler and he's dragging me down the hill. "Mother said," he keeps saying.

When I tell him I ain't never made a cobbler before, he marches me right over to blind Bessie's cabin.

"You need to show her what to do," he tells her.

She's at her wheel, spinning, seeing all she needs to with her hands. Her husband, Ben, has taken ill and lies stretched out on the bed, air rattling through his chest.

"Now, why do you think you deserve a treat?" she asks him.

"Mother said I could," he says. "I rode a horse today."

"Well, ain't that something. You weren't scared?"

"Course not, right Sarah?" he says, looking over to me. "Sarah wasn't either. She rode it too."

Bessie's eyebrows shoot up halfway to her forehead. "Sarah rode a horse?"

"With the blacksmith," he says.

I try to shush him with a finger to my lips that she can't see.

"But you did," he says.

Bessie's mouth pulls down. "That man been sniffing around you?"

"He was getting a horse for shoeing," I explain. "And Master Thomas wouldn't go if I didn't do it first."

Bessie gropes her way over to me and puts her hand to my face. "This here's a good place. You don't got to take no foolishness here. If Master knows about someone trying to carry on his funny business, he'll put a stop to it."

I shake my head. "It weren't like that. He was trying to do a kindness. I rode and then the boy rode. That's all."

She pats my cheek and turns to Master Thomas. "Well, if you really rode that horse today, you best lead old Bessie to the kitchen house so I can teach Sarah how to make the best peach cobbler in Virginia."

I know Maple's going to be mad about us all getting underfoot in her kitchen when she's about to fix food for supper.

Sure enough, she glares at Bessie as she shuffles in, but when her eyes settle on me, she strikes, "And where have you been? You think you're some kind of high and mighty to leave off your work before you hardly got started? I saw the vegetable garden and all the work you didn't do today."

Some slaves would make worse masters than the masters, and Maple is of one of them. She's got so much hate balled up inside her it can't help but leak out.

"Missus told me to stop."

She sucks her teeth and plants her hands on her hips. "You must take me for the dumbest kind of fool there is, if you expect me to believe Miss Martha's going around me to tell you to stop working."

Master Thomas pushes in from behind us. "I get to have peach cobbler and Sarah's going to make it for me and Bessie's going to teach her how."

"In my kitchen? I got to fix your supper."

"Mother said." He drags me and Bessie deeper inside. "'Cause I rode a horse."

"Humph," Maple says, scowling at the child. "You're liable to get hot peppers in your cobbler with these two. And your mother better not start fussing with me when her supper's late."

"We'll be quick," I say.

She just glares at me harder. "I ain't cleaning up your mess. And you better not leave my kitchen looking like no pigsty."

Chapter 15

Henry

At the end of the day, as the sun tucks itself behind the blue mountains in the west, I sit at my forge, staring into my fire. I think of her sitting between my legs on that horse, her back pressed against me, my arm wrapped around her waist. I remember the feel of her hips when I lifted her from the horse's back, warm and soft under my fingers. And the sway of her voice, like the dip and swing of those hips.

That's what I'm thinking of, when I look up and see her walking toward me. I stand, but I don't trust myself to speak.

"I came by to thank you for your help earlier. With Master Thomas. And the horse."

I keep myself from looking at her hips. Instead, I watch her lips pucker and stretch, forming the words. She lifts a cloth of homespun cotton off a plate. The sweet smell makes my mouth water.

"I brought you some peach cobbler. To thank you. For earlier."

I look down at the plate and back up at her. I should say something.

"It's Bessie's recipe," she says. "It's a good one."

She holds it out to me, and I step closer to her, until the plate's right between us. Her eyes are chestnut and hazel flecked together, reflecting the light like smoked jewels. I ease the dish from her fingers.

She looks to the fire, and at the anvil, and then up to the sprinkling of stars spread across the sky like white seeds in a smooth black soil. She swallows once, then twice, and then pulls in a long breath of night air. "Suppose I best leave you in peace," she says.

"Wait," I say, finding my tongue. "Don't you need to take the plate back with you?" I pull the stool over for her. "Will you sit with me while I eat this?"

When she lowers herself on to the seat, I lean against my anvil. I haven't got a second stool. Nor a fork anywhere handy, so I pinch at the food with my fingers. When I place it on my tongue, I am amazed. I could no sooner describe what I'm tasting than name the color of a winter sunrise, or whistle the tune of the forest. I don't mean to, but I groan with my fingers stuck in my mouth.

She laughs at me making a fool of myself, but I don't mind, because I've made her laugh. It's the first time I've heard her do that. If bluebells made a sound, it would be her laugh.

"It's heavenly," I say. "I've never had the like." I eat every scrap, holding back from licking the plate.

She scrunches up her nose and looks at me sideways. "You never had cobbler before?"

I shake my head and drag my finger over the empty plate and suck the last taste from it. "For special days, Ma might have made a meat pie, if we had meat to make it with," I tell her. "I never ate sugar until I got to America. And then only twice. And not like this."

We hear the splash of someone fetching water at the well, and then the clink of glasses being carried across the lawn, probably back for washing at the kitchen house.

"I best be getting on." She rises, brushing at her skirt.

"You'll be needing this." I approach her carrying the plate.

She takes hold, but doesn't pull it from me, and I don't let it go.

"I'm grateful to you," I say, "for coming out here and bringing this for me."

We stand with the plate between us.

"Thank you," I say.

She looks at me with a warmth like the sun. And something else. An invitation. The feeling is like peach cobbler. Sweet and fresh and new and too good to be real.

"Evening, Sarah," says a deep rumble voice that crashes into the moment like thunder. We jump and turn to see Red standing back a pace, watching us. Beside him is the man who drives Jeremiah Keeler's coach and who played so well on the fiddle last night.

Sarah steps apart from me, looking at the floor, at them, at the plate in her hand. Anywhere but at me.

"Evening, Red. Zeek," she says. "I was just bringing Mister Taylor some cobbler for helping with Master Thomas."

I hate that she explains herself. Red stares at her like he caught her misbehaving, and she backs further away from me, putting too much distance between us.

"It's Henry," I say, trying to catch her eye, but she won't look at me.

"I'll walk you back," Red says to her.

She turns to go with him, and he takes her arm, guiding her across the lawn, with Zeek following close behind.

When they've gone a few paces, I hear Red's deep voice asking, "You okay?"

And I see the tight nod she gives him as she says, "I just brought him cobbler"—almost like an apology.

Chapter 16

Maple

I can't get another word out of Kitty about my family. And Zeek's been hiding from me like I'm the law and he got a price on his head. I know they think they're protecting me from something, but I got to know the worst of it. I have a guess that just about stops my heart.

I believe Master Jeremiah sold my little girl. Freddy must have tried to run after her. And Momma must have tried to stop her being sold and got herself sent to the fields. But I need to know for sure and, if Kitty and Zeek won't tell me, I got to go to the one who will.

At the end of the evening, when his nerves've been softened by whiskey, I head up to Master Jeremiah's room hoping to catch him before he's out for the night. I raise my hand to knock, but I'm afraid he'll turn me away, so I grip the door handle, hold my breath and ease the door open.

I peek my head in and I turn to stone.

He's in here and he sure ain't sleeping. He's got Kitty bent over the bed, her blue silk dress crumpled at her feet.

He's got one fist pulling in her hair and the other one squeezing at her neck as he ruts into her, jerking her body with his thrusts. In his beet-red face, his eyes squeeze tight.

Hers are wide as moons. With one hand, she claws at his choking fingers. With the other, she pushes up from the bed to ease the pull on her hair.

As she splutters for air, her wild eyes find me hovering in the doorway. Master Jeremiah grunts, thrusting and jerking and squeezing. The pain twisting her face crumples into humiliation.

I step back into the hall and close the door. This is what it looks like when a master holds you special.

I lean against the wall, my head swirling. I'm sorry for Kitty, but it's Momma I'm thinking about, and all the years she spent choking on the bed.

Chapter 17

Sarah

Most of the morning, I been in the garden on my hands and knees picking out the weeds in by the squash. The brick wall around it runs higher than a man is tall and cuts a body off from the rest of the plantation till you almost feel like you're somewhere else. If I could, I'd be here all day long, digging my fingers in the dirt.

"Lord, have mercy, this garden's fit to burst." Bessie shuffles through a row of carrots with bushy green stalks that spill into the path, brushing at her ankles and tangling in her toes. "Can't a body hardly walk." She wrinkles her nose and sniffs at the air. "Is that onions?"

"They keep the slugs away," I say, sitting back on my heels.

"Well, how 'bout that." She feels through the vegetables with her feet. "You got peas in here?"

"Yonder," I say, pointing, like she could see it.

"Master used to love my peas. Used to say I make the best peas in the whole state of Virginia."

"Bet they were something else."

"Not half as good as my cornbread. Now, that truly was the best in the county. Master's momma won a church prize for my cornbread once. That's how good it was." She bends over to touch the vegetables where she stands, running her hands through the leaves.

"Bessie, you need something from me?"

"Are these here collards?" She feels up and down on a wide flat leaf.

"Turnips," I say. "You looking for something special?"

"Shame we ain't got peach trees. We could make peach cobbler every day of the week if we had a tree. Lord, that Master Thomas loves himself some cobbler, don't he?"

"Sure do," I say. I go back to my weeding while I wait for her to work up to what she wants. Chickweed, cleavers and finger-grass keep trying to come up with the vegetables, but I got them just about beat. Then I check the bean rows, tying up the ones that don't want to cling right with a length of string.

"I hear you gave that blacksmith a taste."

I should have figured that's what this was. "You been talking to Red?"

"He came by this morning, checking on Ben."

I wrap a bean vine around the pole and tie it, though it don't much need tying, waiting for her to say her piece.

"Nothing good can come out of that."

"I just gave the man some cobbler," I say. The strings slip out of my hand and I crouch to pick them up.

"Red's been sweet on you since you got here, Sarah. You want to bring someone cobbler, you think about bringing it to him. He'd make you a good husband."

I twirl the string in my hands, tangling it. "Henry Taylor's the only reason Master Thomas got on that horse. The way I see it, he earned that cobbler. Red don't have a thing to do with it." It's the truth of the matter, but not the heart of it. I move to the far side of the garden against the brick wall, away from her, and pick off stray leaves from the tomato plants.

"I'm telling you, folks take meaning in a thing."

"Ain't you got some spinning you need to be doing?"

She walks the last stretch up to me and puts her hand to my shoulder. "You been spending time with him by the horse field, at the coach house, daytime, evening time. It's more than Red and Zeek that's seen you."

"I fixed his hand is all. And he helped with the horses, so I gave him some cobbler. Folks ought to keep their noses in their own barley sacks and leave off worrying about mine."

She plants her hands on her hips and her feet wide apart. "Standing all cozy last night, is what I heard. Pressed up against an empty plate."

"It wasn't nothing. Don't know why Red even told you."

"'Cause Red knows there ain't nothing that's nothing. You're a grown-up woman. What do you think that white man wants with you?"

"He's not after me like that."

"Oh, Lord, I'm talking to a fool. All the places you could be where they keep you on your back, pretty as you is. But you got lucky coming here and you want to go asking for trouble."

"I'm—" I say, but she holds up her hand to hush me.

"Now, I'll tell you straight. If you start in on some foolishness, Master won't have it. He don't sit for no sin. That's in the Bible. You can't abide no sin in your house."

"Well, I ain't sinning." I turn back to the tomatoes. "Nothing wrong with giving a man a plate of food." I pluck at leaves that don't need picking.

Behind me, Bessie huffs. "As long as that's all you been giving him."

I whip around to face her straight on. I want my words to be like a slap, to knock that kind of talk right out of her head, before it catches and spreads. But what I'm fixing to say dies when I open my mouth. We both know I didn't go in there for cobbler. I hold my tongue and watch her march herself on out, picking through the plants with a sureness to her step like she can see just fine.

Chapter 18

Maple

Master Jeremiah ain't got no patience for staying at Jubilee. After not finding Freddy and two nights of visiting, he's ready to go, and Master and Miss Martha are ready for him to get gone. When Red and Zeek bring his wagon and horses around, I hurry over with a traveling lunch, hoping for a last chance to ask him about my family. He comes out with Kitty trailing behind, carrying his satchel. She's got on her blue silk dress. The high ruffled collar and her dark skin hide most of the bruises on her neck, but not all. She don't look left or right, just sticks her chin in the air staring up into the trees.

I hand Master Jeremiah his food sack and say, "When you see my momma, please tell her I was sorry not to see her this trip. How is she, Master Jeremiah? Is she doing all right?"

Kitty slows to almost a stop before she picks up her pace and climbs in the carriage.

Master Jeremiah's eyes slide off me and land on the far trees. "I don't see much of your mother these days. She's not working in the house anymore."

Zeek ties the satchel down, tightening the rope, looking away from me. Kitty sits stiffly in the wagon.

"Why not, Master?" I ask, playacting like I know nothing.

He tips his face to where the mountains sit smoky blue above the treetops. "I sent her to the fields," he says, studying the horizon.

Miss Martha gasps. "Clemmy, in the fields? What on earth for?"

I hold my breath waiting for the answer.

"Because she forgot her place, and I do mean to remind her of it."

I sink in my bones. She must've been fighting him on selling Rose. Can't think what else she would've dared speak against him on.

"Master Jeremiah, did you sell my Rose?" I can't stop the words from spilling out my mouth. I'm shaking and tears already fill my eyes.

"Father! How could you sell Rose?" Miss Martha takes my hand. "Don't worry, Maple. We'll buy her back. She's like family to us. Isn't that right, Father?"

He glares at his daughter, a warning in his eyes. "I did not sell Rose. She's where she belongs."

It feels like the ground keeps shifting under my feet. I'm light-headed with grateful. Rose is safe at Belle Grove Plantation. But then why did Freddy run? And what did Momma do that got her sent out working the fields? Or not do? Holding thoughts feels like holding fish. Every time I think I got one clear, it slips through.

I think of what I saw in the bedroom, and of all the years of that man prodding at her, and I guess it's a wonder Momma didn't forget her place a long time ago.

Master Jeremiah climbs into his carriage beside Kitty and lays his hand on her lap, tucking his fingers between her thighs. Miss Martha flattens her mouth and turns away. Leaning out of the buggy he says, "You'll let me know if Freddy turns up here. And, Maple, I'll give your regards to Rose."

I still have so many questions, but relief has stolen my tongue. He taps the frame of the trap and Zeek drives the horses on.

Chapter 19

Henry

I hammer out the iron and turn the ends while it's still hot. Reheat and turn. Reheat and turn. It's a foot-high cross. High enough to mark a grave, but small enough for the Johnsons to let it stand.

When I finish it, I take it out to Bessie in her cabin. Ben's laid out on the bed. Today he goes in the ground.

"I thought you might like to have this," I say. I place the iron cross with the curled ends in her hands.

She runs her fingers over the length of it and the height of it, feeling the stretch and shape of the metal. "Thank you, sir," she says. She tears up as she clutches it to her chest. The sorrow and gratitude wrapped in those two words could knock you over.

I turn to leave and find Sarah just outside the doorway.

"That was a kind thing you done," she says.

When Maggie and Beth died on the coffin ship, all I could do was pitch them overboard, sputtering what Bible words I could remember, but, in my mind, they got a proper burial. In my mind, I marked their graves with an iron cross with curled edges. I don't tell Sarah that the cross is as much for my sisters as it is for Ben.

"It seemed the right thing," I say. I want to ask her to step out with me somewhere. Anywhere. I haven't been close to her since the cobbler. But a burying day isn't the day for it.

"She's going to miss him something fierce," she says. "They had a lifetime together."

I hadn't guessed it was otherwise, and I realize they easily could have been sold from each other and never had the chance.

I make my way past the slave huts and the fields down to the burial site. The slave graves lie out of the way, off in a far corner of the plantation. A cluster of forty slaves with long faces and slow movements has gathered in the tall grass.

No one speaks, which seems to me a strange way to gather, even in mourning, but then I see Mister Johnson standing just past the grave clutching a Bible in his hands. He eyes me strangely when he spots me walking up the path, but says nothing.

Bessie soon comes up behind me, with Sarah on one side and Clover's square-jawed wife, Callie May, on the other. Behind them, Bessie's two sons carry the front of Ben's box, while Red takes the back, along with another field hand, all four walking with deliberate steps. It's a rough pine box, but it's solid built, and it's going into the ground with him.

When the famine took my little brother, there'd been so many buried that timber was hard to come by. For his coffin, the wood was cut so thin it sagged with the weight of Dermot's body, which is saying something because he hardly weighed anything in the end. After we lowered him into the grave, and Father Michael said the prayers, Ma didn't want to leave. Father Michael pulled me aside and told me to take her home.

"She'll stay out of the way while they finish burying him," I said. "And you needn't wait with her. We don't want to keep you from your work."

He shook his head. "It's not that. It's the coffin. We'll be needing it back." He flushed like I'd caught him at grave robbing, and I felt like I had. "We can't get coffins as fast as we get bodies," he said. "We try to comfort the families with seeing a proper burial, but, when you go, we'll lay him in the ground and bury him so."

As Ben's procession reaches the grave, Mister Johnson waves them on with a hurry-up gesture. They lower the coffin quickly. Clumsily. I swallow to clear the knot forming in my chest, but it sticks there.

Mister Johnson steps up close and Sarah slips off to the side of the gathering, away from the pack, like she doesn't rightly belong, or doesn't want to. Red sees me watching her and moves to stand beside her. She crosses her arms and angles her body from him, and I mark the tension hanging between them, heavy and charged like the air before a storm.

"We are all sorry to lose Ben," Mister Johnson says. "And, Bessie, I know you feel this blow keenly, but take comfort. Ben was God-fearing and the Lord will raise him up to his rightful place in Heaven."

He opens his Bible and reads from the Psalms, "Yea, though I walk through the valley of the shadow of death, I fear no evil." He talks about Ben's dutiful and obedient life and praises him as a model for everyone else to follow. Then he has the men shovel dirt on top of Ben's box. He says a blessing over the grave, pats Bessie on her back, and leaves for the house.

The rest gather around the fresh grave speaking their own tributes. Giving him a good end. The loss of my family is still fresh enough that it's them I'm thinking of, no matter what's being said about Ben. I try to hide my tears with blinking and swiping. Clover and Samson start up a song of passing, a simple tune and refrain. I've never heard it before, but everyone else knows it. When they repeat the chorus for the third time, I join in. Straight off, the others stop singing. It's like the night of fiddle playing by the fire. This is their grief, and I'm not a part of it. I mean no disrespect, but, in truth, if an Englishman came to Dermot's funeral—even if he hadn't been a landlord; even if he hadn't captained a ship that carried

Irish food to English markets—I'd have struck him before I let him cry at my brother's funeral.

I look at Bessie, clutching my cross in her hands. I know that kind of pain and I've no wish to make it worse. I turn to go, catching Sarah's eye. When I've rounded the bend, a man starts up a song about going to Heaven along the Jordan River. I guess that it's Red's voice and I keep walking.

Chapter 20

Sarah

Folks have been looking at me and whispering about me and I keep my distance from all of them. Red, Bessie, Maple, and even Henry. Whatever thing I might be feeling for him, at the end of the day, he's just a white man passing through.

In front of the kitchen house, I got a basket of peas for shelling, and I'm near about through when Red comes hovering.

"You think those clouds might blow this way?" he says.

I keep shelling. I don't care where the clouds blow.

He swoops down into my bowl and takes up a handful of peas and stuffs them in his mouth.

"Keep your hands out of here," I say. "I'm not doing all this work for you to fill your belly."

"Why don't you set that down and come take a walk with me?"

I shake my head. "Why don't you leave me to my own self?"

"I want to talk to you. Alone."

I know what he's going to say and I've heard enough about how I need to stay away from the blacksmith. I keep shelling and he watches me do it.

When I get to the last ones, he says, "I need your help. Something important."

The way he presses the words out makes me stop and really see him. His tensed-up shoulders and restless moving tell me what his too-big smile is trying to cover up. He's in some kind of trouble.

I nod and he strikes off along the row of huts toward his cabin with me following.

He ducks into his doorway and closes the door behind me. His cabin's almost the same size as Bessie's from the outside, but inside, with him taking up all the air, it's a lot smaller. There's a chair and table pressing in on one side and a rough-carved pinewood bed pressing in on the other, and him and me standing between.

I wait for him to tell me what's wrong, but he hems and haws so long I just ask.

"What happened?"

"You can't tell nobody."

"Who'm I gonna tell?"

"Swear you won't."

"I promise," I say. "What'd you do?"

He pokes his head out the door to make sure no one's around. Then he pulls me further in, right up against the back slat-wall. He huddles close and drops his voice and says, "I found someone."

"What do you mean?"

"He came all the way from North Carolina. Left fourteen days ago."

He means a runaway and I push from him. I don't want to know about this.

"I need you to do something," he says.

"You crazy?"

"He needs food and rest and he'll be on his way. We just got to know when it's safe."

"Why you asking me? I can't help him."

"You sleep in the Big House. You're the only one. You can tell us when Master and all the rest fall asleep. And if he gets up in the night."

I shake my head.

"All we need is a light. In the window. To tell us to go, or warn us to stay." He takes my hands, and I pull them away.

"I don't wish him no harm, but I can't help him. I'm not gonna get peeled open, or sold off, or strung up for some runaway."

"Ain't just some runaway."

A pounding in my ears makes it hard to hear him. All I can think of is that time on Summerville Plantation when a man ran. They gathered up his wife and children and sister and anybody else who might've had a hand in it and, after they whipped them, they chained them together in the smoke house and lit a fire and smoked them. One of the children died before Master let them out. Three weeks later, slave catchers brought back a body so beat up his own wife didn't know him.

"If some fool comes stumbling on to this plantation, it ain't nothing to do with me. The way I see it, he can keep on stumbling till he gets to the next one."

Red runs his hand over his face. The muscles in his neck twitch from pulling so tight. "I'm going with him."

I open my mouth but nothing comes out. I know the yearning I see in him. But the danger. "If they catch you—"

"That's why I need your help."

I take a step toward the door. And then another. "Ask Maple," I say. "Her husband ran. She'd help you."

"I don't trust Maple," he says. "She's woven in too tight and don't know if she's us, or if she's them. It's got to be you. One candle in the window. That's all."

I shake my head. "I can't be lighting safe signals with Master Thomas in the room. I can't be creeping around the house to see who's asleep and who's awake. I can't."

He paces the room and I see the tension in his back cramping his shoulders, stiffening his usual swagger.

"You can, but you won't."

"I can't. And I won't."

He comes up towering over me. There's a vibrating feeling to him, like he's coming loose out of himself. "We're going."

"I ain't trying to stop you. I just don't want no part."

His face shifts when I say that. Like a pond that freezes over in the winter with the same water that was there, but harder and colder.

"If you won't watch out at the Big House for me, maybe you'll just keep that blacksmith busy through the night. That's more your kind of help."

I haul off and slap his face and, when he don't act like he felt it, I slap it again. I charge out of his cabin with him hollering my name after me.

"Hold on," he calls out.

I keep marching.

Maple sticks her head out of the kitchen house to gawk at us. I stomp past her and pull out the carrots for tonight. Sitting down at the working table, I scrape them down with a knife in quick, jerky strokes.

"You're about to scratch the orange right out of that carrot. Something happen in there with Red?"

I'm boiling so hard inside I can't say a thing. Out of the corner of my eye I see Maple's face pulling up stiff, taking it like something against her that I don't talk.

The last thing I need is Red following me into the kitchen house, but that's just what he does. I don't pick my head up for him, but I can feel his eyes on my back. I hear his hand rubbing on his skin. The back of his neck, maybe. Or the cheek where I got him.

"I might shouldn't have," he starts to say, but then he stops. Sighs.

Maple leaves off greasing up a pan with bacon fat to listen in better, giving him all her nosiness.

"I'm sorry," he says. "But can you think on the other thing?"

"I done gave you my answer," I say, scraping. There never was carrots scraped so clean.

"But then, are you—"

"It's your business. I'm not fixing to talk to nobody about your business."

"All right then," he says after a stretch.

When he goes, Maple sucks her teeth and dumps a basket of potatoes on to the table. "That's 'cause you let that blacksmith sniff around you. Men get to thinking you a certain way."

"I'm not in the mood for you being hateful," I say.

"Not in the mood?" She tips the bowl of shelled peas on to the floor. Then she looks around and her eyes light on some herbs I bundled and hung to dry by the cook-fire. She cuts every last one down and tosses them into the flames. "You best believe, I don't care not one dead rat about your mood."

Chapter 21

Henry

There's no denying that blacksmithing is dirty work. The filth settles into your nail beds and into the wrinkles of your skin and the fabric of your clothes. Whenever I'm able, I dunk myself in the slow-moving river that flows just beyond the Johnson property to God knows where.

With my last scrap of soap clutched in my fist, I kick off my boots and wade in, clothes and all. I get most of the soot washed out, but my clothes are not what you might call clean. They need a proper washerwoman to have a go at them, but this trick keeps them bearable. When I think they're more or less presentable again, I peel them off, wring them out, and hang them over the branches of a nearby tree to dry. Then I splash back into the river and wash my body and my hair. The soap is nearly used now, and the little pieces keep floating out of my hands. I have to lunge after them over and over. Soon the soap is gone and I'm just enjoying a swim in the tempting warmth of early summer.

Up the path, I hear the jabbering of a boy and the calm, soft response of a woman. I know that it's Sarah and Thomas. From the pounding of his feet, I can imagine the boy jumping and bouncing in his excitement at whatever Sarah has come up with to amuse him.

I hear them come closer and I'm glad at the chance to see her, but my clothes are in the trees. I won't get to them before they reach me, so I stay put in the water, submerged to my chest.

It's Thomas who spots me first. "Look," I hear him call to Sarah. "There's a man in the river."

I don't want to frighten her, so I call out, "Morning!" and raise my hand in greeting.

Sarah shields her eyes and turns her back to me, but she also waves behind her, returning my greeting. "I'm sorry," she calls out. "We'll come back later."

"No, I can come out," I say, but she's already making her way back up the path, away from me, pulling Thomas by the hand.

I climb out, grabbing my still moist trousers and shirt, and pull them on. They cling to my skin as I work them over my wet body.

"Sarah," I call out, hurrying after them. When I reach her, I'm out of breath, my wet hair dripping into my eyes. "I didn't mean to scare you off."

I guess I look a fright because she takes a step away from me.

"We're looking for special plants," Thomas tells me. He slips his hand from hers and runs down to where my shoes sit by the river.

"Come on now, Master Thomas, we should go," she calls.

He ignores the summons, so we both follow after him. Sarah hangs back from me, keeping her distance.

"They grow by the river," he says. "And they look like… Sarah, what do they look like again?"

"They got thin leaves and they're deep green," she answers reluctantly, "but we can get them some other time."

He picks a limp weed and holds it up. "Is this one?"

Sarah comes closer to where Thomas and I stand.

"Almost," she says. "The leaves should be thinner and less shiny."

In the basket she holds, she's already collected all manner of weeds. The only ones I recognize are the dandelions.

"I want to go swimming," Thomas shouts from the riverbank, already kicking off his shoes.

"No, Master Thomas. It ain't safe," she says. "I can't save you if you start to drown. You got to do that with your daddy."

"But he never has time to take me swimming. I won't drown, I promise," he says, stripping off his shirt.

"I'll mind him," I say, as he goes for his trousers.

Thomas grins and plunges into the water.

Sarah watches him wade in, fingering the necklace she wears at her throat. Two half circles carved from wood. "I can't swim," she says, quiet. Like it's a confession. Like she wants to be saying something else.

She takes a few steps upriver and strips some leaves off a bushy plant. Her back is to me so I can stare brazenly. Her coiling hair is piled on top of her head, exposing the back of her neck, and her dress is cinched tight around her waist, accentuating the flare of her hips.

I come up to her and, peering inside her basket, I ask, "So, what are all of these good for then?"

"That's for fevering," she says, pointing. "That's for coughing, that's for the stomach, that's for pain."

"Are any of those what you used for my hand?"

I flatten my palm and hold it between us. The scar is almost gone, but I want her to take my hand in hers and run her fingers over what remains of the mark.

"No," she says. "That was yarrow." She doesn't touch my hand.

"And the dandelion?" I ask. "What's that one do?"

"That's for Master Thomas. For his stomach."

I'm surprised she uses her remedies on Thomas. I don't suppose the Johnsons would be pleased to know she's giving their son weeds, but I don't mention it. "Where'd you learn all this?" I say instead.

"Momma showed me. She says the good Lord provides when the other one don't." Her hand flies to her mouth and she claps her wide eyes on me, frightened at her carelessness.

"You don't have to guard your words with me, Sarah. I want to know what you really think."

She searches my face, saying nothing. I don't know her looks well enough to know what I see there. Doubt or belief.

Gently, I pull her hand from her mouth. "You can trust me," I say.

She slips it from my grasp. "I should go."

"No, please stay," I say. I want to reach out and smooth the frown lines from between her eyebrows, but I clasp my hands together. No more touching.

"You're not watching me, you're watching Sarah," Thomas shouts from the river. "You're supposed to be watching me."

Sarah looks at me and I smile.

"Guilty," I say. "But, Thomas, you have to admit," I call out to his bobbing form in the river. "Sarah's prettier to look at."

She steps back from me, clutching her basket. "Time to go now, Master Thomas."

"Sarah," I say, not knowing what to say next but wanting to keep her talking. Keep her here.

"Come on and swim out of there."

"I could help you gather when you need more," I say, laying my fingers on her basket. It's between us like the plate on the night of the peach cobbler. I'm desperate to get back to that moment. "You could let me know when you're coming out here."

"Thank you, Mister Taylor, but I—"

"Please," I cut her off before she can refuse me, my borrowed surname grating in my ears. "Please." I don't rightly know how to finish. There's so much I want from her. "My name is Henry," I say. My voice cracks, embarrassing me, but her eyes soften. Then her face relaxes and there is an ease to being there together.

"Henry," she says.

A splashing of water takes our attention. Thomas climbs on to the riverbank, shaking himself like a hound.

"You see. I didn't drown," he says, naked and dripping wet.

He waits for Sarah to help him dress, squirming and making it hard for her. It disturbs me to see her kneeling in front of him, coaxing him into his breeches.

"I guess now I've seen everything," I say.

They both stop and look at me.

"This young man's old enough to get up on a horse, and old enough to swim in a river, but he still needs help putting on his own clothes." I shake my head like I'm considering how absurd it is. "I guess you're not as big as I thought," I say. "You see, I thought you were six, or at least five, by your actions, but now, well, I guess I was mistaken."

"I am six," Thomas says.

"Can't be," I say. "Not if someone else dresses you like you're a baby."

Sarah leans back on her heels, looking from me to him and back again.

"She dresses me every morning. When I wake up."

I frown at him. "You wait for her to come to you to put your own clothes on?"

Thomas shakes his head. "She sleeps in my room."

I take a step back, like the news is knocking me over. "That's just what I'm talking about. I've never heard of anyone but a baby having a thing like that." I can see that I've upset him, and I guess that's what I was trying to do. "I suppose," I say, "you grew so fast your ma didn't realize how big you'd gotten. I guess she needs you to tell her that you've outgrown all the babying."

Sarah pinches her lips to hide her smile. She stands and takes a step away from him. "You want to finish by yourself, Master Thomas?"

"Perhaps you ought to turn around, Sarah," I say. "A young man needs some privacy."

She turns around, and I wink at Thomas and he winks at me and pulls his own clothes on.

Chapter 22

Sarah

I been washing my hands raw, trying to scrape the stains out of Master Thomas's clothes. Missus don't hold with giving the child play clothes and it's my fingers that got to pay the price. I stretch the washing line across two trees in the yard. Pulling it tight, I get to hanging.

I don't get but halfway done when Master comes marching around the side of the house. He's got three men with him and all four are stepping my way. I recognize fat Mister Gantly who's always coming to complain about something, and his overgrown son lumbering behind him. The last man, short and greasy-headed, I don't know.

Master looks like he swallowed a mouthful of sour. "Sarah," he says.

I stop my clothes hanging. "Yes, sir?"

"These men are looking for a runaway. A buck around twenty years old."

"You seen him?" Mister Gantly cuts in.

It must be the one Red was hiding. And since Red's still here, he must be here too. I try to make my face go blank. "I ain't seen no runaway," I say. "I ain't seen nobody here what don't belong here." It's the truth, too. I never saw Red's runaway.

"You sure about that?" Mister Gantly asks, poking me with a chubby finger.

"I swear, I ain't seen him," I say.

"All right," Master says. "If you hear of anything, you let me know."

Mister Gantly's son grabs hold of my face and scowls into my eyes. His fingers dig at my cheeks, mashing them to my mouth. "She knows something," he says. His breath smells like a thing gone rotten.

My heart's racing, fit to burst out of my chest, and I know my eyes are wide and guilty looking.

Master steps up and knocks his hand off my face. It jerks me sideways and I stumble, falling into the grass.

"You may do what you wish with your own slaves, on your own plantation, but I am master here, and you will not touch any slave of mine."

"She knows something, I tell you," Gantly's son says.

As the men argue above me, I glimpse Red running toward the field slave quarters like Beelzebub himself was after him. He's seen the men. If he don't get that runaway out of here, it's both their necks.

"She swore she didn't. I'm satisfied with that." Master turns to me, where I'm still sprawled on the ground. "Finish your chores, Sarah." He walks on toward the slave cabins. "Come on, if you're coming, gentlemen," he calls to the men over his shoulder.

They file past me, glaring at me as they go. The short one, the one I don't recognize, gives me a silent kick as he passes.

"Ouch," I squeal, clutching at my hip just above where he kicked me, so my hands don't cover the mark clinging to the cloth from the greasy man's boot.

Master stops his stride and turns back.

"You kicked my slave?" His sour is getting angry, just like I hoped.

I pretend more pain than I feel, struggling to sit up, putting on a show.

"I let you on to my plantation," he roars, "generously aiding your search, and you disrespect my authority over my property?"

"She knows something," the little greasy one says.

"I don't care if she knows the whereabouts of every damn runaway in the state. You don't tamper with what's mine." Master's near about got fire coming out of his eyeballs.

Red's out of sight, down the other side of the hill, so I stand, careful to limp a little bit, and brush myself off. With long, sure strides, Master marches on, trailing the three men behind him, not waiting for them to catch up.

It's near dinnertime when I come in with the washing finished and head to the stairs to put it all away. At the bottom of the stairs, I hear Master and Missus in the parlor.

"He's exactly the kind of man I'm fighting against. And the fact that he's so rich makes it worse. It's one thing to argue poor rations and rags as a temporary measure until you become profitable, as Parson does, but to have the means and choose to abuse them."

I know he's talking about the men from today and the slave that ran. I listen in, worried for Red.

"Matthew," I hear Missus say, "you can't force people to be better men."

"But don't you see, Martha, that is exactly what this new bill would accomplish. If we could pass legislation regulating slave treatment, we could enforce decency and morality within all the plantations. And fire a deathblow to the abolitionists in the North who claim that we all treat our slaves so barbarously. They would have to give up that cry, and then where would their movement be?"

"I'm sure you're right, but I just don't see how people are going to let a piece of paper tell them how they should behave in their own homes, on their own land."

"Gantly's lost a thousand dollars on that slave who got away. When the planters see that the bill will keep their slaves from running, and keep the North at bay, they'll support me. I'll make them understand how profitable it is to have content and happy slaves, like me. Then they'll listen."

I heft the laundry basket on my hip and climb the stairs. Least I know Red's runaway escaped. Don't sound like Red ran with him, but if he did, Lord, help us all.

Chapter 23

Henry

I wait for her at the top of the hill by the horse enclosure, where I know she likes to come at night when her work is done. I'm bathed and shaved and I feel like a fool, but I also don't care. I've been pacing about and I'm getting myself worked up, so I sit in the tall grass, and pull out the strip of her dress that she used to tie up my hand. I run my fingers along it, rubbing it like it was my Ireland stone, as I stare out toward the Blue Ridge Mountains silhouetted in the distance.

Above the noises of the night, I hear her come up the hill toward me and I jump up and wave, so to not frighten her. She startles and stops walking, so I call out to her. I try to make my voice sound casual, but I'm nervous and I know she can hear it.

"Why you lying here in the grass, Mister Taylor?"

I tuck her dress strip back into my pocket and walk down to her, trying to settle my nerves. "It's Henry, remember?"

"I remember."

We regard one another, both unsure. I want her to trust me and I guess she's waiting to see if I'm trustworthy.

"You come up here for something special?" she asks.

"It seemed like a fine night," I say. "I thought I'd come up here and watch the stars."

She laughs. Above us the stars lay hidden behind a blanket of clouds with a pale half-moon shining through like a dull lantern. All around us the cicadas shout their mating call, sounding like a thousand desperate souls.

We both know I've placed myself here to meet her.

I crook my elbow for her to take my arm and she hesitates. And I wait. I hold myself back from reaching for her. The time drags on until finally, finally she slips her hand into the crook of my elbow. I lead her along the top of the hill, neither of us speaking. I walk with her as if I'm courting her, and I guess I am. I know plenty wouldn't approve, but with Sarah next to me I feel like I could fly.

I borrowed a blanket from Red, and I've spread it out on the grass to sit on.

"That for us?" she asks.

Us. I like the way the word groups us in together and holds us there. I nod at her and we sit.

"Back in Ireland I used to sit outside at night with my sister, Beth. We'd try to count the stars, but we never could. I guess that was the point. We always had a reason to come back out and try again."

"She still in Ireland?"

"No," I say. "She died." The pain of that memory rests under my skin. She spent her last days groaning in agony in the hold of a stinking ship. Coughing until she puked and shat herself from the force of it. And me holding her, willing her to get better, not just for her sake but for mine, scared to lose the only family I had left. "You would have liked her, I think. And she would have liked you back."

I feel the heat from her hand resting close to mine on the blanket and I shift my fingers so that I'm touching her. She doesn't move.

"I used to watch them with my brother, Isaac," she says. "You'd have liked him too."

I know by now that there's no Isaac on this plantation and her sad smile keeps me from asking about him. Whatever happened to Isaac, he's just as lost to her as Beth is to me.

I slide my fingers over hers and take her hand.

At first, feeling her hand in mine is all I can think about, but the longer we sit together, the more natural it feels, till it's like we've been holding hands since always, and her hand in mine is the only place it feels right to be.

She asks me what Ireland was like, and I tell her about the low stone walls and the ocean as far as you can see, and the lush green that's greener than anything in America. But I also tell her about the work and the famine, and about Dermot wasting away from the hunger, and Emily from disease. I tell her about the last harvest that failed and snatched the fight right out of Ma and Da. And how, soon as they were in the ground, me and my sisters left for a better life that killed Beth and Maggie before they could start living it. She leans into me, and it's like I've passed a kind of a test.

I trace circles on her hand with my thumb as we stare into the sky, and she tells me that she used to have a doll named Star.

"Isaac named it," she says. "I called it Doll for the longest time and he said it needed a name, so when we were out looking at the stars he named it Star. Momma sewed it with burlap from a cotton sack and stuffed it with pilfered cotton. It had two mismatched buttons for eyes sewn into its head. I took that doll with me everywhere."

As she speaks, I can't believe my own joy. I'm happy just to hear her saying things meant only for me to hear. Us.

Above us the clouds shift and hide the moon and around us the cicadas sing on.

It's late and she's tired, and I guess I am too, but I'm not ready for her to go yet. I lie on my back and ask her to join me. When she does, I wriggle closer to her until we're side by side, hand in hand.

"Sarah, can I ask you something?"

"I guess so," she murmurs.

I turn my head to hers and see her eyelids drooping. "Are you going to slap me if I kiss you?" I say it soft and quiet and close to her face.

She blinks a few times, becoming alert again. "If you kiss me?" she asks. She turns to look at me and I kiss her gently.

"Like that," I say.

"I ain't gonna slap you."

"Good." I reach up and stroke her cheek. "I'm going to kiss you then."

She smiles at me. "You just did."

I shake my head. "That was just for permission. This is the kiss." I kiss her then. I let her feel my longing and my need, and when I'm afraid I've shown her too much I pull back. I search her face as her mouth slides to a shy grin.

"Was that the kiss?" she asks. "Or was you still practicing?"

I'm grinning too and I squeeze her hand because I can't help myself. "That was it."

"Well, I didn't slap you."

"No. You didn't."

I walk her back down the hill past the big house and over to the slave cabins. She's been moved from Thomas's floor to a pallet in Bessie's cabin. We stop outside the door. We.

"I have something for you," I say. I'm bashful, though I want to be bold. I ease a green scarf out of my pocket and offer it shyly.

She takes it in both hands and strokes it. "You get this for me?"

I nod. "I was in town and I saw it, and I just thought…"

"I ain't never had nothing this soft before," she says, and caresses it to her cheek.

I feel ten feet tall. She looks up at me with gratitude and affection and lifts on to her toes to kiss me on my cheek.

"Thank you, Henry."

Then she ducks into the cabin and I'm left floating in the clouds.

Chapter 24

Sarah

I been waiting weeks to find the right time to ask, or else to find the courage, but, come one Saturday, I do. Missus is in as good a mood as I'm likely to find her, fed with her favorite food, sitting in her favorite parlor that I done cleaned three times over when it weren't even dirty, so she don't have cause to say no.

I knock at the door and come slinking on in. "Sorry to bother you, Missus, but can I ask you something, ma'am?"

"Of course, Sarah. What is it?"

I shuffle my feet as I try to find the words even though I practiced a dozen times. "Well, ma'am, I was wondering. I have my free afternoon coming up. Tomorrow. And Missus Welleby, when she had her baby last month, she said she'd have me back on my free afternoons to do some cleaning and extra washing and all. She said she'd talk to you about letting me hire out."

She pinches her lips and I know already what her answer's going to be. "Missus Welleby spoke to me about this, but I let her know it was a foolish notion. I let you work there out of Christian kindness. I knew she couldn't cope with that new baby on top of the other three, and barely a house girl in sight. But the Lord's Day is not meant for scavenging around for pennies, Sarah. I would have thought you had enough Bible in you to know that."

"Yes, ma'am."

"Besides, you don't need money. You're well provided for here."

"Yes, ma'am."

"You want for nothing."

"Yes, ma'am."

She cocks her head watching me. "I know what this is about," she says with a voice like skipping stones. Bouncy and light, but heavy all at the same time. "I see you're wearing a new scarf."

I touch my head thinking of Henry giving it to me. My smile flashes out before I can pull it back in, but she's seen it. "This here was a gift."

"And I can guess where it came from."

The bottom drops straight out of my stomach. Maybe Master and Missus ain't so blind as they seem.

"Oh, Sarah. I'm not angry," she says, seeing my worry. "I've seen the way Red stands close to you and talks right up in your ear. Smitten, I'd say."

"You seen what?"

"He must have bartered for it the last time he drove his master into town. Well, no harm in that, I suppose."

For a second my mind goes stupid, thinking to correct her with the truth. I mash my teeth together to keep the words in.

"And I can understand you wanting to buy him something in return." Standing, she walks over to me and I grip at my skirt, staring at my feet.

"You're at an age where you should be paired up, and Red's a good choice for you. I'll have a word with your master."

"Please don't say nothing, Missus. Please don't." I wish, for both our sakes, he'd gotten away with his runaway.

"You leave it to me." She pats me atop my head. "And let's have no more talk about earning money on a Sunday. He'll hardly expect you to come with a dowry."

Chapter 25

Maple

On Saturday afternoon, Willa catches me in the kitchen house staring off into nothing, thinking on Rose and Freddy and Momma.

"Master wants to see you in his study," she says, pulling me out of my thoughts.

My belly twists like a worm on a hook. Master never wants to see me.

His door's wide open and I shift on my feet waiting for him to look up from the papers scattered over his wooden desk. When he does, he waves me into his room that has books for walls. The air is stale and suffocating. He leans toward me in his high-backed chair and folds his hands. I stand in front of him fidgeting.

"They caught Freddy," he says. "Trying to get up North. My father-in-law had him whipped and sold."

"Sold?" I say, my breath coming up short. That ain't right. We gonna be together when Master Jeremiah passes on. He can't be sold. "Maybe, can I talk to Master Jeremiah? Freddy ain't never been no trouble before this. I know he'll get right again."

Master's mouth sags low. "It's too late, Maple. He's already in a coffle headed to Mississippi."

"I can't see him?" It's a fact pretending to be a question, and a question pretending we got hope. I start to cry, but my eyes stay dry. My back stays straight. It's just my breathing that shudders and gasps. My heart hurts thinking of him shackled in a line, marching down Mississippi way, leaving me and Rose for good. Sold for money Master Jeremiah don't even need.

Master gives me a minute to put myself together, but when I can't quite do it, he says, "All this could have been avoided if only he hadn't run."

I ball my hands into my skirts at my sides. I won't blame Freddy for wanting to be free. There ain't a slave alive who don't want that. I only blame him for leaving Rose. "It don't make no sense that he'd just up and leave," I say.

"I suppose he's changed from the man you remember. I'm told he'd grown obstinate and aggressive. He got a severe whipping for attacking a gentleman. A relative of the household, in fact. I know this is unexpected, but I hope hearing what sort of fellow he's become will help you put him behind you."

I'm so mad I shake with it. At Master Jeremiah, at Master, at whoever bought my husband, at whoever caught him. But mostly I'm mad at Freddy. He's the one who promised he'd look after my baby when I left, and he can't do that chained up in Mississippi.

"Best you forget about him. We'll find you someone new. Maybe Samson."

I go to suck my teeth and scowl but catch myself and pull my face back to quiet.

"Well, we'll think on it," he says.

I bite my cheek so I don't say nothing about how you can't change out a husband like changing out a horse.

"That's all, Maple. You can get back to work."

"Master?" I say. My mind's churning. Something ain't right on Belle Grove Plantation. And now there ain't no one round the house whose looking after Rose. "You know I got a daughter?"

He nods, pulling some papers to him, half-listening.

"You been teaching us about God and the Bible and all that, and I been thinking, Master Jeremiah don't do some things like you preach them."

He folds his hands on the papers with a look like sucking on a lemon. "I'm aware."

"My Rose is a good girl, Master. And it sure would be nice if she could learn the good teaching like you tell us."

Master's eyes soften. "The good news of the Lord."

"That's it, Master. I pray she could hear you preach about it every week like you do. If only she could be here at Jubilee, she'd learn so much from a good master like you."

I chew at my lip and hold my breath.

He sighs. "I can't go around buying up every slave whose master doesn't stick to scripture."

"I know, Master," I say. "But I sure wish you could. Especially my Rose, my only child. It just breaks my heart that she won't get no salvation."

He purses his lips and frowns, but he don't say nothing, so I start in to singing, "Mary had a baby, oh my Lord." Singing soft and rocking with it like I got the spirit of God moving me. When I get to, "The people keep a-coming but the train done gone," I say, "The people keep a-coming, but not my Rose."

Master waves at me to quiet down, and says, "I suppose I could write to my father-in-law, see if he'll send the girl."

"Oh, bless you, Master," I say. "God bless you. You're gonna get a good one in Rose. Obedient like she is. And hardworking."

He shoos me away, and I back out of the room blessing everything I see. "Bless you, Master, and bless your house, and your books, and bless your furniture, and bless your paper." Whatever it takes to get my daughter away from Belle Grove.

June 1849

Chapter 26

Henry

Seems like there's no end to the things Mister Johnson wants mended or made, which suits me just fine. Every time I turn around it seems he needs another hoe or horseshoe. Today, I have half a dozen neck rings to mend and a new set of chains and wrist shackles to make. He's particular about how thick they need to be so that they can't be pounded through.

It's the start of June, and while blacksmithing can be counted on to keep a man warm in the winter, it'll bake you in the summer. I'm dying to get done with the day's work and jump in the river.

I match my breathing to the steady rhythm of the hammer. Three pounds for a breath in, and three for out. It keeps me from rushing. Steadies the blows. I try to focus on the iron getting nudged into shape with my hammer, but Sarah's face keeps floating through my mind. And the way kissing her melts my insides. I feel my swing going uneven. Stuttering when it should flow.

That's what I'm thinking about when Sarah turns up with a blueberry pie. She's got the green scarf tied around her head. When I see her, I stop mid-swing of the hammer.

"Afternoon," I say, getting up and coming over, wiping my hands on my rear because my apron is too dirty to get me clean. "I'm glad to see you," I tell her. I want to tell her more, but I don't know how to say it.

"Hello, Henry. I baked you a pie." She hefts it higher like an offering.

I pluck off my apron and lean in to smell. I'm close to her now, so I put my hand on her hip because it feels wrong not to touch her.

"It's blueberry," she says. I can feel her breath on my skin and the heat of her closeness. "I picked them this morning."

"Smells delicious," I tell her, but I don't want pie. I duck around the dish and kiss her cheek. "Thank you," I say. I take it from her hands and set it down on the workbench. "I'll get us a knife to cut it up. You'll eat it with me, won't you?"

I go to my wagon searching for my knife. When I find it, I see it's not been cleaned in a while, so I reach for my water pouch and a rag to wash it. The rag hangs on its peg but the water pouch is gone. I know I hung it here earlier, just before Annie called me out to the Big House to get Mister Johnson's newest assignment, and I wonder if she might've taken it. With no water, I wipe the knife down with the dry rag as best I can. When I get back to Sarah, she's looking over my work from the morning. The neck rings and the wrist chains.

"I had to clean the knife," I say

She jumps when I speak and takes a step away from me. "You made these?"

The tone in her voice makes me want to say "no," which would be a lie. Instead, I point to the neck rings and say, "Those ones I only fixed."

She doesn't say a word. Just stares at them.

"Mister Johnson hired me to do a job," I say, carefully. I can see the way she's looking at them, at what they must mean to her. I hate that I have them here. I hate that I made them, but what can I do?

"You know what they are?"

"I do." I take a step toward her and she backs up, bumping into the anvil.

"Sarah, I don't agree with the use of them."

"But you made them," she says.

"They pay me to make things."

She shakes her head with a look in her eye like I'm not who she thought I was.

"This is how I live," I say. "I have to feed and clothe myself. I take the work I can get and how I feel about what I make doesn't matter. What matters is getting paid."

She shakes her head at me. "You're a free man. You take whatever jobs you want. You can say no."

I clasp her arm, needing her to understand, but she cringes away from me like I might hit her, and I know I've made a mistake by grabbing her. I force myself to let her go and walk up to the workbench, picking up a neck ring. "I don't agree with this." But I can see something has shifted for her.

She stares at the ring and places a hand to her throat. "You ever have one of those around your neck?"

I can't answer her. I can't look at her.

She snatches up the shackles and thrusts them into my chest. "Or one of these around your ankles?"

I lay my hand over hers and she pulls it away, leaving me holding the cold iron.

I feel the shame choking me, but also the anger, because she doesn't understand what I've been through, or why I need to keep working no matter what.

"I've had shackles my whole life," I tell her. "Being poor is like a chain that squeezes tighter every time your empty belly rumbles, and I'll not be its victim again."

"It's like a chain?" she says. "Like the ones that cut your skin making your ankles bleed when they march you down to the auction block. Does it feel like that? Or like being hooked to the man in front of you and the woman behind you, keeping you hunched up, taking half-steps all the way from Charlottesville."

"You don't understand."

"And when a man down the line takes up a rock and hits at your poor-man chains, does he get whipped till he can't hardly stand? So everybody knows never to try to touch them chains again?"

"You've never known what it means to starve. To see your family shrink to skeletons and die of hunger."

She lays her hand over the links of metal on the table, like she's checking that they're real, and I can see she's trembling. She doesn't look at me as she says, "I know about dying of other things." She wipes her hand on her skirts and backs away. "I have to get on back to work now, Mister Taylor, before they start to miss me. Enjoy your pie."

Chapter 27

Sarah

Master's got a dozen friends over so I can't go to bed. My feet hurt from all the standing. I shift my weight and pick one foot up, barely off the ground, and curl my toes and circle my ankle. I sway my weight back and do the other foot, moving slowly so no one will notice.

"Why should we try to appease people who will never understand?" that Congressman Bocock with the chin beard asks.

Don't know why he thinks a snatch of billy-goat beard flapping around when he talks makes him look good. He holds his glass out and gives it a shake, and I come scrambling over with the bottle. They been drinking wine all night and now they done moved on to whiskey. Nearly got that bottle beat too.

"Congressman Bocock, you can't just dismiss the claims," Master says.

I slink back into my corner. I don't know what feels heavier, my arms or my eyelids.

Master holds his glass out for more and I know I'm going to be here a while. With a drink in his hand, Master can go on all night enjoying the sound of his own voice and the cleverness of his own thoughts.

"The critics are getting louder," he says, "and what they say has merit."

"No, it don't," shoots in Clayton Ridgemore. "You sound like my Boston brother-in-law, not a Southern planter, born and bred."

Master frowns. He don't like to be interrupted once he gets himself going. "The way some plantations are run is simply not Christian." Master looks at Mister Gantly when he says that, 'cause everyone knows at least five of his slaves are his own children.

"But why should we let Yankees have a say in the way we run things when they have no vested interest in the livelihood of the South." Congressman Bocock drinks down the rest of his glass and holds his hand out for me to come by again.

"Here, here," a few of them call out, and all dozen men nod their heads.

Master heaves himself up from his low-slung chair and steps into the center of the parlor. I can tell by his swagger that he's fixing to give a speech, so I risk leaning back against the wall to ease the tightness in my legs.

"Friends." He holds up his hand for quiet. "Forget the abolitionists for a moment. We are God-fearing Christian men. Southern landowners. Gentlemen. We have standards of acceptable behavior in our business dealings and in our society, and, I tell you, we must have clear standards in the way we deal with our property, especially our slaves." As he speaks, he catches the eye of each man, making sure he's got every one of them hooked on his words. "Now, our Yankee abolitionist countrymen have been making a lot of noise about the mistreatment of the Negro slave. We cannot ignore them as their cries grow louder. I say now is the time for legislation to silence them. We cannot count on President Taylor to side with the South, even if he is a Southerner. We must act, gentlemen. Before more territories become free states, and we're outnumbered in Washington. Am I right, Senator Hunter?"

A plump man with a long nose and angry eyes nods. "Maintaining a congressional voting balance is crucial for Southern concerns."

"That's why we need legislation that assures the righteous Christian treatment of slaves. With these laws, new territories cannot be prevented from becoming slave states on moral grounds. The other side will have nothing to complain about."

"They will always find something to complain about."

"And I'm not letting some Yankee get me to shackle myself with a lot of rules and regulations that will decrease production and profitability on my own plantation."

"Here, here."

Master holds up his hand for quiet again. "I understand your concerns, but look at this plantation. We do not whip slaves, except for the gravest of crimes. We do not separate families, unless absolutely necessary. My slaves are clothed and fed sufficiently. They have their own homes, hell, some of them even have a garden. My slaves are happy. In return for being well cared for, they work diligently and amenably, with the proper respect, and my plantation is prosperous." He waves his crystal glass full of expensive whiskey around the room, and their eyes shift from the framed oil paintings to the carved wooden moldings, to the marble fireplace I hunch beside, to me. I straighten up from the wall.

"This one's Sarah. She can tell you herself how true that is."

I tense up and almost drop the whiskey bottle. My eyes slip down, focusing just in front of my feet where the dark oak floor meets the Oriental rug. The edge of the rug throws a thin shadow on the wood and I try to put all my attention to that shadow, but I still feel the roomful of men staring at me.

"Sarah, tell these men what you think of working here."

I look over at Master, who nods to me to start talking, and twelve men lean in to hear me tell them how much I love being a slave.

I can't speak. I know what he wants to hear, but I can't make myself say what I'm supposed to say.

"Go on. They won't bite." I hear the impatience under his soft words.

"Oh, I don't know about that, Matthew." Mister Gantly steps closer to me, crowding me, looking me up and down. "I might like to sink my teeth into this one."

The men laugh.

I hate that Mister Gantly is close enough to hear my breathing change, coming out short and fast. I got the whiskey clutched up close to my chest and Master comes over, takes it out of my hands and sets it down on the fireplace mantle by his snuff box. Then he draws me forward, his grip clamped tight on my arm, and plants me in the middle of the room.

"As you can see, she's well dressed and well fed," he says.

He has me turn around so they can all get a good look at me, and it feels like being back on the auction block. I tremble and clutch my skirts to still my hands some.

"Sarah, are you beaten or harassed in any way here?"

"No, sir," my voice scratches out hardly more than a whisper.

"Are we good to you? Do you have food to eat? A blanket for the winter?"

I swallow at the lump building in my throat. "Yes, sir."

"And are you happy here?"

My heart's beating so hard my ears pound with it. There's only one answer allowed, so I say it, "Yes, sir."

"Thank you, Sarah, you may go."

I head straight out of the room before he figures out he didn't want to send me off, 'cause it's me who's supposed to be serving in there all night. I make it outside into the night and grab my head. My green headscarf slips off as I gulp at the air, feeling dirty and ashamed. *Am I happy?* I want to spit. On top of all the bowing and scraping and yes-siring, now I got to like it too? *Am I happy?* It's no kind of question to be asking. I sink to the ground. Am I alive? Am I surviving? That's all I been hanging on to.

Annie comes up from the kitchen house with a tray of ham and biscuits and sucks loudly at her teeth when she sees me hunched on the grass. "Why ain't you in that room? Maple gonna have your hide when she sees you out here." She turns back from where she's come, and calls out, "Maple. Ain't she supposed to be in that room?"

Maple peeks her head out from around the kitchen house and, when she sees me, comes storming up to us, hissing for me to get up.

"You supposed to be in there serving."

"Master said—"

"Don't you come at me with Master said. Your missus wants you in there, so you better get on back where you supposed to be."

From the corner of my eye, I see Annie balance the biscuit tray with one hand and swoop down and scoop up my green headscarf with the other.

As she tries to slip it in her pocket, I lunge for it and rip it out of her hands. "Get your thieving hands off my things."

Annie sucks her teeth at me again. "Can't nobody know whose it is if you leave it lying around like that." She turns and marches inside with her tray.

I smooth my hair and retie my scarf. "Master said I can go," I tell Maple.

"He did? Well, you left. And now you can get yourself back in there and serve the ham and biscuits like your missus said." She plants her hands on her hips.

All around us the cicadas belt out their call. I think of the last time I lay back listening to them, with Henry on the paddock hill.

I was happy on the hill that night.

Maple pokes at me. "Get on, now. I ain't gonna be blamed for your laziness."

The ache of tired in my arms and legs flares as I peel myself off the grass. At the door of the parlor, I hesitate, hearing the men even louder and drunker than a few minutes ago. I brace myself and walk back in.

"There is no way forward but secession. I don't know about you all, but I won't have Northerners telling me what to do on my own plantation." Mister Gantly has gotten red-faced in the time I was gone.

Annie is busy at the far end of the room, putting ham and biscuits on little plates. I cross over to her, pick up the plates and begin to offer them around.

"We are a fledgling nation. We should not speak so recklessly of dissolving what we have built." That's that Senator Hunter with the angry eyes.

"Agreed," Master says. "Splitting the country is a type of failure."

"Not if it preserves our values and our way of life."

"That would weaken the nation."

"It would weaken the North. The South will be fine. Seventy percent of American exports come from our plantations. We will be fine."

"We have to come to a compromise as a nation. If we leave, there will be war."

"It will be brutal. Brother against brother."

"I don't know about you, but my brothers are all in the South," Jesse Morton says, and the men erupt into laughter.

"I've got a sister up North," says Clayton Ridgemore. "But I'll tell you what, I wouldn't mind an excuse to have her husband at the other end of my Brunswick."

The men laugh again as I squeeze by Mister Gantly, who reaches out and grabs my bottom, pinching hard. When I jump and struggle away from him, he joins in the laughing with his deep chuckle, slapping his knee.

Across the room, Annie walks to the fireplace where I left the whiskey. She slides her hand over the snuff box next to it and slips it into her pocket. Then she takes up the whiskey bottle and fills every man's glass, easing through the room with no more notice than a shadow. I look over at Master, who's laughing with the rest of them, all of them joking about going to war.

Chapter 28

Henry

I'm working at my station with the sun beating down on my back when I see Sarah and Thomas go by. She doesn't glance my way as she usually would. I watch them walk toward the pasture on the hill where the horses will be.

My anger comes through in my blows, as I strike too hard at the chains I'm making. I hate the chains, and I hate what they will be used for, and I hate that she sees me differently because I make them.

But she's never had to earn money. She doesn't have to feed and clothe herself. If she did, she'd understand.

I finish the chain and lay my hammer aside, wiping the sweat from my hands and forehead. Then I stride up the hill to the horse enclosure. I see them as I reach the crest. They've brought apples for the horses and she places the fruit in Thomas's hand, holding his fingers flat and out of the way, encouraging him to feed them.

They're concentrated on the apple and the horse and don't hear me come up to them, until I'm right behind them.

"They're sure enough getting a grand treat today," I say.

Sarah's shoulders jerk at the sound of my voice, but she doesn't turn around.

Thomas, however, wriggles away from her and bounds up to me. "I can feed them. They like me and they don't want to hurt me," he announces. "Watch. They won't bite me." He scurries back to Sarah and takes an apple from her bag, then holds it out in the flat of his hand, glancing first to her for her approval and then to me with pride.

The horse nuzzles into his palm, taking the apple. Thomas turns to me and beams.

I smile at him, and then at Sarah, but she refuses to look at me. Her hair is tucked into the green headscarf I gave her and I'm longing to have things between us like they were the night I gave it to her. I need her to forgive me and understand that it's my living, and I don't choose what they hire me to make.

"Afternoon, Sarah," I say.

"We'd best be getting back, Master Thomas," she says.

"But we still have apples left." He reaches into the bag to show her. "Here," he says handing me an apple. "You can feed them too."

I take the fruit and sidle up next to Sarah.

We feed the horses in silence and when the bag is empty she tells Thomas again that it's time to go.

"It's such a fine day," I say. "Maybe Thomas wants to get on a horse. What do you say, Thomas?" I pat the smooth neck of the brown mare in front of me.

"Yes," he cries, jumping up with excitement.

"Take care he doesn't hurt himself," Sarah says. She turns from us and strikes off away from the paddock.

"Aren't you staying?"

She glares at me over her shoulder, but she stops walking. "You can take time whenever you like to do what you want, but I can't."

"Come on, Henry," Thomas calls from the mounting block, though the horse is on the other side of the enclosure.

I take a step closer to Sarah and lower my voice, "I don't get to choose my jobs, same as you. I make what they tell me, if I like it or not. It's how I survive."

"You do it for money."

"Making money is surviving. It's food and medicine, and coal to burn in the winter, and a home to live in. Money is life, and I know because I've been poor. Being poor will kill you like it killed my whole family, and thousands more besides."

"You're a free man. You could make something else for money. If you make chains, it's 'cause you choose to make them."

"Would you have me starve?" I say.

She's stares at me with the fiercest look I've yet seen on her, puffing angry breaths through her nose with me doing the same. "If you make shackles and chains for money," she says, "it makes me wonder what else you'd do for money."

In the humid air my clothes stick to my skin. His clothes. The dead man from New York. I shake my head. Clear the memory. "I need to live."

"Henry, I'm ready," Thomas calls from the block.

"Master Thomas's waiting on you," she says. She turns her back to me and storms down the hill.

"I need to live," I repeat to myself, watching her go. I tamp down my frustration and dig my hands into my pockets. Behind me, Thomas calls for me to get the horse.

Chapter 29

Maple

Standing in Master's study is like being in a cage with books on every side of you trapping you in. I once knew a slave who could have read them. A reading slave. Master Jeremiah bought him that way and, when he found out, he blinded him.

Master sits at his desk and points me to the chair across from him. I stand behind it, figuring he forgot himself, and I don't want to be sitting there when he comes back to his senses. He picks up a letter and puts it back down again.

"I've heard back from my father-in-law about buying your daughter."

From the flat line of his mouth, I know what he's gonna say, but I still clasp my hands, hoping.

"I'm afraid he's not inclined to sell."

There's a dropping in my stomach like falling from a cliff.

"It seems Rose is held in particular fondness." The pulled down line of his mouth says he don't think much of that.

My dropping feeling shoves outward, pushing up the hairs on my arms. Fondness ain't always a thing you want Jeremiah Keeler feeling for you. But he's her grandfather. Much as he don't want to admit that, he surely wouldn't forget it.

It feels like I got a fire blazing in my head, but my voice comes out soft as spring leaves when I ask, "Master Keeler take a shine to my Rose?"

He turns two shades whiter than his natural-born white, seeing what I'm asking. He shakes his head. "His nephew, Nathaniel Keeler, has become a frequent visitor. My father-in-law tells me that your daughter is a particular comfort to him." He dips his chin, looks at his desk.

I grip at the high-back chair in front of me, clutching with both hands. Nathaniel Keeler is the worst kind of no good. Hearing his name splits me open like gutting catfish. I want to scream. I want to pound my fists and tear the walls down. Time was, he made me his special comfort. I get hot and cold with the shame of thinking about those days. How he liked to grab at me when folks turned their backs. How he'd laugh when he scared me, springing out from behind the smoke house. How he smiled when he called me and I came, trembling. How he made me look at him when he did what he did.

That last winter he came to stay, he'd wait for me to lay the morning fire in his room. When I got it going, he'd close the door and lay me down on the cold floorboards. One hand on my mouth in case I howled.

I never talked to Freddy about it but, when Rose came out dark brown, he lay his cheek to hers and called her "my child" and cried over her. And he thanked God.

I thanked God that after Rose, Master Nathaniel stopped coming around the plantation. Maybe he didn't like that she was my husband's baby. Maybe he just got busy somewhere else.

Or maybe he was waiting on Rose. "She ain't but thirteen years old."

Master's got the good grace to squirm in his seat. "I know this is disappointing news," he says, "but I've done all that I can. It's in God's hands now. I recommend you pray."

"Master," I say. "Who was the white man Freddy put his hands on?"

He shakes his head like he don't want to answer, but then he sighs and says, "Nathaniel Keeler."

My mouth is dry as a stone. Freddy. Whipped and sold trying to protect his girl. And Momma. That's what she nagged her way to the fields about.

"Can you ask Master Jeremiah again?" I say. I feel like my bones are melting. I lean against the chair to keep me from tipping over.

He scoffs, snatching up a pen and tossing it back down. It skids across his desk, over the edge and falls to the floor by my feet. "My father-in-law is grooming his nephew to take over Belle Grove Plantation. An inheritance that should be mine, by right of my wife. He'd disinherit his own grandson so as not to oblige me," he growls.

I swallow past the choking in my throat. Master Nathaniel might get Belle Grove. My heart near about stops and I can't help the noise that rises up in me like someone dying. I ball my hands so I don't scratch his face. All his fool-headed talk about treating slaves better ain't worth a damn if this is what it gets me. My Rose owned by that devil. I swipe at my eyes and blink hard. I will not cry in front of this man.

"He's a spiteful old man and he means to control me with this. He thinks he can stop me from pursuing my legislation."

I'm breathing so hard my head's starting to spin. "Maybe," I say, my words weightless as air, "maybe Miss Martha could talk to Master Jeremiah?"

He shoots me a look fit to burn through my head. "I will not send my wife to argue on my behalf."

"But she could—"

"You're not listening, Maple. The issue is much bigger than Rose." He leans forward and stabs at his desk with his finger. "This is a chance to unify the nation in a slavery compromise. If we can silence abolitionist criticism in the North, we can hold new territories for Southern interests. Why can't he see that?" His anger is like a bad odor. He runs his hand across his mouth. The stubble on his face makes a scratching noise against his palm. "I will not be manipulated by my father-in-law."

On the rug, by my foot, lies his favorite pen. I step to the side and crush it. I hear the shaft crack under my weight and the metal tip snap. That's for Rose. But it's nowhere near enough.

Chapter 30

Sarah

Sunday morning we're all underneath the big walnut tree at the back of the house. Before he goes off to church every Sunday, Master comes out here and gives us his gospel. We stand there a spell and, when he's good and ready, Master comes striding on down the back steps of the Big House and across the yard to the edge of the garden where we all wait.

I know he's still thinking on Red's runaway because he done pulled out the old Philemon sermon again. He tells us that a Bible times slave ran away, but he became a Christian when he met Paul and came on back to his rightful master, Philemon. It's the one he likes to tell whenever there's talk of a runaway slave, in case anybody starts getting ideas. "You see, the Bible tells us all how to live," he says, waving his fat, brown book around in the air. "It tells us how to be a good wife and a good husband. A good father and a good child. A good master and a good slave. It gives us all the instruction we'll ever need. Now," he points at us with his old, tired-looking book, "can you guess why that slave went on home to his master?"

We stare at him, but don't say a thing. Far as I can see, he was a fool.

"When the slave became a Christian, he learned to do what was right. He was the rightful property of his master, Philemon. By leaving, he had stolen from his master. He had become a thief. But, by returning, he stopped being a thief. He did what was right and God forgave him all his sins."

The sun's shining in my eyes so I ain't much looking at him, but I feel when the attention shifts. I look up to see Henry coming around the house. He strides right on up to our gathering and then right on up to me. I stare straight at Master's feet, trying to pretend I ain't seen him come.

Master stops his sermon and asks him what he's doing there.

"I heard you talking about forgiveness, Mister Johnson, and I thought I'd like to hear about that."

"This is the service for the slaves. There's a service for us in town, Mister Taylor. Reverend Bates will be delighted to have you join us."

"Oh, no, sir. I'm not one for jockeying about on the Lord's Day of rest. This will do me just fine."

Master looks like he wants to say something to that, but he just shakes his head at Henry and gets on back to his sermon.

I can feel Henry standing beside me and I can't help stealing little glances at him. And he steals them right back at me. Master don't seem to notice, but Annie and Maple and Red and the others sure do.

Master's talking about how much God wants to forgive everybody, and how God loves it when a sinner repents. Seems to me if God loves forgiving so much then Philemon's slave should have lived a good free life and asked for forgiveness at the end when it was all over. He may have done what he done, but I know for sure, if I ever get free, I won't be marching myself back to bondage because some other free man thinks I ought to. How's a free man gonna go tell a slave he ought to go back to that? Now, if Paul said, brother, I'll take this burden for you and go back as a slave in your place, now that would be something.

I keep that to myself and I nod at Master.

Standing on my left, Henry leans in closer. "You've been avoiding me."

I inch away till I bump into Bessie on my right.

"We need to talk," Henry whispers.

I shake my head. "Ain't nothing to talk about, Mister Taylor."

"Sarah, please."

Bessie, standing on my right, gropes her way around me and puts herself in between Henry and me. Master don't pay her no mind at all. Then Red steps up from where he's been standing, close to Henry's left, and leans in like he's straining to hear. They're warning him off.

I should be feeling grateful, but I'm angry. This here's between Henry and me. Ain't got nothing to do with Red, or Bessie, or nobody else. I look over Bessie's head at Henry and he's looking back at me. I see how much he's been missing me, and, truth be told, I've been missing him too.

"Now, you all may have heard about a runaway slave from over on the Gantlys' plantation. Well, that there runaway slave is just like Philemon's slave in the Bible. A slave who ran away from his lawful master." He stops and looks round at us. "Now, I'm not going to pretend that he didn't have cause to be unhappy. Arthur Gantly is a hard taskmaster. And he doesn't believe in sparing the rod. But the slave had no right to run away. By running like that, he has stolen himself from his legal master. That was wrong. It was a sin. And God punishes your sins by throwing you in the fires of hell." Master looks around the gathering, lingering on anyone he thinks might have gotten it in his head to run. "Now, if he thought he had it bad as a slave, he's going to think he was in heaven when he gets to those hellfires. There'll be a lake of fire and brimstone. That's a burning hot stone. And when a sinner gets thrown in they burn forever and ever and ever. He'll be screaming and weeping and gnashing his teeth like a rabid dog, but he'll never burn up. He'll just keep on suffering forever." He looks around, lets that sink in.

Back behind him at the house Missus comes out on to the back porch and stands between the first two pillars. She's got a wide pink dress on and lace gloves with no fingers. Church clothes.

"You about done there, Matthew?" she calls to him.

He turns to her and waves that he'll be right over. "But there's good news," he carries on to us. "Because if that slave comes on back, like in the Bible, God will forgive him and he can go on up to the Promised Land. In fact, that's why God made him a slave in the first place, so he could hear about the gospel of Jesus Christ and be saved for all eternity." He nods his head as he scans the crowd. "So that's good news, right there. Good news from a good God."

Forty-eight blank faces stare back.

"All right, now. I'm going on to church. You all should sing a song."

There's a moment of hesitation. A silent shuffling. Resistance. Then Jim clears his throat and sings out in his honey baritone, "Swing low, sweet chariot."

We all join in with, "coming for to carry me home."

We're singing with all our heart and soul. Master looks pleased and hurries on off to his wife. He's pleased because he don't hear the anger and the longing and the determination. He don't know we're singing for that runaway. He don't see the tears on Jim's face when he sings out the last part. "If you get there before I do, tell all my friends I'm coming too."

He don't know it's a freedom song and we're singing it for the slave who got away, and for all of us left behind dreaming of the promised land.

Chapter 31

Henry

The chains are done. And the neck collars and the shackles. Mister Johnson is pleased with them and I am glad to have them out of my sight.

The new piece I'm working on is a decorative fireplace grate that he's asked me to make for the dining room. If I do a good job with it, it being the first decorative thing he's asked me to make, he'll have a lot more work for me. He's mentioned gate doors for the walled garden made of twisted iron vines, and a new handrail full of iron roses for the stairs.

I'm awkward with my hammer strokes. I should be tapping, coaxing the metal into shape, but my mind is stuck on Sarah and my frustration makes me clumsy.

The children who usually supply me with fresh water buckets haven't turned up, and I can sense that something is different on the plantation.

I stop my hammering and snatch up my bucket, meaning to head to the well, but the sound of a sharp crack down by the fields catches my attention and makes me curious. I strike off that way, just to see, and find a crowd gathered around a sycamore tree that grows beyond the overseer's cabin and the field slave huts. It looks like a Sunday church gathering, except those are held under the walnut tree on the lawn behind the main house, and it isn't Sunday.

As I draw up closer my ears prick at the swish and lick of the lash. I've heard about these plantation whippings, but in all my months down South, I've never seen one first hand. I hold back on the paddock hill and hear another blow. And another. I don't want to stay up here, hovering like a spy, but it seems cruel to go on about my day as if nothing were happening. There's a chance, I think, that another white face might keep the overseer's anger from getting too excessive with his punishment, so I make my way toward the gathering.

In the middle of a sea of black and brown, clad in the dull tan of homespuns, I can see the billowing white shirt and blond head of the overseer. There's a rhythm to the blows he's meting out. His body surges forward and back like a wave. This time, when he rears up for another blow, I get a view of a mahogany back, slashed and slick with blood. The slim waist and shoulders tell me instantly he's striking a woman and my stomach turns at seeing his brutality.

He pulls the whip back and when it crests in the air he brings it down again. Her wail is terrible.

Then I notice the green headscarf. The one I gave Sarah. The one she's worn every single day since, even though she's been angry with me. My breath stops.

When the overseer's arm arches back again and his whip dances in the air, I move. I don't remember dropping the bucket, but I'm aware I'm running without it. Sprinting to the overseer. The whip arches down again, clawing at her back, making her scream out in a pitiful howl of agony, seconds before I crash into the brute. He cries out as I tackle him. I rip the whip from his hands and jump up. Swinging it back, I bring it crashing down across his prone body. His shriek of surprise and terror eggs me on and I slash at him again, harder, ripping through his shirt and drawing blood. He rolls into a ball, shielding his head with his hands and I whip him again. I hear Sarah's voice begging me to stop.

I look up and I see her in front of me, arms outstretched, fingers splayed. I can't understand it. She's dressed, and there's no blood. I look over to the woman chained to the sycamore tree with her back open and her blood staining the skirts around her waist. I can see now, even from behind, that she isn't Sarah, but I walk around the side of the tree to where her face is turned anyway. It's Annie. The one I'm certain stole my water pouch.

"What the hell is wrong with you?" the overseer blusters and bellows from the ground. "I have every right to whip this thieving nigra, you son of a bitch! Mister Johnson said so." He throws a silver snuff box at my chest that I don't move to catch. It falls to the ground, spilling the snuff in the dirt. "You're going to pay for this, Taylor." He labors to his feet, shaking with rage. I can read the hate in his eyes and in the twist of his mouth as he shouts at me, his bellowed words mixing with his spit, "You hear me? You nigra-loving son of a bitch!"

Beside me, Annie whimpers. The bloody lashes crisscross her back. And Mister Johnson has allowed this. I can't stop it; this is Southern law and plantation justice. I feel Sarah's eyes on me, but I can't look at her. I drop the whip in the grass and walk away.

Behind me, I hear the overseer demand that Annie be stripped of her skirts.

"Now, we're gonna have a real whipping," he says.

When the lash cracks again, her scream scrapes at my bones. I force myself not to turn around. I keep walking with guilty, helpless steps, knowing that Annie will pay for what I did. And I can't let go of what I felt when I thought it was Sarah chained to the whipping tree. I'm breathing hard, walking fast, trying to get away from the sound of it: the whipping and the screaming.

I don't stop until I'm far from what's happening under the sycamore tree. At the river in the woods, I hear chirping and buzzing and the burble of the water, and I stand still, pulsing with feelings I can't put to words. I've known starving days and fever nights and waking up next to dead kin, but I've never known this.

I stay in the woods, staring at the river, until the daylight drops away.

Chapter 32

Maple

By the time Master Mulch tires himself out and hands Red the key to the shackles, Annie ain't got strength to stand. She hangs alongside the trunk of the whipping tree, her arms strung around a low branch, her naked body slick with blood.

Red unhooks her and Samson and Clover catch her and carry her to the cabin she shares with Willa. Callie May picks her clothes from the dirt, and then runs ahead to put a soft quilt on the bed and cover it with an old sheet so the blood don't stain it. With her back ripped to pieces, they lay Annie on her stomach. He got her from her shoulders to her knees. In some places, her flesh hangs loose. I ain't never seen a slave whipped so hard at Jubilee. A time or two at Belle Grove, but never here.

"We should tell Master what he done," Callie May says.

"You crazy, woman?" Samson scratches his fingers through his thick hair. "If Master Mulch finds you been talking on him, he'll get you good."

Callie May hugs around her own waist. "Red, you should say something. You ain't up under him in the fields."

"He don't need to be," Clover says, slipping an arm around his wife, pulling her to his side.

"We ain't saying nothing to nobody," Red says. "We ain't making this worse."

Willa comes in with a bowl from the kitchen house and a rag floating in it. She kneels next to Annie and dabs at her back. Annie's whimpering turns into yells.

"Leave her be," I say. "It's too raw to be touching on it."

"This here's from Sarah. She says we got to keep the infection out. She's brewing up something else for the pain and to help her sleep."

Red holds Annie's hands as she quakes and jerks and moans and whimpers every time Willa takes the cloth to her. Samson, Clover and Callie May leave for the fields and I leave for the kitchen. Whipping or not, I can't be late with supper.

In the kitchen house Sarah bends over my pots, brewing up her potions and mashing up a paste.

"That stinky mess for Annie?" I ask.

She nods, mashing and mumbling to herself. I leave her to it. Annie needs all the help she can get.

I take up the basket of collard greens and wash and cut them myself. When Sarah's done, she carries her pot and her paste out to Annie and I finish the meal on my own. When it's ready to serve, I go by the cabin and see Sarah and Willa hunched over Annie, dabbing paste on her back and laying soaked cloths over the top. They got her drinking some foul-smelling mess, but she's quieter.

I say, "I need someone serving with me," and they both look up. I take Willa and leave Sarah where she is.

When we walk into the dining room, Miss Martha looks at me surprised. I ain't come serving in a long time.

"Where's Annie?" she asks. "And Sarah?"

I cut a look to Master, who's got his scowl-mouth on, but she asked me, so I tell her, "Annie got a bad whipping, and Sarah's tending to her lashes."

"What's this?" Miss Martha says, looking to her husband. Worry lines wrinkle her forehead.

Master flicks open his napkin and lays it on his lap. "Her ten lashes were well deserved."

No one counted those lashes, but I'd wager it was closer to fifty.

"Thieving is against the Ten Commandments and the laws of Virginia." He reaches out and pats her hand. "Annie's been justly dealt with."

After supper, me and Willa leave the dishes stacked up and the dining room half cleared to check on Annie. Sarah's not there, but Bessie is, laying damp cloths over mounds of paste on Annie's back.

"Where's Sarah?" I ask.

"In the woods," she says, feeling her way from Annie's backside to the bowl.

She must be finding more herbs and weeds for her concoctions. For Annie. I let her be; me and Willa can take care of the dishes.

Chapter 33

Henry

In the woods by the river, the night sounds rise with the moon. The owls compete with the bullfrogs and, through the chorus of cicadas, I hear her call, "Henry."

I turn to see her coming up behind me. She's been pushing me away for days, but when I sweep her up into my arms she lets me, and thank God she does because I don't think I could let her go. She holds me tight against her and I am so relieved I cry.

"It wasn't you," I whisper.

She shakes her head and tucks it against my neck, wetting my collar with tears of her own.

"Oh, God. I thought it was you," I say, and I hold her closer. It's too tight, I know, but I can't think what to do but hold her tight. We stay like this for a while, until I can slowly loosen my arms. But I can't let her go. I've stopped my blubbering and I'm just trying to get my breathing back. "If that bastard ever whips you, I'll kill him."

She lays her fingers on my lips. "Don't talk that foolishness."

I take her hand in mine and kiss her fingers. I'm afraid she'll pull away, but she doesn't, so I place her palm on my cheek and lean my head into it. "I won't let him hurt you," I say.

When Sarah looks at me, I see the trace of her tears on her cheeks and I reach up and wipe the wet away with my thumbs.

"It ain't gonna be up to you," she says. "You don't own me, Henry."

I bend down and kiss her. I don't want to own her. I just want her to be mine.

She wraps her arms around my waist, and I sigh, feeling the weight of her body against me. The disjointed clanking that's been vibrating inside me since she found me making those chains and shut me out is finally quiet. I pull in a deep breath of sweet air. A lungful of Sarah.

She tucks her cheek on to my chest and it's like all the tightness inside me is melting away. I rub her back with one hand and hold her close with the other.

"You can't never stop a whipping like that again," she says into my chest.

"I know," I tell her.

She looks up at me. "You made it worse for Annie, and if that'd been me—"

I shake my head at her. "It won't be you. It will never be you."

"Henry—"

"That would kill me."

She raises her eyebrows at me and stares hard. "Starving ain't the only dying we know about."

"Sarah," I say. I don't want her to bring up our argument.

She pulls back from me and says, "You remember you told me about your family back home? And how you worked the land but didn't own it?"

I run my hands up and down her arms. I wish she would stop talking and just let me hold her, but I say, "Yes. I remember."

"That man who owned everything, would he come by your hut sometimes?"

"Lord Edwards lives in England," I say. "He's only been to Ireland once. Another man manages it for him. A little like an overseer, I suppose."

"Then imagine he sent that other man to take your brother from your hut because your Lord Edwards got a mind to sell him. Maybe he got debts, or too many hands, or the overseer's been telling lies on him, saying he's trouble. Or your Lord from England just got a notion to, 'cause he don't need a reason."

"They couldn't sell us," I say. "They could starve us. And take the land back. Leave us homeless with nothing."

"But imagine he could," she says. "And imagine your daddy tries to stop them from taking his boy and gets himself whipped bloody."

I know this happens here, but it sounds like a new horror when it could be Dermot getting taken from our home, and Da being whipped. It's a terrible thought.

"And imagine your Lord Edwards comes up from England that one time, and sees your sister and decides to take her for the night. When your daddy stands in his way he's whipped again, and this time it's weeks before he can walk. Then, as extra punishment, your Lord Edwards keeps your sister for a week instead of for a night, and when he comes back he takes your momma, just to show your daddy his place. To show all of you. And when he don't like the look of your stink eye, showing him just what you think of him, he sells you too. One day you're hoeing in the fields and the next someone puts shackles around your wrists and ankles and an iron collar around your neck, leading you God knows where. Only thing you know is that your family and your home is gone forever." She reaches up to cup my face. "I know you been through a hard, hungry life," she says. "I want you to understand that slave suffering is a different thing. When somebody owns you, there ain't nothing they can't do to you."

I hadn't thought it possible that I could hate Lord Edwards more, but the thought of him doing this to my family sends me into a twisting rage. It's an evil thing to own another man. Even if a master chooses not to torture and abuse someone, it's enough that he could. I am in a land of smiling villains, and I want nothing to do with them.

"Master Mulch put Annie in shackles and ran the chain over the tree branch on the other side so she don't fall down when her legs give out." Sarah watches me, waiting for a response.

"I saw," I tell her.

"Were they yours?"

I'm sickened to be part of this. The chain maker. I shake my head. "I don't know." But I know I can't claim innocence no matter how small a cog of the wheel I am. "I'm sorry," I tell her.

I will never make another chain.

Chapter 34

Sarah

The days drag by slow as molasses and I'm itching to get into the cool shelter of the woods and off the plantation. I ain't seen Henry since after the whipping the other day, but I hear him out by the coach house pounding on his metal. Most days, one chore just follows after the next, with no time for anything else. But today, when I finish in the house, Thomas is with his momma learning his letters, Willa's looking after Annie, and Maple's left for town with Red, so I take my chances and slip away for a spell.

I snatch up my herb basket and make for the woods, looking in the places Momma taught me—near the rotting logs for bindweed, and in the sunken wet soils for turtlehead leaves.

I head toward the river, expecting to find Joe-pye weed growing by the banks. Instead, I see Henry coming up alongside the river. My hand goes to smooth my hair. Annie's still got my headscarf and, after the extra whipping she got on account of Henry and me, I don't have the nerve to demand it back. A slip of hair has fallen out of my bun and hangs beside my face. I tuck it behind my ear.

Henry walks straight up to me, picking his way between the wild growing plants. Sunlight peaks through the leaves overhead, playing across the two of us standing up to our knees in ferns and mayapple. In the distance a woodpecker hammers on a tree.

"Afternoon, Sarah," he says, just like he's expecting to see me here.

"Henry," I say. I been missing saying his name.

There's a moment when we're stuck, like we're back to where we don't rightly fit. The air's so still it feels like the whole world's holding its breath for us. But then he takes a step closer to me and I take a step closer to him, wading through the sprawling leaves, and it's like we just crossed right through whatever was keeping us apart.

He glances at my basket. "Are you gathering plants?"

I nod.

He bends down and picks a mayapple leaf. "What will this one do for me?"

I shrug. "Probably make you sick."

He tosses it aside and holds out his bent arm for me to take, like he's fixing to walk out courting with me. "We can look together if you'd like. You can show me what to look for."

My heart's thumping in my chest like a rabbit with the hounds after it, and I'm breathing heavy like I'm the one just got finished being chased.

He got his arm out waiting on me. "I'll wager I'm better at this than you think. You should give me a chance."

I take it. "Ain't you supposed to be hammering out some horseshoes, or something?"

He grins on over at me and I smile right up into my cheeks. Lord, he does get me to act a fool.

"Aye, I am," he nods. "But I saw you going into the woods, so I decided my blacksmithing could wait."

There's a thing I learned to do when I was little, where I tell myself I don't feel what I'm feeling. I don't miss what I'm missing. I don't want what I can't have. If something hurts, it's only 'cause I'm thinking about it. Lately, I been telling myself that this thing with Henry weren't all that much anyway.

Now, here he be, and there ain't no way I can keep on pretending. This here with Henry is a onetime thing.

I pull a turtlehead leaf out of my basket and hold it up for him to see. "How about you help me look for some more of this."

Here and there he points out what he thinks he found, but it ain't right. One looks almost like it, but it's too shiny. Another looks close, but it's got some red on it. I never thought gathering was hard, but Henry sure don't take to it.

I'm picking whatever I see that's useful as I go, not just the turtlehead I told him to watch out for. When my basket's near about full, Henry asks me if I want to see something. He's looking at me all excited and he's making me a little nervous, but I say "yes" because it's Henry.

He leads me up the stream a ways more, to where there's an old door propped up against a tree.

"Do you trust me?" he asks.

I nod, because I do, but I'm thinking maybe I shouldn't. Red's and Bessie's voices get mixed in with my own and I'm not sure who's telling me to be careful. Me, or them.

Henry kicks off his shoes and pulls the wooden door into the water. He splashes in after it, holding it steady at the bank.

"Climb on," he says.

I don't move 'cause I can't swim, and I know he wants to pull me right into the middle of the river.

"I promise you'll be safe, Sarah. I won't let you go."

I step on to the door and it wobbles under my feet, so I sit, clutching on to the sides. Henry pushes me on out and wades alongside me, until we get into the middle where he starts to swimming a spell, all the while keeping one hand on the door, and then he's wading again and we're at the other side.

He climbs out of the water dripping wet and holds out his hand for me like his soggy clothes clinging on him don't bother him one bit, and I take his hand like I ain't even noticed. He sloshes along the woods in his bare feet, making wet slapping sounds with every step, until we get to a clearing. I catch my breath and squeeze his hand, because the whole clearing is covered in wildflowers, and flitting around from flower to flower are at least a hundred butterflies. I ain't never seen nothing so beautiful.

We walk in among them real slow, so they don't get to worrying we're gonna bother them. Then we stand in the middle. They're just flying around us, like maybe we're some new kind of flower.

Two bright yellow ones come right up and land on Henry.

"Could be they're thirsty," he says, and we both laugh, scaring them away.

"How'd you know about his place?" I ask him.

"I like to walk," he says. "Especially when I'm frustrated." He steps in closer and brushes aside my hair that's fallen into my face again. "Lately I've been walking a fair amount." He pulls back his hand. Tucks it in his pocket. "Anyway, when I found it, the first thing I thought of was showing you."

We sit ourselves down in the middle of the field and watch those butterflies fly. Between the flowers and the butterflies, seems like there's every color there that God created. They ain't even a little bit scared of us, and they're especially sweet on Henry. Before I know it, I got my head on his shoulder and he got his arm around mine.

The afternoon dips into the early evening, and though I hate to go, I've got to get back. When I tell him, he leans over and kisses me.

"I know," he says. He plucks a pink coneflower and threads it into my hair. Then he gets up and pulls me to my feet.

He tucks his arm around my waist and I slip mine around his like we been doing it all our lives, and back we go, hugging each other close. At the river bank he slips in, getting his dried-out clothes wet all over again. I climb up on the wooden door and he eases me across the river. He pulls on his shoes, while I collect my basket, and taking my hand he guides us through the woods toward the plantation. On the narrow path, before we leave the cover of the trees, I stop him.

"Thank you for showing me," I say.

"I'm glad you liked it, Sarah." He says my name like it's a precious thing.

I step in close to him. I reach up and take his face in my hands and I kiss him. I don't care about Bessie warning me to keep my distance. I don't think about all those people who've got something to say about me and Henry. I know he ain't going to be around here forever, but I kiss him because I want to, and I keep kissing him because I want to. In a minute I got to do a mountain of things I don't want to do, but right now I'm doing this because I choose it.

When I step back, I'm wet all up and down my front where we been pressing together. He's breathing hard and he's glowing, and I'm amazed that I have the power to do that to him.

We come out of the woods hand in hand, but as soon as we get clear of the trees we get a cold taste of Virginia reality. Propped against the old sycamore tree, the overseer sits slumped with a bottle of hooch. As we step out into the open of the plantation, he sees us. Our fingers linked together. The flower in my hair. My feet stop moving. I can't get no breath.

We drop our hands and put some space between us.

"Just keep walking," Henry says.

I do. I try. But he's seen us. "Henry," I say.

"It'll be all right." He steers us away from Master Mulch, toward the stables and the yard, and I stumble along beside him. "I won't let anything happen to you."

I look back and the overseer's got his eye right on me, putting a fear in me that sits deep in my bones. Henry's jaw is clamped so tight he's cramping up his whole neck, and now I'm scared of what Henry's going to do to the overseer, and of what the law's going to do to Henry once he's done it.

Chapter 35

Henry

The overseer is a shiftless man. He sits atop his Quarter Horse with his whip coiled at his hip, his pistol glinting in the sun, and his back to the workers in the field. His focus, I see as I draw near, is trained up the hill—to where Sarah and Thomas feed grass to the horses.

My arms are full of hoes and shovels I've been mending and making that I carry into the cotton shed. When I come out, he's still watching Sarah. The water runners, four children too young to pick, but too old to be allowed to sit idle, have brought buckets of water for the workers' water break. They stand holding the buckets, waiting for him to give permission for the field hands to drink.

I approach him without a clear idea what to say, but I'll not have him lurking around hounding Sarah. If he has a quarrel, it's with me.

"It seems to me we got off on the wrong foot," I say. "I bear you no ill will."

Mulch pulls his attention from the hilltop and rolls up his sleeve. His forearm is marked with the wound of the whip. "I can't say as I feel the same."

I step forward and take the bridle of his horse, who drops his head and nuzzles my chest, docile and affectionate. The more his horse relaxes into me, the more nervous Mulch becomes. It is an effect I'm counting on.

"It's not good for either of us to keep bad blood going," I say. "I saw you," he says. "I can tell Johnson any time I want and get you thrown out of here."

I run my tongue along my teeth like I'm distracted by something in my mouth, as if this doesn't worry me, or hasn't been keeping me up at night.

"Based on the word of a drunkard overseer he's already thinking of firing?" I say it casual. Nice and slow. I haven't got a barns-arse of an idea if it's true, but he knows I saw the dressing down he got for whipping Jim without permission. And he didn't report about me stopping Annie's whipping and slashing him with the whip, which I guess means he's not sure of Mister Johnson's reaction. Mister Johnson'd be angry with me, sure, might even fire me, but he'd also be furious at Mulch for taking his anger out on Annie and over-whipping her as he did. Especially after he'd already been warned with Jim.

"I saw you," he says again. "Johnson don't keep with slave whoring."

"You should mind your own business," I say. "Seems to me, Matthew Johnson doesn't care for people who overstep." He says nothing, and I spit on the ground by the foot of his horse. "If you have a quarrel with me, for what I did, then let's settle it like men. Right now, if you like."

Mulch scoffs. "Some of us got to work."

I look over at the slaves toiling in the field and the children waiting to bring them water, and then at Mulch, sitting on his arse. "If you're too busy," I say, "name your time."

He juts his chin out and yanks his horse's head up, off my shoulder, where it's been nuzzling. "You'll know when I'm ready to settle it." He turns from me and looks back up the hill to Sarah and Thomas leaving the pony in the enclosure.

"Master Mulch, you want us to give the water now?" one of the children asks.

He ignores her, tracking the progress of the two on the hill until they've gone down the other side out of view. He wants me to see that he's got Sarah in his sights. It's all I can do not to drag him from his horse and pound his head in. He turns to me and smirks, and only then am I aware of my hands curled into fists, my clenched jaw, my heaving chest. I want to rip his face off.

"Keep away, or I'll come for you." I don't mention her name. I don't have to.

He's pleased with himself. He wanted to get a rise out of me, and he's got it. "Ain't you got work to do, blacksmith? Idle hands is the Devil's work." He digs his heels into the horse's flank and trots into the cotton rows. "Get that water out in the fields," he shouts to the children.

They heave their buckets and spread out from worker to worker while I stand there grinding my teeth.

By the time I turn and leave the fields, I'm tight as a bowstring. I find her in a cellar room off the carry-through, fetching apples with Thomas.

"Are those for the horses?" I ask. "You're going to make them sick with too many apples."

She holds her apron full of fruit. "He wants to feed them."

"Thomas, go down and see Red," I say. "He can help you give them a sack of barley. It'd be better for them."

Thomas rushes out without a further thought to the apples in Sarah's skirts. She turns to the crate shelf to replace them. I step up behind her and, when she's finished, I press in close. She stills and leans back into my chest. I run my hands down her arms, and weave my fingers between hers and feel myself ease, just from touching her.

Chapter 36

Sarah

"Look, Sarah! Look at me," Master Thomas yells from up on top an old mare.

He grins from ear to ear and I grin right along with him. Henry jogs beside the boy, his face a mask of concentration.

"Don't lean forwards, stay upright," Henry calls out. "And keep your legs strong."

Henry slows the horse down before Master Thomas bounces himself clean off the seat with his trotting.

Behind us we hear clapping and spin around. Master stands there watching. My heart thumps and my palms prickle with sweat. I think back, hoping there weren't nothing going on here that he shouldn't see.

"Well, this is a happy sight," he says. "Thomas, you look like a natural up on that horse. Like you were born to it."

Henry and me don't say a word, but I reckon we're both thinking the same thing. You can encourage the boy without outright lying.

"Doesn't he look fabulous up there?" Master asks us, and we both agree. Ain't like we're gonna say no. He comes over and shakes Henry's hand. "I can see you are a man of many talents," he says. "Sarah mentioned you were helping with this."

I'm glad he remembers and this looks normal to him. Glad he hasn't seen how me and Henry been looking at each other all afternoon. Glad the overseer didn't talk to him about the other day.

"I've come to collect you, Thomas. We're riding into Fredericksburg. Your mother too. Your aunt and uncle have bought a new house, and we're going to go take a look."

He turns to me. "We'll be back the day after tomorrow, in time for supper."

"Yes, sir," I say.

Henry helps Master Thomas down from the horse. He runs to his daddy who hefts him up on to his shoulders and carries him down the hill.

"And put that horse away," Master calls over his shoulder.

Little Master Thomas turns back to wave at us and then, nearly losing his balance, clutches his daddy's head with both hands. I smile after him.

"He's a sweet lad," Henry says, coming up to my side.

"Sure is," I say. "It'd be easier if I could hate him."

Henry looks at me, shocked.

I wait for him to understand and, when he don't, I explain. "One day that little boy's gonna own me. Wouldn't you be ashamed to love someone like that?"

He's quiet for a minute. Then he says, "The man who owned our land back home ground us into the dirt without even using his own heel. His manager did that for him, with Lord Edwards back in England somewhere getting fat on it. The hating was more straightforward."

With no one watching us, I slip my hand into his and twine our fingers together. It's a powerful thing, feeling understood.

"The loving was straightforward too," he says, squeezing my hand.

We step apart, afraid to linger, and he takes the horse's reins as we walk out of the enclosure. Stroking its neck, he says, "So, if the family's away, does that mean you've got some time?"

I look at him sideways. "Means I don't got Missus checking on everything I do, pretending she ain't. But I still got Maple."

"Because I was hoping, maybe this afternoon, if you can get away, you might like to come with me into the woods. We could go for a swim."

It's the craziest thing I ever heard.

"I can't swim," I say.

"I'll teach you."

I picture the two of us stripped down in the water and feel the blood rushing to my head, pricking my face. I glance away, biting my lip, wondering if I dare. He looks at me intense and pleading and, before I know it, I'm nodding.

"All right," I say. "Let me put the horse away and finish sweeping out the house, and I'll meet you at your forge." I can't believe myself.

He smiles. "I'll be waiting."

I bring the mare into her stall and since Red's gone with Master and all them, I take the bridle from her mouth like Red and Henry both showed me. I fill up her water and fetch the brush to run over her flank. I brush too fast but I don't want to slow down. I want to hurry up and get my work done and meet Henry.

I'm getting her hind legs when I feel a hand grab my waist.

Then I'm off my feet and I kick and flail, hefted like a sack of corn out of the stable door and into an empty stall full of hay across from the mare. There's a smell of stale sweat and whiskey and I know before I look that it's the overseer. He throws me down. My panic tastes like bitter rust as he closes the stable door behind us.

I hear Henry, out by the forge, pounding rhythmic and strong on his iron.

"You been whoring around with that blacksmith," Master Mulch says, unbuckling his belt.

I sit up and shake my head, backing away from him, sliding across hay that pricks at my legs.

"If you lay down for him, you can lay down for me."

I'm trembling and mute. I want to scream, but all I can do is shake my head. He grabs my ankle and yanks me forward.

When I kick at his hand and claw at the hay, he smacks me across my face, knocking the seeing out of my eyes and a ringing into my ears. I pitch to the side, gasping.

"You need to learn your place." He grabs my leg and flips me over to my stomach.

I whimper. I squirm and flail. Finding my voice, I say, "Master won't like this." I try to slide away.

He holds my hips and plants his knee where my legs come together, pushing them apart till his knee sinks through to the ground. I hold my skirts down behind me and he laughs.

"I'm your master right now. You hear?"

His second knee crashes on to my leg and pushes it farther apart. "Me and no one else."

He grabs my hands and lifts them above my head, holding them in place, trapping them against the ground. He leans forward and I feel his hot breath in my ear, "You tell that blacksmith, from now on, we're gonna share."

"Please don't," I try to say, but my sobbing chops the words into grunts.

With his free hand, he gropes at me, pinching and bruising, like he's trying to leave marks for Henry to find. I pretend it's not happening and that I'm somewhere else, far, far away. I'm with Isaac in our old cabin and Momma's cooking yams and collard greens.

Then the overseer shoves my skirts up and I'm back in the stable, face down in the hay.

Screaming.

Chapter 37

Henry

The fire's not hot enough, but I'm impatient. I get the bellows going and throw the iron in. It seems to take forever to heat, but, when it's ready, I grab my tongs and pull the iron out of the glowing coals and slap it on the anvil. I pound out in a rhythm, not thinking much about the hooks I'm making. My mind is on her, coming with me to the river.

Then I hear a scream.

I jump up, run to the stable, burst through the door, and rush to a back stall where all the noise is coming from. There I find Ralph Mulch on top of Sarah. I grab him by his head, digging my fingers into his eyes and ears, and throw him against the stable wall where he crumples to the ground. The horses thrash and bray. He tries to stand, but trips on his trousers round his ankles. I punch him where he lies. As he scrambles for the door to the stall, shrinking from my blows, I kick it shut. It swings closed on its hinges, slamming his hand in the frame. He howls in agony. When he draws back into the stall, I punch him again and again until he's slouched down on the floor, unconscious.

Sarah's pulled herself upright, watching the whole thing, looking like a rabbit in a trap. I kneel in front of her and hold her. Her heart's racing and her breath is coming in little pants.

"I have you now. Put your arms around my neck," I tell her, "and hold tight." I lift her and carry her in my arms to the coach house.

I climb the ladder to my loft space one-handed and lay her down on my hay bed. I hold her hand and lie next to her. The whole time I'm whispering to her that I'm going to get her out of here. That the two of us are going away together and we're going to leave all this behind us. And I mean every word of it.

Chapter 38

Sarah

I spend the whole day hiding out from the overseer. Tomorrow, Master'll be back to keep him in line and Lord knows what lies he's gonna tell. He's already been boasting up and down the fields that he had me on my back yesterday. He's saying I did it for a yellow ribbon. I been saying it ain't true, but seems like everybody knows I spent the night up with Henry. So now it don't look like it ain't true.

"Guess you're open for business now," Maple says when she sees me in the morning. She don't talk to me for the rest of the day. Just scowls, looking mean. Willa won't come near me, and Annie elbows past me saying, "Never thought you'd go so low." Bessie turns away from me when I try to talk to her.

I know they think they know what happened, but at least one of them should have asked. They got it all figured out between them enough to be judge and jury over me.

I work all day preserving and jarring runner beans and tomatoes from the garden so that they'll keep for the winter. It keeps me from having to talk to any of them and far away from the overseer.

When I go back to the cabin I share with Bessie at night, she's got my pallet rolled up and set outside the door. She done pulled her bed into the middle of the floor with her table and chairs spread apart and her spinning wheel taking up the last of the space. There's no room for a pallet.

"You got to put all that back," I say. "I got to sleep here."

She grunts at me and keeps combing through her cotton, spinning on her wheel. For someone who can't see, she sure knows her way around that wheel.

"Where I'm supposed to sleep?" I try again.

"You can find a white man around here to hire yourself out to. Get yourself some more ribbons and sweets and headscarves. I know you don't want to waste the night."

I'm so shocked I can't find the words to tell her she's got no cause to turn ugly on me.

"It's only decent people I share my cabin with," she says. "You got to go."

"You can't kick me out. Master put me in here with you."

"Then when he gets back, you can go tell him why I throw'd you out. Master's a Christian man. He don't want no bed wenching around here."

I march over and grab her wheel, stopping it. "I ain't done nothing wrong."

"Oh, no? Where was you sleeping last night?"

"You don't know what happened. Henry was—"

"Henry? Ain't that supposed to be Mister Taylor? Well, you go on back to your *Henry* and let him take care of you some more. I don't keep company with no Jezebel."

I storm out of the cabin, hurt and angry, and go to the coach house. I'm tired right through to my soul. Sitting down on the floor at the bottom of the ladder, I lay my head on my knees.

Don't know how long I sit there like that before Henry comes back from wherever he's been and sees me.

"Bessie won't let me stay in the cabin," I say.

He kneels in front of me and wraps his arms around my shoulders. My head tucks into his neck like I been doing it for years. I cling to him like he's all I got left. But I don't have him at all. Not really.

"It's going to be all right," he says, and I nod.

That's a new one for me. A white man promising me things and me believing him. He kisses me like on the night we looked at the stars. Like the day at the river. Like a man kisses a woman.

When we climb up the ladder, the whole world shrinks to the loft above the coach house. We lie on his bed and he puts his arms around me. He waits for me to be ready to be touched any more than that, and I'm not ready, so we fall asleep to the crisp song of the cicadas in the humid night air.

Chapter 39

Henry

I watch her sleep, careful not to move to wake her. I've dreamed of having her in my bed. Now she's here and I dare not touch her. Her eyes fly open and she startles when she sees me.

"It's just me," I say, and she eases a little.

I feel like smashing Mulch's hand all over again. That and more.

I want to keep her squirreled away up here, out of Mulch's reach and away from the hatefulness of Bessie and Maple and all of them. But I know the more time she spends with me, the harder they'll make it for her. And, like it or not, she has to go out and face them.

Maple puts her to work with a broom and a rag, having her clean the house, getting it ready for the Johnsons coming home this afternoon. When they get back there'll be a reckoning. I'm just not sure for who.

When Sarah walks in the house, I shift the position of my forge so I can have a clear sight to the fields and the paddock hill that Mulch would come over if he came this way. It's only morning, but the humidity mixed with the heat has already got me perspiring. I take out a kerchief and wipe the beads of sweat from my top lip and from my neck.

Around about midday I see him. Mulch. Atop the Quarter Horse he rides through the cotton fields, headed over the paddock hill toward the house. I douse the iron I'm working on in a bucket of water, bank my fire, and hurry over to the house, slipping in through the carry-through and up the cellar stairs. I hear Sarah above me, so I climb the main staircase with an ear out for Mulch. I have the clear sense of being where I shouldn't. Each squeak of the steps is like an accusation of trespassing, but I walk on. I pass a large bedroom that I guess is where Mister and Missus Johnson sleep, but then I come to another one just as big, with dark wood instead of yellow and blue flowers, and I realize they sleep alone.

In the dark-wood bedroom, with her back to me, Sarah sweeps the floor. She hears the thud of my step over the scratch and swish of her sweeping and spins around, clutching the broom.

Her features soften when she sees it's me. "What you doing here?"

I don't want her to feel like I'm crowding her, or following her. And I don't want her worrying about Mulch before she has to, so I say, "I thought I'd check the fireplace grates." I glance at the grates I made three weeks ago that sit unused, waiting for the summer to pass and the cold weather to come.

"Master won't like to find you up here."

We both look out of the window. Instead of the Johnsons coming home, we see Mulch turn his horse down the drive, riding away from the plantation toward the road. The look she gives me tells me she knows why I've come rushing up here. And the look I give her back says I'm not letting him near her ever again.

She takes a step toward me and I clasp my hands behind my back to keep from touching her, waiting for her to come to me the way I would with a spooked horse. She takes another step. When she's close, I lean in, slowly, laying my forehead against hers. We stay there, breathing in each other's air. It's just our foreheads touching, but as she eases toward me I can sense the jitters in her calm. I clutch my hands tighter to keep from folding her into my arms. I want so badly to comfort her, but I know I need to wait for her to want me to.

"Humph," we hear from the doorway.

The thinking part of me knows it can't be Mulch, but I spin around, fists up, ready to fight him just the same. It's Maple that's standing there, scowling at us with fire in her eyes, looking like she'd like to take a lash to the both of us. She sucks her teeth and shakes her head and marches on.

"Are you going to be in trouble with her?" I ask.

"She can't do much except set me to cleaning the privy," Sarah says.

"Does that mean you don't mind if I stay with you a while longer up here?"

"I don't mind, but I got to get this done," she says, lifting her rag and her broom.

"Then I'll just keep you company."

She nods and takes my hand and leads me to the room next door with the yellow and blue flowers. She talks to me as she sweeps, and the more she relaxes the more she talks. She tells me about how her ma hated sweeping because the dust stuck in her nose and made her eyes water. Her ma's talent, she says, was healing. And her ma's ma could smell what a plant could do for you. She tells me how her ma's ma had been a midwife in Africa and, in her hands, even the backward-facing babies all came out breathing.

"That's how she got taken," Sarah tells me, as she sweeps under the bed. "Everybody knew about staying in at night, away from the snatchers. But a baby ain't gonna wait for morning, so she went. Snatchers got her on her way. The whole boat ride over she kept wondering if that baby came out alive without her."

I guess I thought the African slaves crossed the Atlantic in the stinking hold of a coffin ship like the Irish did, but they didn't. Sarah's grandma was put in a stinking hold, true enough, but the slavers stacked them like books on a shelf, with rows of human cargo above and below, to piss and puke and shit where they lay, chained to captives from other tribes with other languages they couldn't understand. They were force-fed when they wouldn't eat and exercised now and again to keep the dying to a minimum.

I can't imagine surviving it.

By the time the Johnsons turn into the driveway, with Red coaxing the horses on with the rhythm of his voice, the house is swept and dusted and the windows have been shined with vinegar and water. I squeeze Sarah's hand and dart down into the carry-through and out the back. I build the fire again, take up the cold shapeless iron from the water bucket and thrust it into the hot coals. And wait for the reckoning.

Chapter 40

Sarah

Master, Missus and Master Thomas are all tired from their trip and wanting an early supper. Maple doesn't want me near her, so it's Willa who has to help her in the kitchen house. She has me unpack the travel cases and then go get the dining room ready.

I'm changing the tablecloths in the dining room when I hear an angry voice in the front hall. I freeze. Mulch is back and he don't waste no time before coming to talk to Master. I poke my head into the hall, and I see Master leading him into his study. His face has puffed into a blue-black mess.

I strain to listen from where I stand in the hallway, but I can't make out more than a loud rumble. When Maple comes by and sees me, she grabs my arm and yanks me outside. She's hung rugs on the line and sets me to beating them. The dust flies in my face, making me cough, and she smirks. I swear, she'd set me to work in the fields if she could.

As I'm pounding and coughing, Annie rushes out of the house and over to the forge. In a minute, she's leading Henry back to the house. I stop beating, watching him go. Maple comes back out threatening to have me whipped for laziness.

I've walloped two rugs when Master bellows my name. I freeze for a second and then I come running, scurrying into his study. Master sits at his desk with Henry and the overseer standing in front. I hover by the door clutching the rug beater.

"Yes, sir," I pant, out of breath.

"I understand there was an incident here in my absence." His neck is splotching red, which means he's already angrier than what's safe.

I drop my gaze to the floor and feel the eyes of all three men on me. "Yes, sir," I say.

"I told you what happened," Master Mulch says. "What are you asking her for? She's just a slave, for Christ's sake."

Master glares at him with flashing eyes. You can't be taking the Lord's name in vain with Master.

"She's just a slave," the overseer grumbles, correcting himself.

"You'll want to watch your tone and your words, Mulch. I won't have that in my house."

"This man attacked me unprovoked." The overseer waves his ruined hand, straining to keep his composure. "For the second time." He pulls back his sleeve to the lingering whip scar on his arm. "He's out of control and dangerous."

"You deserve worse than you got," Henry snaps.

"Sarah," Master says, "did you see the blacksmith attack Master Mulch?"

I open my mouth and close it again. I won't say yes. I bite my lip, thinking.

"Was Master Mulch instructing you in the stable? And Mister Taylor struck him from behind?"

I look over at Henry. Either he didn't tell his side of it yet, or Master already decided to believe the overseer.

"Master Mulch was trying to sin in the stable and Mister Taylor stopped him," I say.

"Lying whore," the overseer cries.

I shrink away from him and Henry steps between us.

Master studies the three of us. "In what way did you think he was sinning?"

My mouth is sticky with thirst. Words swoop and dive in my mind like bats I can't get hold of.

"Tell me!" He thumps his hand on the table and I jump.

"After you left," I say, but that's not part of the story. "In the stable," I say. I shake my head. It don't matter where. "He pushed me down and pulled up my skirts and climbed on top of me," I say in a rush. Like that, it don't sound so bad as it was. "It weren't right what he done." Talking about it I can feel his hands on me again and I blink back tears threatening to spill.

"I was disciplining her, is all," Master Mulch says. "For being lazy. She was hiding in the stables when she should have been working."

"What were you doing in the stables, Sarah?" Master's voice strains like a rope pulled too tight.

I push my fingernails into my palms until the stinging bite in my hands settles the whooshing in my ears. "It was when you took Master Thomas, sir. I went to put the horse away, like you told me to."

His head snaps over to the overseer. He don't like nothing to get between his orders and folks following them. Henry sees what I'm seeing and speaks up.

"I understood that you're a Christian man of rules and principles," Henry says to Master. "And that you don't tolerate that kind of behavior."

Master drums his fingers on the table. "But was it necessary to surprise him from behind, slamming his hand into a door, breaking the bones?"

"Yes, sir, it was," says Henry, bold as you please. "He didn't see me coming for him because he was pulling his breeches down with the one hand and holding her still with the other."

"He smashed my hand!"

"I'm just glad it was me that walked in on him, not Thomas, or Missus Johnson. I hate to think they might have seen what I saw."

"Liars! Both of them are in cahoots against me. This man is wild and brutal. He attacked me twice for no reason.

I'm telling you, he shouldn't be here. You got to send him packing."

I look at the overseer and see he's gone tomato red and his bug eyes look ready to pop right out of his head. I hold my breath, gripping on to the rug beater.

"This is my plantation, Mulch. I decide who stays and who goes. And I have had enough of you questioning my authority and, frankly, going around my back to defy me. The blacksmith's right. Suppose my son walked in on you, with all the time he's been spending with the horses. I'm trying to raise him up to be righteous and you defy me by sinning with my slave on my land."

"It wasn't like they said. These two would say anything. They been sneaking off. I seen them. I'm telling you, you don't know what's going on."

"Do you think you know more than me? About my own plantation? If there is something I don't know, it's because you've been hiding it from me. You're fired, Mulch. I can't use a man with a ruined hand anyway, and even without it I think you've outstayed your welcome. Get your things and get off my land."

The overseer glares at Master, then he turns his hate over to me and Henry. He spits at Henry's feet, right there on the rug in Master's study, and shoves me as he storms out of the room. I right myself, clutching the rug beater so hard I'm surprised it ain't broke in two by now. We all stand there listening to the stomp, stomp of his boots on the floors and the slam of the front door.

Master gets up from his chair and walks around the desk to Henry. He lays a hand on his shoulder. Henry shifts his stance.

"Taylor, you were right to stop him. And I'm sure there's no truth to what he claims."

I see the muscles working in Henry's jaws and his eyes going hard. He flicks his gaze to the window and keeps it steady, staring at the western woods.

"I'm sure you know how wrong that would be," Master says. He takes his hand off Henry's shoulder and crosses back to his desk. "That will be all. You can both get back to work."

We leave the room and walk through the hall, out the back door to the porch and down the steps.

"You all right?" Henry asks when we get to the lawn.

"He's leaving," I say.

He brushes the back of my hand and turns left across the yard back to his forge.

Chapter 41

Henry

I sense her before I see her, standing off at a distance, watching. I'm at my forge, banking the fire, finishing up for the day, when she comes by. I smooth my hair back and stand.

"Evening," I say.

She keeps back and doesn't say anything. Instead, she glances toward the overseer's cabin behind the hill. I can see she's still wound up tight.

"He's really gone," I tell her.

She nods and takes a step closer to the dying fire. The glow of the embers makes her skin shine like polished wood.

"I keep thinking I'm gonna see him coming round a corner," she says.

I shake my head and move to stand beside her. "I watched him go myself."

"Bessie heard about what he done," she says, flattening the folds of her skirt. "She says she's sorry for sending me out last night." She looks at the coals as she speaks. "She says I can come on back tonight."

My gut clenches.

"So," her voice is soft and uncertain, "I come by to say you don't got to put up with me taking up your sleeping space no more."

I should give her up. It's been dangerous enough for both of us already and if we keep it going, there's no telling what it will cost us. This job, for sure. And who knows what for her. I should wish her well and let her go, but I say, "I'm already used to you there next to me. I don't think I can get comfortable again on my own."

I brush my fingers along her hand. She weaves them in between hers.

I reach into my pocket and pull out the bracelet I made for her. It's a copy of the connected half circles she wears as a wooden necklace. Instead of wood, this one is iron. I hold it out to her in my palm and wait for her to take it. Instead, she looks up at me with a question in her eyes.

"I made this for you," I say.

She touches her wooden necklace. "Isaac made this for me. The broken loops is supposed to be broken chains for freedom."

"I saw it as being linked together," I say. "That's what I had in mind when I made this for you."

She takes the bracelet and slips it on her wrist. It fits her exactly. She runs her fingers over the metal, tracing the interlacing loops. "Thank you," she says.

"If I'd known about the chains," I say, and she looks up at me. I don't know how to put to words what I'm trying to say. "I'm done making chains," I tell her.

She takes my hand and squeezes it.

"I want you to stay with me," I say. I feel her still in the quiet way she has of considering things.

"I don't know if I should."

"Sarah," I say, "this isn't wrong."

She doesn't move, so I lean in close and lay my forehead against hers. "Don't listen to what anyone else says. They've nothing to do with us."

She takes hold of the front of my shirt and balls it in her hands, like she's considering to push me away or pull me close.

"How much longer you gonna stay?" she asks.

I slip my hands over her fists. "As long as I can."

She nods, her forehead rubbing against mine.

"I know I can't give you near what you deserve," I tell her, "and if this thing with me is costing you too much, I'll understand. But I want to be with you, Sarah, for as many days and nights as I can get." Everything in me wants to hold her tight, but I let her go and step back. I reach out my hand to her.

Her fingers trace over the bracelet and grasp her wrist. I can only imagine what Maple and Bessie have been saying to her about being with me these last two nights. Or what Mister Johnson would say if he saw us. What I know for sure is that I need her to come with me.

"Please," I say. "Stay."

She takes my hand and follows me in, and I vow, then and there, that I won't ever let her go.

Chapter 42

Maple

Sarah's trouble with the overseer, and whatever's going on with that blacksmith, keeps me thinking on Rose, even when I try to put her out of my mind. And that leads me to thinking on Momma in the fields, and Freddy marching to Mississippi in chains. I'm mad at Freddy for running from Rose when he couldn't help her, 'cause she still needs him. And my heart breaks for Momma, who never talked about her times with Master Jeremiah, but I know she must have had her days of choking on the bed. I hope she's learned to pick fast enough to keep the whip off her back. At the Keeler place they whip you to make your hands dance. Whip you if you come up short. Whip you to see if you can pick more the next day. Whip you if you can't.

Sitting at the table in the kitchen house, I hear shuffling behind me. When I look over, the blacksmith's walking in.

"Something I can do for you, Mister Taylor?"

His gaze swims around the room like an eel. "I came by to return this," he says, holding out an empty plate. I don't like his up-to-something shiftiness.

"Well, you returned it." I take it from him and face away, showing him he should go.

"I thought Sarah would be in here washing dishes."

I suck my teeth and shake my head. The filthy man's come back to get himself some more of her. Bile climbs up my throat.

I want to tell him to leave her alone. Leave all of us alone. Just 'cause that girl don't know to hold herself more precious don't mean he ought to take advantage, dipping in and out like drinking at a well. He ain't no different from the rest of them.

I keep my back to him and speak to the coals. "Master don't like folks acting a certain kind of way here." I go to the fire and take up a stick, poking at the dying embers. Red sparks flare and float and cool into ash. "Not here."

He comes close. Stands behind me. "You don't understand about us," he says.

I grip the poke-stick tighter. "You leave her be," I say. My voice shakes.

"Maple, look at me," he says.

His words take me back to Belle Grove Plantation with Master Nathaniel standing behind me, waiting for me to finish with the fire, laying me down and gripping my chin to turn my head from facing the flames. "Look at me," he'd say before he covered my mouth.

I'm miles away from him and trembling. And I'm breaking into pieces for Rose, there, on the floorboards, looking at him while he covers her mouth. My only child. From the bottom of my soul, I weep for her.

"Are you all right, Maple?" Henry Taylor asks from behind me.

He puts his hand on my shoulder and I jump like I been shot through with lightning. I scoot away and whip around, holding out the fire-stick. "You stay away from me," I say. "If you touch me, Master's gonna throw you right out of here."

He holds his hands up and takes a step back. "I'll not hurt you. I was only asking what's wrong."

"You think you can do what you like. You take and take and think you can just keep on taking. Well, you can't." I'm crying hard and sloppy till I can barely get the words out. "Master don't have that here." I back against the wall shaking the stick at him. "Master don't have that here."

I know it's Henry Taylor, the blacksmith, standing in front of me, but it feels like it's Master Nathaniel come for me again. But Master Nathaniel's with Rose, laying her down, hiking her dress up, covering her mouth. I gasp for air and push into the rough wooden slats of the kitchen house wall that trap me in here with him.

"You leave us alone," I scream at him. "You leave us alone." My nose drips from crying.

"I swear, Maple, I mean no harm," he says. He backs out slow, moving like I'm a wild thing he's trying not to startle.

When he's gone, I sink to the floor, my breath in hiccups, my own hand over my mouth.

Chapter 43

Henry

It's like there are two worlds. The one with Sarah and me alone together, and the other one with everybody else in it. Every morning I wake up happy because she's next to me, but Maple and Red and the others wake up hateful, pointing fingers and calling names. They've stopped blaming her for Ralph Mulch attacking her, but they're still blaming her for me.

When we climb down the coach house ladder, Annie's hovering just outside by the forge, no doubt checking if Sarah's here. When she sees us together, she turns and scampers over toward the kitchen house and the house slave cabins, ready to report what she's seen to the others, I'll bet. I pull Sarah in close, wanting to give her strength for the day to hold up against their meanness.

"Shout if you need me," I say. "For anything."

"I'll be fine. All they do is look at me sideways."

It's not true. They call her names and get in her way, but they don't when I'm near. I hate letting her from my side.

I watch her walk down to the kitchen house, ready to take her instructions from Maple, who'll no doubt give them with a slathering of spite. Then I collect the morning's iron, lay to a bucket of water, and set my wood around yesterday's embers. I reach for my bellows, but they're not where I keep them. I can't find them anywhere, though I had them yesterday and put them away last night. Like I do every night. It's just been me and Sarah here since then.

And Annie this morning.

After the whipping she got for stealing I can't see her doing it again, but my bellows are missing, and she was over here. I need them to work, so I make my way to over to her cabin, for a look around.

She must have seen me pass, because not long after I go in, she turns up huffing.

"What you doing, Mister Taylor? Ain't nothing here for you."

"Did you take my bellows?"

She makes a face like I've lost my mind. "No, sir. Not me. I didn't take nothing."

I keep looking.

"I'm telling you, it ain't here. You must've forgot where you put it."

"I need them back," I say. "I can't work without them." I search under her bed and feel around in her mattress. It's lumped with bits of cloth, probably taken from Missus Johnson. I'd wager Sarah's green headscarf is in there. I run my hand between the mattress and the wall and there, shoved into the crack are my bellows, pressed as flat as they go and covered with her blanket.

I pull them out and hold them up. "Weren't you just whipped for this?" I say. I don't mean to shout but my frustration makes me loud.

She drops to her knees and cowers at my feet. I'm sick when I see that, but I feel worse when she speaks, "Please, Master Taylor. Don't whip me for this. I'm sorry. I won't never touch it again. Please, don't whip me."

I lower my hands and my voice. I would never take a lash to her. But that's not what she sees. She sees a white angry man. To her, I'm one of the masters.

I want to tell her I'm not like those others.

I'd never do those things to her.

I'm Irish, not American; the oppressed, not the oppressor.

She looks at me the way I used to look at the English. All of them the same and none of them good. She won't believe me different until she sees me acting different. I can't expect it otherwise.

"I'll not be having you whipped," I say.

She doesn't look like she trusts me, but she stops her yammering.

"And I'll not report you for taking them." I reach down and help her to her feet. "But why did you?" I ask. "They're no use to you."

She pinches her lips together, but she's got the look of someone itching to speak her mind, consequence be damned. I wait her out until she does.

"Ain't about using something," she says. "It's about having it be mine."

In her cabin, there's almost nothing. It's as bare as the hut of a starving tenant farmer. We're not so different, her and me. She steals just to have it. For someone who's been told she can't own anything, not even herself, filching is a kind of victory.

The one time Lord Edwards came up from England to survey his land and see for himself what "all the fuss over starving Irish" was about, he came by our place on his fine horse with his glossy dogs yapping at his heels. There was nowhere to tie his horse since all the shrubs and trees were long cut down for wood—for ages we'd mostly burned moss and dung—so he handed me the reins and told me to hold her. As Da explained about the years of rotten potatoes, and how the work gangs weren't enough, and the disease-filled workhouse a death sentence, and that people were evicted from land and homes they'd held for generations, and how homeless families slept in ditches, his lordship's dog started barking and didn't stop. To shut it up, he reached into his saddle bag, took out a bread roll and tossed it to the dog. Then he turned back to Da and told him to keep explaining, but Da couldn't say a word more. When you've seen that, there's nothing more to say. Riled up by his silence, Lord Edwards called him lazy and ungrateful and said we deserved what was coming. That's when I slipped my hand in the saddle bag feeling for food. Instead of bread, my fingers wrapped around a silver flask. I slipped it under my shirt. When I handed his horse back, I looked him right in the eyes. He slapped me for being "an impertinent oaf," and I thought, if he comes again, I'll steal the whole damn horse.

The flask paid for Ma's and Da's funeral and three tickets to America, but, when I took it, I wasn't thinking of what it could buy. I took it because Lord Edwards had wronged us, and he owed us more than I could ever steal.

"I can't let you keep the bellows," I tell Annie. "I need them for my work." But I take from my pocket a leather pouch where I keep the strip of cloth ripped from Sarah's dress the day we met. I take out the cloth and lay the empty pouch on Annie's bed atop the mattress stuffed with her stolen treasures. It's old and worn, but that's not the point. It's a thing to be owned. And it's hers, free and clear.

July 1849

Chapter 44

Sarah

Night after night, I stay up in the coach house loft. Everybody knows about me and Henry. Not at the Big House, but everybody else. Bessie don't like it, though she's less ugly about it now, but Maple'd spit at me as soon as look at me, and Red's been acting like I'm something from the bottom of his shoe.

But Henry and me, we just look over all that.

Laying side by side, I feel Henry's want and his patience. Truth be told, I feel my want too. It's only fear that stops me, and the memory of Master Mulch. When I reach for him one night, he doesn't trust that I mean it until I show him that I do. I won't let what happened in that stall keep me trapped more than I already am.

He's careful and sweet, like I knew he'd be, and he caresses the memory of that day right out of my skin, till when I think of the weight of a man pressed on me, or a man's hands running up my thighs, or a man's hot breath on my neck, I think of Henry and I go soft with wanting.

The sun scorches hotter day by day in a humid heat that's sticky and heavy. I try not to notice about how the weeks are slipping by.

When we wake, Henry's got his arms all wrapped up around me, and I got mine all wrapped up around him. When he opens his eyes to me looking at him, he breaks into a grin. I can't help smiling back.

"I dreamt about you," he tells me.

I scooch closer till our noses are almost touching. "What'd you dream?"

"That you were next to me when I woke up."

I shake my head. "That ain't no dream. I'm right here."

"Yes, it was," he says. "It just came true."

I know how I feel about him now, but it's better not to talk about it, because one day he's going to have to move on. And I'm going to have to stay. And that's going to be that.

I hear someone at the well pump and know I got to pry myself out of his arms and get to work. He reaches out and grabs me back.

"I got to go before they wake up over at the Big House," I say. I lean in and kiss him. The way he looks at me makes me feel like I could float right up to the clouds.

Soon as I take two steps into the yard, Master's there with his dander up, ready to bite my head off. I got no business being over here when my quarters are clear over on the other side of the yard.

"What are you doing over here?" he shouts, fit to burst.

I don't know what to say. I can't think why he's out so early. Normal times, he ain't even started on his breakfast yet.

"We looked for you last night," he says, mad as the Devil. "Where have you been?"

I open my mouth like I'm fixing to give my excuse, but I can't think of the first thing.

"You weren't in with Bessie and she couldn't say where you had gone."

"Oh. Well, sir," I stammer. My eyes is hopping around the yard trying to light on something that will give me an idea what to say. "I just…uh…"

"She was with me," I hear Henry say from behind me, and everything goes real still.

"With you?" Master spits out. His face goes right through red and straight into purple.

"Yes, sir. That's right," Henry says. He steps up next to me with his chest out, his head high. I could faint dead on the spot.

From the stables behind the coach house, Red comes striding over. I shake my head for him not to get mixed up in this.

"Master," says Red. "It was the horses."

We all turn to look at him and not one of us know what he's talking about.

"You see, Master, one of Mister Taylor's horses is sick and Sarah knows about the healing herbs."

"A horse?" Master says, which is what I'm thinking too.

"Yes, sir." He lies like he was born to it. "I was in and out half the night myself fetching water and making up a fire for boiling."

"Boiling herbs?"

"Yes, sir. That gal can make all kind of ointments and healing drinks with them plants of hers."

Master looks over at me again, but now he's only red. "I don't want you giving herbs to my horses, you hear? You could make things worse."

"Oh, no, sir," Red says, 'cause I still can't find my tongue. "It was just Mister Taylor's horse. Your horses're just fine."

I nod at what he's saying. Can't do much else, and I wait to see what Master's going to say to that. And I pray Henry don't say nothing else.

"Well, Thomas needed you," he says. "And you should have left word with Bessie what you were up to so that we could have fetched you."

"Yes, sir," I say. "Sorry, sir." I don't let my eyes go no higher than his knees.

"Red, ride out to the doctor and ask him to come by today to see Thomas."

"Yes, sir," he says, bobbing and backing away.

"You want me to go to Master Thomas now?" I ask, keeping my eyes lowered. I feel Henry standing behind me. I can hear in his breathing that he ain't happy.

"Yes," says Master. "Yes, I do. And you'll stay with him tonight, horse or no horse."

"Yes, sir," I say, and scoot on out of there before he want to ask something else I can't answer.

When I glance back, I see Henry watching me go. His shoulders sag and he stands crumpled staring after me, and I can tell he don't want to accept this. And I wonder if this is the thing that's gonna make him want to move on.

All day long I tend to Master Thomas. In the evening, he messes up his bedsheets with his sick, and I strip the bed and give him fresh sheets and set the old ones out in the hallway before they stink up the room.

Before long Missus comes in asking what I think I'm doing stinking up the house. I tell her Master said I have to stay with Master Thomas, but she tells me to get rid of the sheets, so I do. I take them down the back stairs into the carry-through and near about jump out of my skin when someone darts out toward me. It don't take me but a second to see it's Henry, and I drop my stink sack and throw my arms around his neck. He kisses me like it's been a month since he last could, instead of less than a day. I pull away to tell him he shouldn't be here, and he just kiss me harder, like he's claiming me.

He's got me all wrapped up in his arms, and I got my head on his chest and I can't say a word because there's a ball building up in my throat. I want to stay like this with him, but I got to hurry back upstairs, and he's got to get out of this house before someone sees him. Something's breaking in me and the only thing I can do about it is cry.

"I wanted to defend you and I almost made it worse," he says. "This is…I can't stand not being able to protect you. And I don't want to hide." He holds me tight and says, "It's not right."

He's right about that because it ain't, but the law says what the law says. And what it says is that me and Henry ain't got no kind of chance.

"We had it bad in Ireland. We had rot and fever and more dying than living, but a man's woman was his woman."

I circle my arms around him. That ain't never going to be how it is with us.

"I want you to come with me," he says.

I shake my head. "I got to get back upstairs. I'll be in trouble for sure if I disappear again."

"No," he says. He weaves his fingers in between mine, looking at our hands folded together. Then he pulls our fingers up to his mouth and kisses them. "I mean, I want you to leave the plantation with me when I go. I want us to stay together. I mean to make a life with you."

I feel like I got all the happy in the world mixed up with all the sad. I close my eyes against the tears but they spill out anyhow.

He rubs at the wet on my cheek with his thumb and cradles my face in his hand.

"How we gonna do that?" I say. "They ain't gonna let me go."

"I'll figure it out," he says. "But I'm leaving here with you. That is, if you'll have me."

I reach up and kiss him right on his mouth. "Henry Taylor," I say, "I would go anywhere with you."

Once I would have thought it can't never be, but, the way Henry's talking, he's got me believing in it too and, Lord, if it don't feel good to be hoping for it. Seems like between Henry and me we could almost wish the stars down from the sky.

Chapter 45

Henry

Lying alone in the coach house, missing Sarah next to me, I come up with a plan. But, like everything else in the world, it needs money.

First thing in the morning, I go to see Matthew Johnson. He doesn't understand me wanting to move on when he's still got work for me here. I don't explain to him that I need it faster than I can earn it. I pack my supplies and harness my horses. I'm ready to go, but I wait for Sarah to get a chance to break away.

When she comes, I lead her into the coach house. Tucking her against me, I rest my chin on her head. I feel the weight of her arms against my back and the rush of her breath into my neck.

"I won't be long," I tell her.

She nods, but when she looks up at me her eyes are shining.

"A week. Maybe two," I say.

I'm selling my forge and horses. With that plus the money I've got saved, I can get her free. Then we'll get the hell off Jubilee Plantation. Go back to New York, maybe, or keep heading south.

I take her hands in mine and kiss her fingers. She opens my palm and presses her lips to my healed scar.

It's time to go, but instead of leaving I pull her back into my chest. "I'll be as quick as I can," I say.

"I know," she says so quiet I don't so much hear it as feel her saying it.

When I bend down to kiss her, she hooks her hand around the back of my neck, making me want to carry her up to our hayloft, or smuggle her into my wagon and ride off with her right then and there.

We step apart. I mount my wagon, and set my horses trotting off at a determined pace. She watches me go from the coach house door. It's not like the last time I sold everything I had. Back then I was leaving home behind, but now there's a different kind of desperation driving me. Not a running-from but a running-to. Sarah's my home now.

I ride first to Fredericksburg, looking for a buyer, but all I get there is a drunk fool wanting one horse. My best chance is to sell the two horses and forge together, so I take the road up to Washington hoping for more luck in the capital city. I spend too many days asking around and getting nowhere. I try at the guest houses, and down by the docks, and in the shops. I've been gone near on two weeks when I ask a blacksmith, hoping he's nothing like Mister Reardon and that hearing I'm a traveling smith won't make him want to take a hammer to my head.

He has no interest in buying my traveling forge, and no knowledge of a blacksmith looking for one.

"But there was a guy," he tells me, "looking for forge and smith."

I ask where I can find him, and he says, "Georgetown. Below Bridge Street. Down where the Irish stay."

I bristle when he says it, wondering if he knows I'm Irish, and if he won't buy my forge because of it. I wonder if there really is *a guy*, or if he was just building up to tell me to get where I belong. Below Bridge Street. My eyes flick to the doorway, looking for the *No Irish* sign, but it's not there. Maybe he's not being hostile. Puzzling through people's prejudice is maddening.

I do go down to Georgetown the next day. Even if no one's looking for a forge and smith, even if it was a way to tell me I don't belong, it'll be good to be around my fellow countrymen. I stop into a tavern and ask, again, if anyone's interested in buying a traveling forge and two good horses, or knows someone who is. It turns out there is an Irishman down from New York looking for a blacksmith and forge who'd surely like a word with me. I hadn't expected it to be true. The barkeep says he'll get word to the man to meet me there that evening, and when I come back the person waiting for me is none other than Ennis Flanagan.

"Jesus, Mary and Joseph. I can't believe it," Ennis says, wrapping me in a bear hug and patting at my arms like he's making sure I'm flesh and bones and not some trick of the light.

We take stools at the bar, grinning at each other like boys.

"When you disappeared, I thought the Dead Rabbits got you for sure," he says.

I feel a sliver of guilt. He took me in off the boat and I should have let him know I was all right when I got the job with Mister Reardon. I'd been too afraid of the Dead Rabbits to go back to the Five Points. And too afraid it'd get back to Mister Reardon that I was Irish.

Ennis has left Bridget and the boys in New York to go off and make his fortune. He sees my face when he says it and adds that he'll come back for them in a year or two. "It'll be worth it when we're living like kings," he says. "Soon as I heard about the gold, I took the first train down here. When I get supplies together, I'll take the C&O Canal to Cumberland."

"Are you saying there's gold in Cumberland?"

He lifts an eyebrow, excitement in his eyes. "You haven't heard? They found gold in California. The trail west starts in Cumberland, Maryland."

It doesn't seem likely to be true. But, true or not, Ennis believes it.

"I swear it's just sitting in the ground for any man who can swing a pickaxe."

I stare in amazement. "You're talking about gold. There for the taking."

"I'm telling you, Henry, this is a hell of a country."

"Then why are you looking for a blacksmith?"

"See now, that's the beauty of my plan. Men'll be fighting over every patch of ground, stabbing each other in the back to lay claim to a stake. But first, they've all got to get west. Every gold prospector and every west settler will strike out from Independence, Missouri, the last settlement before the westward trails lead through bears and buffalo and Indians and wilderness.

"By the time a man gets to Independence, he's going to have a strong appreciation for his wagon wheels," Ennis says. "He'll want them fixed up, new ones bought and a few spares to take with him. That's where we'll come in. I can make a wheel, but I need a smith for the runners." He leans into me and presses me hard with his stare. "Think of it. If you come out there with me, we'll be rich as Solomon."

"It's a good plan," I say. My mind floats to a picture of what that could be like. To the open road and striking out to Missouri with Ennis, making my fortune in wagon wheels at the tail of civilization. A man can't help where his mind goes, and that's where mine went. To the wide-open possibilities. But it comes back to Virginia soon enough, and to Sarah's eyes, and her shoulders, and that spring rain smell of hers, and the way her voice curls around my name when she says it soft in my ear and the hairs on the back of my neck poke right up. With all that holding me, a fool scheme making wheels can't stand up. "I wish you luck, Ennis, but I'm selling my forge for the cash."

"Jesus, Henry. What'd you do, drink too much whiskey at the gambling table? I met a man who gambled his whole farm away after a bottle too many. Had to go home and tell his wife to pack up the family."

"It wasn't gambling," I say. I don't tell him the story. It seems too much to tell. And not likely he'd understand if I did.

He claps me on my back. "Whatever it was, I respect a man who settles his debts. And I'll be honest with you, I'd go out there with any blacksmith willing, but I'd rather it be you." He lowers his voice. "I'll tell you what I'll do." He's got the look of a man ready to do what it takes to get his stake in the world. I bet every man who ever got rich had that look on him. "I'll buy your forge myself," he says.

"And the horses too?"

"I'll buy the lot. Go settle your debt and come west with me, Henry. This is the chance of a lifetime."

"Partners down the middle?" I ask, seeing the possibilities.

"With me coming up with all the money to start us off? And the whole idea mine in the first place? Twenty percent is all I'll be offering you. But you wait till we get there. Folks'll pay a pretty penny for a good wheel at the last sight of civilization. Twenty percent of a fortune is still a fortune."

"I suppose it is." I shake on it, and hope that Sarah will see the sense of it. "There's a woman," I say. "I'll be taking her with us."

Ennis drags a hand over his face. "Women make things complicated, Henry. They slow you down and they talk too much."

"I won't go without her," I say.

He drums his fingers over the rough wood of the bar. "The thing is, you'd have to explain to her family about our plans for going west, and there's no accounting for who they'd tell."

"Why would that matter?"

He leans close and drops his voice. "Right now, there's one fellow out there doing what we'll be doing. One man. And not the sort most folks like doing business with, if you catch my meaning."

He means he's a cheat, I guess, or else his work can't be trusted.

"If we get there, folks will come to us, see? But not if you go running off your mouth and giving us competition."

"We won't be telling her family," I say.

Ennis looks at me, surprised. "I'm getting the lay of it now. You mean to run off with her."

I do, but not in the way he's thinking of it. "In a manner of speaking," I say level and even.

He rubs his beard, considering. "I'll not get in the way of you and your girl, but don't think you'll come to me when her da comes hunting you down with a shotgun."

"Well, he won't be doing that," I say. "So you've no need to worry on that account."

"And I won't have her slowing us down. It's a rough road for sure, and a rugged life. She better be use to hard work because it's no picnic heading west."

"She can handle the work," I tell him. "She's used to a no-picnic kind of life."

"Well then," he says, "I guess it's settled." He knocks the bar for the keep to bring two more whiskeys.

"I guess it is," I say.

"To Flanagan and O'Toole. Wheel makers to the pioneers."

"Flanagan and Taylor, it'll have to be," I say. "Henry Taylor's what I go by now."

He sets his drink down and pulls his face into a frown. "What's wrong with O'Toole? Are you ashamed to be Irish?"

I look into my glass, at the clear brown whiskey sloshing at the bottom. I drink it down and wait out the burn running through my throat and chest. "I saw one sign too many telling me not to apply," I say. "I didn't leave the hunger in Ireland to come here and starve for being Irish."

"But your name. Your father's name."

"My father'd rather see me use a borrowed name than follow him to an early grave."

Chapter 46

Sarah

It's been two weeks since Thomas got sick, which means it's been two weeks since Henry left. Every day feels like a month.

Thomas can't keep the medicine down that the doctor gives him. Seems to me the man should know better than giving him something to swallow when he throws up everything he puts in his mouth. After the third time he comes back giving the same no-use medicine, I can't stand it no more. I go dig up a yam and cut a snatch of red cedar. I boil up the yam with the cedar to make a mash that I spread in homespun.

When I come in his room, he don't even lift his head from the pillow. He's gray and wet through with bed sweat, and when he breathes it's only wheezing.

"I made something for you," I tell him.

He opens his mouth to say something, but a coughing fit takes him and, when it's over, he collapses back against his pillows.

I wrap his chest with the warm yam.

"You smell that?" I say, when the crisp scent of the cedar coming out of the yam cloth starts to fill the air. "That's going to help you breathe better. It has to be good and warm to ease your chest with all your coughing. When it cools off, I'll get you a new one."

I soak two cloths in cold water and put them on his calves, wrapping dry cloths around them, holding them in place. That gets a moan out of him.

"That's for the fever," I tell him. "We got to bring it down. You been burning up for too long."

A while later, when his momma comes in to check on him, she gets right up close to the bed and starts working her nose.

"What's that smell?"

"It's just some cedar from outside," I tell her. "He rests better with it."

She bunches up her high forehead and at first I think she's going to tell me to get rid of it, but then she sees that he's laying quieter than he has for a long time. She leans over and kisses him. "It's good to see him sleeping." She picks up the bottle from the doctor. "Are you giving him the medicine?"

I tell her I am, but I don't mention the other things I got him wrapped in, and she don't see them under the covers, so we leave it at that.

I spend the night in his room again, like I been doing for the past two weeks, and in the morning the fever breaks, but I don't let up. I keep him wrapped with cedar and yam mash on his chest and cold water on his calves.

When I duck into the kitchen house to cook up some more yams, Maple's in there. I hoped to miss her, coming in before she needs to start cooking. She's sitting down at the work table doing nothing at all.

Straight away, she's angry I caught her being idle. "What you think you're doing in here?"

I set my yams to boil. "Just something for Master Thomas to get his breathing straight."

"You got this whole place smelling wild."

"That's just cedar," I tell her. "It helps him."

She watches what I do, and when I take it off the heat she sucks her teeth at me. "The doctor's looking after that boy. He don't need none of your potions."

I scoop out the yams and mash them with the cedar.

"Guess you got to find something to do with yourself now that your blacksmith's had his turn and moved on."

I don't look at her. Don't even act like I heard. I scoop the mash on to fresh homespun.

"They out there saying, 'Poor Sarah, poor Sarah.' Well, I say it serves you right. You should have known better than to be taking up with a white man."

"He'll be back," I say, too mad to pretend I don't hear.

She comes over and stands by me, crowding me. "You the worst kind of fool there is and that's the dumb kind. Everyone can see he done left you, but you. He ain't even thinking about coming back."

"You're wrong," I say, but that wobble in my voice tells her I'm scared. It's been two weeks. "He wants to be with me."

Maple sucks her teeth and shakes her head. "He said that? Well, he done been with you now. He had his good time and he's gone."

"You don't know him. You don't know anything."

"I know plenty. I know my granny momma had to take it when her master let his friends borrow her at night. And my momma couldn't say nothing when her master came for her over and over and over. I know about white men pulling me behind bushes and taking what they want. Even my little girl knows how it be." She points her finger right up in my face. "And now, here you go, laying down with whoever comes smiling at you."

"That ain't how it is with Henry and me."

"You and him makes all them times like it wasn't nothing. Like what they done weren't wrong, and it's us got the problem for not liking it like you do. You wanting to be with him is telling every white man he should just keep on."

"Those men that done that weren't Henry."

"They was him. When he comes taking what ain't his and moving on, it's them all over again."

Chapter 47

Maple

Now that Master Thomas is on the mend, Sarah's got to split her time between checking in on him and her regular work, but really she spends it between moping and fretting. When I fix a pitcher of lemonade for Miss Martha and go to carry it across the yard, who do I see still sweeping the back porch, slow as a snail on sand and barely looking at what she's doing? I already caught her twice poking around the coach house, pining for that blacksmith like a pet dog waiting at the gate for its master. That girl's the most shameful creature I ever seen.

I suck my teeth and pass her by, dipping down into the carry-through and up the cellar stairs into the house. Miss Martha sits in her drawing room, flipping through the same book of poetry she been picking up for weeks.

I set the tray down and pour the lemonade.

"Thank you, Maple. Just what I need."

"You look plum worn out, Miss Martha. You feeling all right?"

"It's this suffocating heat. And to think we've still got August to get through. It's going to be unbearable."

"Just summer, I suppose," I say, though I been wiping sweat from the back of my neck all day. "You sure you ain't sick?"

"My feet are bursting out of my shoes." She twists her body sideways and swings her legs up on to the settee. "Rub my feet, will you, Maple?"

I swallow the smart-mouth answer I want to give her and bend over her feet, taking off her silk shoes. Her ankles are big, and her feet are swollen. I rub them as she sips her lemonade.

"Feet like this and tired as you've been, could be you're with child."

She shakes her head. "I'm sure it's just the heat."

"Momma was always the best one to have around when somebody was carrying. Maybe your daddy would let her come here early."

"Early?"

"You know. Before he pass on and leave everything to you," I say. "She could help you get through your time. And Rose could come over to care for it when it comes, like I did with you. Wouldn't that be fine? Almost like a tradition."

"It's a lovely idea," she says, "but I'm not having a baby." She props up on her elbow. "I know what you're doing, Maple. I told you to wait until I inherit Belle Grove. You'll all be together soon enough. Except Freddy, but that's his own fault."

There's no guile in her face, so I know Master ain't told her. She don't know that "soon enough" is much too late, and if Master Nathaniel has his way it could be never.

"Not so hard," she says, kicking at my hands.

I unclench my fingers from around her feet and start up again with gentle kneading.

"I hear Master Nathaniel's been visiting your daddy a lot," I say.

"My cousin?"

"Un-hunh." I know Master'd say it ain't my place to tell her about this, but I don't care. I ain't telling her for him. I open my mouth and step right into that snake pit 'cause I got to try. "From what I hear, Master Nathaniel's trying to get Master Jeremiah to give Belle Grove Plantation to him instead of to you."

"That's ridiculous. Where'd you hear that? Did Kitty say something when she came with my father? Or Zeek?"

I put my hands on my back and straighten up. We both hear it crack as I move.

"Could be it's just talk. Could be there's something behind it," I say. "If you want to ask without asking, I'd see if he'll give you Momma and Rose early. That ought to tell you what you want to know."

Chapter 48

Henry

After three days of walking, I make it back to Jubilee just after the sun's gone down, worn out, but shot through with joy. It's too late to try and see Mister Johnson, but I'm burning to see Sarah, so I creep into her cabin where I find Bessie spinning at the wheel.

"Evening, Bessie," I say.

She starts when she hears my voice. "I thought you was gone."

"I came back for Sarah," I say.

She cocks her head like a hound picking up a far-off noise she's not sure she heard.

As the evening stretches on, I go from standing to sitting to pacing to peeking out the door. It feels like I've waited an eternity, and then, finally, she's in the doorway. She rushes toward me and flings her arms around me. I catch her up around her waist and lift her off the ground, spinning her in tight circles. We're laughing and she's crying and my heart's trying to tear out from my chest.

Neither one of us wants to spend our first night together again in a cabin with Bessie, so we slip through the far trees under the cover of darkness to the coach house and climb up to the hayloft. There never was such a sweet reunion.

I tell her about meeting Ennis and about the wagon wheels plan in Independence, Missouri. When I've told her everything and we settle down to sleep she starts crying. Quiet, so I won't hear, with her head turned from me.

"What is it?" I ask her.

She shakes her head and pats my arm.

"If you don't want to go to Missouri, we don't have to go," I say. "We can go wherever we like."

She turns to me then, her face streaked wet.

"Please, Sarah. What's wrong?"

She takes my cheeks in her hands, in that way that she has, and says, "Tomorrow, I'm gonna be free."

We sleep clutching on to each other like two drowning souls. In the morning, the sun can't get up fast enough for me. When she leaves to do her duties, I slip out to the river and wash myself, as much to make the time go by as to make myself more presentable. I circle around outside the property to the road, and I walk up the drive, up to the front porch, and I knock.

Sarah opens the door for me, beaming bright as the sun. She squeezes my hand as she lets me in. I touch the wallet on my belt again where I have the money. Over a thousand dollars. Much more than he paid for her, but it means I'm ready if he tries to drive up the price.

I sit on the bench in the hall while she goes to tell Mister Johnson that I'm here with some business to discuss. My knee jitters when I sit down. I straighten my leg and pull it back, but it starts jumping again, so I leave it. I rest my hand on the cash at my belt and wait.

Mister Johnson's smiling when he comes in, holding his hand out to shake mine.

I stand as soon as I see him.

"Good to see you back so soon," he says. "Missus Johnson's still eager to have you make that gate. You can set up where you were." He pumps my hand as he talks, looking almost relieved to see me.

"Sir," I say, "I've come for something else."

His confusion stills him to a careful considering. "Sarah mentioned business. You have some business other than blacksmithing in mind?"

"Yes, sir."

"I see. You'd better step into my office."

He leads the way down the hall to his study and sits behind his wooden desk, offering me a cushioned armchair. He pushes the books and ledgers to the side and folds his hands.

"So, tell me," he says, "what's on your mind?"

"Sir, I've come to buy Sarah."

He stares at me, confused.

I pull out my wallet and hold it between us. "I know how much you paid for her and I want to give you that money. I want to take Sarah with me."

Mister Johnson sits back and considers me. "What on earth do you want with my slave?"

The question pulls me up short and I can't answer it. I open my wallet. I've tied off the seven hundred and eighty dollars and I pull out the cash, placing it on the desk. "I have the money," I tell him.

He ignores the pile of bills and steeples his fingers, leaning forward in his chair. "I see a young man before me with no plantation and no house, and yet you want a house slave."

He's wrong. I don't want a house slave. I want Sarah. The jiggling comes back to my leg, so I adjust my backside on the seat and shuffle my feet.

"We'd go west," I say. "There's an opportunity in Missouri."

"I don't generally like to sell my slaves, Mister Taylor. It creates anxiety and unrest in the quarters. But in a situation like this, you seem to be asking me to sell you a bed wench. I have to tell you I find the suggestion unconscionable."

"No, sir. It wouldn't be like that." I want to stand. I feel trapped sitting here. I shuffle forward on my seat. "Sarah wants to go with me."

He raises his eyebrows inviting me to explain. "You know that how?"

"She told me as much." My leg jitters again. I shake it to stop.

His lips pinch and his eyes flatten. "When did you have occasion to discuss striking off west together?"

My dry mouth sticks when I open it. "I'm very fond of her, sir. As she's fond of me. I've seen much of her in the time I've been here and…and…"

"Now you want to take her with you."

I lay my hand on the bundle of money and inch it forward. "Yes, sir."

He taps his desk first with one finger and then drums with all four. "I gave no credit to what Mulch said about you sneaking off with her. Now I see I may have been hasty to dismiss him."

"No, sir. Mulch was a bad apple. Abusive and—"

"I believe I told you when you first arrived that I don't condone slave bedding, but all this time you've been whoring with her right under my nose."

"No. That's not how it is. I mean to marry Sarah, Mister Johnson. I need you to take this money so we can be on our way."

His mouth hangs open as the color drains from his face.

"That's seven hundred and eighty," I say. "But I can make it eight hundred, if you like, and we'll just go quietly." I pull more money out of my wallet.

He watches me do it, finally looking at the money and then back at me.

"Tell me how much." I add another twenty dollars to the pile.

"Good God," he says, "you actually want to make my slave your wife!"

My stomach drops and I go cold. I see in his face that I've made a terrible slip trying to get him to understand. I should have told him I was buying a house.

A blotchy red creeps up his neck and into his face. "Your wife!"

"I know it isn't as if we could marry," I say. "I didn't mean—"

"Have you lost your mind?" He slams his hands on the desk and stands, sending the chair toppling.

"When I met Sarah—"

"This is the most immoral proposal ever put to me!"

I stand, facing him eye to eye, both of us puffing. I am panicked, feeling this slip from me. "I love her," I say. "Please."

His eyes are wild and I think he's going to strike me. "You are a vile and depraved man."

His insults roll off me. They don't matter. I need to stay calm or I've lost. "Mister Johnson. Sir. Sarah and I—"

"Damn you!" he shouts. "There is no Sarah and I. God made the races to be separate. Each after its kind. He smote them at the Tower when they tried to mix, and, by God, Virginia will smite you with a lynch rope if you try that here."

"Please. We'll leave. You'll never see us again."

"You may not buy my slave, Mister Taylor. I will not sell her to you at any price."

Chapter 49

Sarah

Seems like everybody got an idea about Henry and me. From the ones that can't believe he came back for me, to the ones who say he should have known better than to try. All their talking makes me want to plug up my ears. Fact is, I'm still here and he can't get me out.

When Sunday comes, I go out to the church tree wanting to just get Master's sermoning over with so I can go down to the river. I need to get away from all the staring. And I can't stop myself from hoping Henry might be there.

"I hear he tried to buy you free," Jim says. It's the first thing he's said to me since I fixed his back.

I nod, but I move away from him.

I've had enough of the questions. It's like I'm walking around with my insides hanging open for anybody to come by and pick through.

Master steps outside, fanning himself with his hat. It's only morning but the heat's coming on strong. He walks over to us under the church tree. Standing in front of his forced congregation, he looks at each face till his eyes get to the back row and rest on me.

Then he starts.

"Babylon was an evil place with a lot of sin."

I flick my eyes past him and on to the house. I got too much hate in me to look at him.

"The people thought they knew better than God. You see, God made some people to be servants and some people to be masters, but in Babylon they tried to mix the people together."

I hate his face and his voice and the way he stands with his feet planted wide. I hate how he uses God against us and tries to make us think this is all we deserve.

"So, what did God do? He destroyed what they built up and made it so the races couldn't talk to each other, so they'd stay apart."

He slaps his brown leather book in his hand. "Stay apart. That's what God wants."

I hate him.

We all stand still, waiting for it. There's not one of us that don't know what's coming. My muscles draw in tight bracing for whatever he's going to say. But, no matter what comes, I know me and Henry ain't wrong.

In my mind, I leave him standing there waving his Bible at me. I pick my feet up and go. Through the woods, to the stream. I get on the door and float across and go to our butterfly clearing where Henry's waiting for me. He takes my hand and we walk all the way to Missouri. Maybe when we get there we just keep on walking.

"That blacksmith," I hear him say, and I'm listening in spite of myself. "Tempted one of my sheep into sin." He waves his brown book at us. "He caused Sarah to break God's law, and man's law."

I feel like someone threw a bucket of ice water on me. We all know that's his way of calling for a whipping. I search his belt quick for the overseer's whip. When I don't find it, I search over by the house for one of the town whippers who might've come to do the job for him.

"Now, I've been thinking about your punishment, Sarah."

Master's still got his eyes fixed on me, and I take a step back. The shaking starts in my hands and moves up my arms and then down my legs. I bite down on my tongue so I don't open my mouth and beg.

"But your missus is a tender-hearted woman. She urged me to consider how a white man, who you know to be your superior, whispering lies into your ear, could get you to do almost anything. Like that serpent whispering to Eve. He chose Eve because she was weak, and that devil chose you, Sarah, because you are weak too. He twisted your mind, tempting you to the sin of fornication with lies and false promises, not unlike the serpent in the Garden of Eden."

My breath comes in shallow pants and his voice grows muffled under the buzzing in my ears.

"The Lord is a good master. He forgives when we repent our sin and he shows us mercy."

Over at the house, Missus steps on to the back porch in her peach Sunday dress, resting her hand on one of the thick pillars.

"And I try to be a good earthly master to all of you. I forgive, and I show mercy. That's why we're not going to have a whipping for this. Instead, Sarah, you'll work in the fields this next week. It is my hope and my expectation that you will take this time to remind yourself of your place. And I expect all of you to take a lesson from these unfortunate occurrences. And I never want to hear about this sort of thing again."

I look up to Missus on the porch and she nods, and I know she's just saved my hide. A wave of relief steals my strength and I feel like I need to sit down. When I sway on my feet, reaching out for something to hang on to, Clover steps up to take hold of my arm, steadying me.

Master puffs out his chest and spreads his arms wide. "God wants loyal, obedient servants," he says. "And He rewards them in Heaven."

I lean into Clover as he props me up by my elbows.

"And when I find a loyal obedient servant here at Jubilee, I can do no less."

Everybody starts looking sideways at each other, to see if somebody else can make sense of what he's saying, but everybody there's got the same look that says, "What now, Lord?" I feel the tension creep back into the group. There's a buzz of excitement at the chance of a reward, mixed with fear, because a master's reward isn't always good. That man could be talking about anything.

"Bessie has served my family since before I was born. I've never had any trouble with her. Isn't that right, Bessie?"

"Yes, sir, Master. Ain't never given you no trouble."

"That's right. So, Bessie, for your loyal and obedient service, I've decided to set you free."

"Master?"

"I'll draw up the papers and get them validated at the county court when I'm in town next week. And then you can go."

"Go where, Master?"

"Wherever you like. 'Well done my good and faithful servant,' that's what God will say, and that's what I say. You've been a good and faithful servant. All right now, let's have some singing."

We look at each other like we all been struck stupid on the head with a pan. Ain't no song for the likes of all that. He won't sell me, but he's gonna set blind old Bessie free. It's a different kind of lash.

"Momma," Clover says from next to me. Now it's him that wobbles. And Bessie too. Samson steps over to her and puts his solid arm around her, keeping her standing.

Nobody sings, and after a time Master looks like he's about to get upset. One thing about blind Bessie is she can feel what other folks can see. She clears her throat and steps forward, and Master's good and faithful servant lifts her weedy voice. "It's me, it's me, it's me, O Lord," she sings, her voice straining to hold the tune, "standing in the need of prayer."

Don't nobody join in with her, even with Master looking on.

Chapter 50

Henry

I haven't dared sneak back on to Jubilee since Matthew Johnson refused to let me buy Sarah and threw me off his plantation. I'm afraid of what he might do to her if he finds me there, so I keep my distance and worry. Truth be told, I'm afraid of what he might have already done. The not knowing is eating me up, but all I can do is wait by the river.

It's been two days. But today is Sunday and she's got the afternoon off. Today she'll come. If she doesn't, I swear I'll go mad. I've been sleeping in the clearing, but I get myself over to by the river just past sunrise and sit, thinking. Since that day, I'm always thinking, trying to come up with a new plan. And trying not to panic when I come up blank. I've gone over that conversation with Matthew Johnson at least a hundred times in my head, cursing myself for all the things I should have said. I trusted too much in having the money. It never touched my mind that having money wasn't enough. Mostly, I curse Matthew Johnson and his goddamn Tower of separate races. I guess Father Michael would have had a thing or two to say about that. According to him, Jesus was always flapping on about loving people. Enemies and all. I'm sure I'm not a very holy man, truth be told, because I can't muster a bean of love for Matthew bloody Johnson.

The sun is straight overhead when I hear a rustle on the path. I look up and Sarah is headed toward me. I rush over to her, catching her up in my arms. Neither one of us says a word for at least a minute. It's a relief to hold her and to feel her wrapped around me.

"I wasn't sure you'd be here, but I was hoping," she tells me.

It hurts me that she could think one setback would turn me from wanting to be with her. "I told you I'm taking you with me, and I mean to do it."

She tucks her head up into my neck. Right up into her spot. "I ain't never getting off this plantation, Henry. And you can't come back on." She steps back from me and looks into my face. "Maybe you should move on."

"No," I tell her. "We're moving on together."

"Master says God don't want us together."

I trace my fingers around her brow and down to her chin. "And do you believe that?" I ask.

"No." Her eyes well up, squeezing my heart. "But if Master believes it, God might as well be against us."

I lay my forehead against hers. "When I'm with you it's like God's breathing life into me," I tell her. "I'm stronger and smarter and a plain better man. The way I see it, that could only happen if God himself had a hand in it. I think he's telling us he wants us together." I take her hands in mine. They're cool despite the heat. "He made you special for me. And He made me special for you. It wouldn't be right to turn our backs on that just because Matthew Johnson doesn't understand about it."

She lays her head on my chest and it about melts my heart because I know she's crying and she doesn't want me to see. When she's wiped her eyes, I lead her up the river to where I hid the door. I hold it steady for her as she climbs on. Then I push her out into the river and swim her across. On the other side, she climbs off and presses in close against my side, even though I'm soaked through. Her arm snakes tightly around my waist, and mine around hers.

Goddamn Matthew Johnson.

I want us to always be like this, pressed close to each other, wanting everything from the other and wanting to give everything too. I want to pledge myself to her before God and hear her pledge herself to me. I want her to never doubt I'll be waiting for her, no matter how many setbacks and how many days.

We come out on to the wildflower field where a hundred butterflies dance and flit, like God's made us our very own heaven. I don't hesitate. I lead her into the middle of the field and drop down on one knee.

"Will you marry me?" I say.

"We can't," she says. "How can we?"

"Never mind about that," I say. "I want us to be man and wife and build a life together. I want for you to know that I'll never give up on being with you. I want to marry you, Sarah. Will you have me?"

She looks at me like I've gone daft in the head, but then she says, "Yes, I will," so it doesn't matter how she's looking at me.

"Wait here," I say. I run to the trees and fetch a fallen branch. I lay it down in front of her. "Almost like a broom, wouldn't you say?"

I've surprised her again and she laughs, taking my meaning. "You want to do it now?"

"No better time," I say.

Her face lights up and she scurries off around the field picking wildflowers and bunching them into a bouquet. When she comes back to where I'm standing, I bend down and pick a blue cornflower and put it in her hair behind her ear. From my pocket, I pull out the strip of cloth from her dress that she used when we met to wrap my hand.

"I know the broom is your tradition," I say, "but we have traditions too."

I take her hand and twine her fingers between mine. Then I wrap the strip of cloth around our clasped hands, and with our free hands we clumsily tie it together.

"We don't have anyone to speak over us so I suppose we should speak for ourselves." I press our hands tighter together under the cloth and say, "I promise." I pause, thinking. There isn't that much I can promise her. I'm a simple man with not much to offer except myself, so I settle on that. "I promise that I'll be yours if you'll be mine."

She lays her free hand on our joined ones. "I promise that my heart is always yours, no matter what."

We grin at each other and, counting to three, we jump over that branch broom. There's not a state in America that would say we're a legally married couple, but I know, and Sarah knows, and God almighty knows that she's my wife.

We lay down in the middle of the field by the broom and we take our time because its Sunday and we have until the morning, and because it's our wedding day and I want to savor every second with her. I strip off her clothes and she peels off mine, and in among the butterflies on a bed of flowers we lay as man and wife. Overhead, the sun shines straight down on us, warming us with God's blessings.

Chapter 51

Sarah

When I come back from the woods, it's near on morning. In the cabin, Bessie and her sons, Samson and Clover, sit round the table Ben made, on the chairs he carved, looking like they been up all night. On the bed Ben built sits Clover's wife, Callie May, with her four children curled up asleep behind her. Since Ben died, Bessie's told and retold the story of how he wouldn't marry her until he finished carving that bed, saying he wouldn't bring his bride to a pallet on the floor.

I cross over to my own pallet and lift the corner, laying the flower Henry put in my hair and my clutch of wildflowers beside the iron bracelet. Bessie tips her head my way so I know she's heard me come in, but when she speaks it's to her sons.

"You think Master'll let me come visit you all when I go free?" she asks.

"Course, Momma," says Samson. "Course he will."

I never heard of no freed slave coming and going around a plantation, keeping everybody longing for freedom, but I keep my tongue.

"You could ask him about that," Callie May says with her out-loud words, but the twist and pull of her face says, somebody's got to stop lying to this old woman.

I stand to go, leaving Bessie with her family, when Callie May says, "Maybe Sarah knows someone you can stay with when you leave here." Callie May darts her eyes over to where I've lain my flowers under my pallet.

It about knocks my breath out that she knows I've been with Henry. Silence slides around the room as they wait for me to say something. Clover's little girl wakes in the stillness and climbs on to her momma's lap. She sucks her thumb and closes her eyes with her head on Callie May's chest.

"Don't you all know anybody?" I say.

Bessie reaches for Clover's hand. "Everybody I got's right here on this plantation."

"Don't you worry about that, Momma," Samson says. "You can go into town and hire out."

Callie May glares at him. "Doing what? Who's going to hire a blind old lady?"

"She can spin," he says.

Callie May rocks her little girl and turns her face away.

"Momma, you got your freedom," Clover says. "You been wanting that since you was old enough to know you didn't have it."

"It ain't the same now. I done gave all my good years. I nursed that boy from a babe and when I get to where I'm no use to even my own self, he goes and turns me out like an old barn cow."

"But, Momma, you'll be free. You'll die a free woman."

She pats his hand. "I want to be buried next to your daddy. That's all I want now."

"Momma, you need to get your head right," Samson says. "This ain't just for you. This here's for all of us."

Callie May's eyes bore into me over the top of her little girl's head. "She's just going to need a little help out there."

I look from one expectant face to the other. "Maybe you could stay with," I glance at the door, nervous of being overheard, "someone I know. For a little while."

"Maybe she could," Callie May says.

Bessie reaches for her cane and shuffles over to me. "You still seeing him?"

I don't answer. Just watch their faces and sense the air getting thinner with Master's threat pushing in from every corner of the cabin.

Bessie reaches out feeling my shoulder, my neck, my jaw, my mouth. "You ain't gonna stop till you're both hanging from a tree."

I pull away from her pawing at me and cross to the door. Outside the sun's coming up east, peeling back the dark.

"I need to get into the field," I say. "First light's already come."

Samson leans back in his chair. "Ain't no overseer down there now," he says. "Master don't check the field till he eats breakfast. We'll be on over there by then."

I go to the cotton shack by the fields and find a large burlap bag that I tie to my waist. The end of it tangles with my feet when I walk. I take myself off to the far end of a row of cotton where a few others have gathered. I reckon we're the cautious ones who can't afford to be caught out if Master comes down first thing after all.

I pluck at the white wooly bloom, but the cotton don't come out clean. When I pick at the clumps left in the dry hull, the sharp points of the pod stab at my fingers. I pull them away, shaking my hand and sucking at the blood drops.

I work down the row, hunched and slow. My near-empty bag seems even bigger than when I tied it on.

In the time it takes Samson and Clover and Callie May to get out to the field, my back is hurting and my fingers are raw. And in a little more time, when Master comes out and checks on us, they've already picked as much as I have. It's going to be a long and painful week.

Chapter 52

Maple

When I go up to brush Miss Martha's hair, she's waiting on me, drawn up tight and tall, with smoke near about pouring out of her ears. "Was it my husband who told you about my father's plans?"

Here we go.

"Were you trying to have me go behind his back?"

I think about lying, but she already knows, so I give her a corner of the truth wrapped up in honey words.

"You told me enough times I should never keep secrets from you, Miss Martha. Didn't seem right not to say something."

"I see." She takes up pacing the room.

"You want me to start keeping secrets, ma'am?"

"Of course not, Maple. But you should have told me the whole story. We've stumbled into a real hornet's nest."

I make my face go blank and stand beside the dressing table, picking up the hairbrush, waiting for her to sit.

"Father is feuding with Matthew. And he won't hear sense from the likes of me. Apparently, I should concern myself with *matters appropriate for my sex*." Her nostrils flare. She looks like her momma when she's fired-up angry.

"Seems to me," I say with a voice smooth as silk, "it's a woman's place to be looking out for her family."

She sinks into the chair of her dressing table and looks at herself in the reflecting glass. "I just don't have it in me for this fight, Maple. Not when they're both set on keeping me out of it."

I dig my thumb into the bristles on the brush. She ain't even started fighting yet. "What'd your daddy say when you asked for Momma and Rose?"

She turns in her chair to face me. "That a real man doesn't send his wife to beg for him, and that he'd already given Matthew his answer and my asking for more wouldn't change his mind. He said it's stunts like this that make my cousin look a worthier heir."

The back of my skull draws up tight. Master Jeremiah's not letting them go.

Her jaw tenses as she stares me down. "You should never have inserted yourself into my business. Your prying has made everything worse, for all of us."

I want to sit down. Instead, I lean heavy against the dresser.

Fuming, she sits back in her chair and unpins her hair, letting it fall dark and full down her back. I don't brush it. The tightness across my head creeps down my neck and sits in my shoulders. It climbs down my back and pulls at my insides.

"Maple?" Miss Martha turns to look at me.

"Rose can't stay there," I say. Momma may be lost to me, but I can't leave Rose to him.

Through the looking glass she watches me like a field rabbit watches a meadow. She smells the wolf in the air. "That's not something I can fix," she says to my reflection. She runs her fingers through her hair, like a carefree southern belle, but her nostrils flare, giving her away.

"Did he tell you she's a special comfort to Master Nathaniel?" I say. I won't let her pretend not to know.

She puts her hand on my arm like comforting a sister. Then she says, "I can't interfere again. Father and Matthew will work it out in their own time."

I pull away from her, my sister and my mistress. Family that ain't no kind of family.

Chapter 53

Henry

I telegraph Ennis to let him know that I'll need a little more time before I can head west, and I find work in Liberty Valley breaking big stones into small. The work is hard and familiar. Breaking stones was one of the work-gang jobs Da and I did back in Ireland, but I manage it better now that I'm not starving.

Three days into my new job, I strike off as the bell rings at quitting time. There's nothing like dirt and rock smoke and hard labor and the stench and swearing of other men to make you long for your woman.

She won't be at the river tonight, so I pick my way through the woods to the plantation. The night is dark and moonless, but with a thousand silver stars. I plan to creep to her cabin unseen and lead her out before blind Bessie knows I've been.

I crouch from tree to tree, picking my way closer and, checking that no one's about, I dart into her cabin. Sarah's not there, but Bessie is, and so are Annie and Willa. I curse my impatience as I try to think what to do. They've seen me. Now they've got a way to make trouble for Sarah.

"Is that Red?" Bessie asks from the table where she sits.

I don't say anything. Looking from one to the other, I put my finger to my lips wondering if I could sneak back out.

"No. That's Sarah's blacksmith," Annie says.

My stomach flips for Sarah.

"Mister Taylor?" Bessie says. "Come on and have a sit-down. I reckon I need to talk to you."

Maybe I could bribe them into not telling that I've been here. I make my way to her table and sit opposite, trying to think of what I could offer for their silence.

"Do you have a home, Mister Taylor?" Bessie asks.

I blink at her, gaping. A house is a lot to ask for, and not much use to her here.

Annie and Willa lean in for my answer.

It feels like there's a trick to this question.

"Where's Sarah?" I ask instead.

"She'll be by," says Annie. "But we was wondering if you got a place." She glances at Bessie and says, "Somewhere a freed slave woman could stay with you?"

My heart jumps, hoping maybe Mister Johnson changed his mind about Sarah. "I can. I will. We're heading west," I say. "To the head of the Oregon Trail. I'll build her a place when we get there."

"That ain't no good," says Willa.

"No," says Bessie, as her sons come bustling in with Callie May. "That don't help me none."

Samson, Clover and Callie May hesitate when they see me, but then Clover and Samson both say, "Evening," and walk on in.

"How you doing, Momma Bessie?" Callie May says, going to her side.

When I see this, my first thought with them pawing around her so concerned is that Bessie's sick. Maybe Ben's dying has pushed her to her end, like Ma's dying did to Da.

My second thought is that now with the six of them knowing I'm here, the bribing's getting trickier.

"I'd appreciate if you wouldn't mention to Matthew Johnson that you'd seen me," I say.

Bessie reaches across the table and pats my hand. "Ain't nobody gonna say nothing about you being here."

"Where's Sarah?" Annie asks the three of them who've just come in. It's what I want to know as well.

"Making something to soak her fingers," Samson says.

I don't like that he knows this. It seems too familiar that he should.

The door opens again and I expect it to be Sarah, but it's Red, and I tense when I see him. At every gathering it's always Red who makes it clear I'm not welcome. I expect him to rail at me that I've been kicked off Jubilee and I ought to stay away, but he tips his head to me and comes and puts his hand on Bessie's shoulder.

"He ain't got no place a body could stay," says Willa. It's like they've been discussing this between them.

"Wants to go out west," says Annie.

Red pats Bessie's shoulder.

"We'll come up with something," Samson says.

"Would one of you please tell me why you're all so interested in my having a house?"

They look at each other. Bessie gives a nod, and Annie blurts out, "Master freed Bessie."

I stare at her. I can't be hearing right.

"Least, he says he will, soon as he gets around to going by the courthouse for the papers," she says.

"Freed?" is all I can manage to say.

"For a lifetime of being good and faithful to her master," Red says with bitter scorn.

"She ain't got no place to go," says Callie May, "so we was thinking she might could stay with you."

"Me?"

"You ain't like most white folk," says Annie. "We thought you might help."

I could rip Matthew Johnson's head off, the bastard. He won't free Sarah for love or money but then turns around and does this. I should say something kind to Bessie, but the bitter disappointment gags me.

"We know what you tried to do," Callie May says, sitting beside her husband on Bessie's bed. "It was a good thing."

"I still mean to do it," I say. "I just need to find another way."

"See, that right there makes you different," she says, studying me with bright eyes. "Folks thought you'd move on, but here you be. Sticking by your woman."

"Not just sticking by. Selling up to buy her free," Clover says, taking her hand. "How a man gets his money and what he does with it shows the soul of him."

I'm surprised at how grateful I feel to be praised and welcomed. "What's between Sarah and me," I say, running my nails along the wood planks of the table, "it's not something you move on from."

Samson hands me a bottle of something clear and claps me on the shoulder. Whatever it is burns all the way down.

"I still say, he ain't got no business messing with her," Red says.

"Leave it, Red," Annie says. "It don't got nothing to do with you."

"No. I'm gonna say my piece. It's his fault she's out there."

"What's he talking about? Where's Sarah?" I stand, anxious.

Red points his finger at me, and I brace for what's coming. "You got her put in the field," he says.

By the faces of the others, I know it's true.

"That ain't on him," Callie May says.

"Who else it on? You? Me? He needs to leave her be, or it's gonna get worse for her."

In the tense silence, Sarah walks in carrying a bowl of floating leaves. The sight of her goes right to my bones. When she sees me standing in the crowded room, she lights up. I twine my arms around her, holding her, feeling a flood of relief, like cold water over a burn.

"Henry," she says, and it's like music.

When I dip my head she lays her cheek against mine, and I breathe in her scent, earthy and sweet like honeysuckle and thyme.

The room's gone quiet watching us, and I step back from her. She looks exhausted but beautiful.

I take the bowl from her and notice the scabs and scars on her swollen fingers that weren't there when I saw her on Sunday. "He's making you pick?" I say.

"Just for a week," she says.

A rage flashes in me. I want to burn his precious fields to the ground. But Sarah will pay the price for anything I do, which just makes my blood boil hotter. I have to get her out of here.

She settles into my vacated chair, soaking her fingers in the water. Even the backs of her hands are marked with scratches.

I touch my hand to her shoulder as light as I can and, with my heart in my throat, I ask, "Did he do anything else?"

She shakes her head. "Nothing else."

It's a strange kind of relief I feel as I let my hand rest heavy on her shoulder. An angry relief. This should never be something a person worries over. I rub her back in circles, my nervous energy needing release.

"It ain't right to keep her hanging on for something that won't never be," Red says to me.

"Already is," Sarah says, sharp as a slap. "We jumped a broom. We mean for it to stick."

"What's that?" Bessie says, reaching out to Sarah across the table.

"Good on you," Callie May says from beside Clover on the bed. "Folks should take whatever happy they can find wherever they find it."

"Maybe, but that broom don't make one lick of difference," Samson says. "It sure ain't gonna keep the whip off her back, or stop Master selling her Mississippi way if he catches lover-man creeping around here."

The back of my head throbs thinking about all the evil that bastard could rain down on her. "I won't let that happen," I say. "I'm getting her free."

I think of the man killed in New York whose clothes I took, and of Mister Reardon bludgeoning the blacksmith to death, and I wonder if I could kill a man if it came to it. To keep Sarah safe, I believe I could.

I rest my hands on her shoulders. The feel of her quiets my insides. I lean into her like a moth searching for light.

"You leave them be," Callie May says. "Don't none of us know what's coming next, so you got to grab the good thing you got and hang on as long as you can."

August 1849

Chapter 54

Sarah

Coming back to housework after my week in the fields, I mostly try to stay out of Master's sight. I don't want to give him cause to send me back out there. It takes Maple three days to notice what I'm doing and then, hateful as she is, she sends me to him every chance she gets.

"Bring this pitcher of sweet tea out to Master and his guest on the porch," she tells me with a look of trying to stir up trouble.

Master sits on a rocker waving his hat in his face to fan the heavy air. A second man sits beside him perched on the edge of a chair like a chipmunk testing the branch for its weight. He's a tall man, and hungry-thin with worn-out clothes that droop near about as much as his jowls.

"Ah, good, yes," Master says when he sees me with the glasses and the pitcher of tea. "That's just what we need."

I fill the glasses and set the pitcher down and turn to go.

"Sarah, get the fan and give us some air. It's far too hot today." He takes a big drink.

"Yes, sir," I say. I duck down to the carry-through and back to a side room searching for the wicker fan with the long wooden handle. I find it leaning next to a fishing pole and hurry back. Stepping up to the porch, I wave it at their heads. Maple's going to be spitting coal that I'm not back to help her get the meal ready, but I guess it's her own fault for sending me.

"I'm not too concerned that you've never worked as an overseer, Mister Laramie, though you understand your pay will reflect your lack of experience. My slaves are well behaved and compliant. I don't anticipate a problem."

"You seem to have them under control, sir," Mister Laramie says.

"The secret to keeping slaves is righteous rules. When a horse is ill-treated, we aren't surprised when it bolts at the first opportunity. And when a master insists on arbitrary beatings and starvation rations, we shouldn't wonder that his slaves long to be free of him and cause mischief at every opportunity. My slaves are well-treated. They are fed and clothed. I encourage pairings and I almost never break up families. If they work hard, they can expect a peaceful life. It makes rebellion unnecessary."

"Yes, sir. They look right peaceful. But I never heard of a slave who don't need a whipping now and then."

"We whip when it's necessary, but I prefer to reward good behavior. Take cotton picking. It's reasonable for a prime hand to pick two hundred pounds of cotton a day. If someone picks more, I might lay on some meat at the end of the week. Or a traveling pass on Sunday. You draw more bees with honey, Mister Laramie."

"Well, I'll take your word for that."

"Yes, you will, sir. If you work for me, you certainly will."

The sun bakes my skin and the sweat runs down my neck. I swipe at it and draw Mister Laramie's attention.

He watches me as more sweat beads up and rolls along my skin. I don't dare touch it. Just let it crawl on down my throat.

"I believe in rules," Master says, and Mister Laramie snaps his attention back over to him. "I set up rules and I expect them to be followed." He waves at me to refill his glass. "My last overseer, and others," he glances at me, "chose to break my rules. I don't tolerate that."

"No, sir. I wouldn't do that. Believe you me, I'm a stickler for rules myself."

"Good. Because we all have to follow rules. Laid out by God and government."

"Yes, sir. Amen."

"My last overseer, and others, committed the sin of fornication."

"Sir?"

"God's got a rule against that. I expect you know that fornication, even with a slave, is against God's law."

"I suppose it is."

"Now, the Devil's always at work."

"Yes, sir."

"He can send a lust on a man," Master snaps his fingers. "Like that. But on a sanctified plantation, and that's what Jubilee is, we have to renounce the Devil and his temptations."

"Amen, sir."

"And I'll tell you something else. God didn't ordain we should be masters over the Negro race to teach sin. We're to teach them the righteous gospel of the Bible."

"Well, I sure am a God-fearing man, sir."

"That's good. Christian slaveholders and overseers have to bring light into dark minds."

The aching in my arms spreads around my shoulders and crawls all down my back till I'm burning up with tired. I roll my shoulders but keep the fan waving, hoping Master won't notice me shifting about. When Bessie comes feeling her way around the side of the house and Master shifts his attention over to her for a minute, I tuck the long handle under my shoulder to try to ease the heavy in my arms.

Bessie tests the ground and inches forward. Watching her makes me think on a timid bird. She's nothing like the woman she was when I first met her less than a year ago, all sure steps and swagger.

"This one's Bessie," Master says. "Come here, Bessie."

She gropes her way up the stairs.

"I set Bessie free last week. I'll bet you thought I forgot about that."

"No, Master."

"I haven't had time to sort out your free papers yet, but don't you worry. They're coming."

"I been meaning to talk to you about that, Master."

"Something on your mind?" He lays his cool glass against his face.

"I was wondering. Well, I was hoping. It's just that my Ben's buried over yonder, and Samson and Clover's here. And Callie May and the children. Little Patsy and Shine and Tally and Hep."

"Bessie, I know my slaves. What's this about?"

"Well, Master, I appreciate you giving me my papers. I do. But I want to ask you if I can stay put."

"Stay?"

"Don't got that many days left no more. This here's the only home I know. Please, Master. I won't make no trouble."

"Well, I'll be damned." He slams down his drink and turns to the new overseer. "Do you hear this, Mister Laramie?"

"Don't mean no harm by it, Master. I'm grateful for what you done."

Master straightens tall in his seat with his chest puffed out. "I gave this woman her freedom, and you hear what she says? She wants to stay here." He jumps up out of his seat, knocking over his glass of sweet tea. It spills from the small table on to the white painted porch.

"Bessie, you are my proof. And, Mister Laramie, you're my witness. I've been saying this all along."

"Don't mean to make no trouble," Bessie says, shrinking from Master's excitement.

"Bessie, you're the best slave I ever had. We've got to get this in the papers. Treat your slaves right and they don't want their freedom."

She shakes her head, backing away from him. "No, Master. I...I—"

Master throws an arm around Bessie's shoulders and squeezes her into him, making her stumble to catch her footing. "Let's see what those abolitionists make of that!"

I don't know if Bessie meant to give back her freedom, or just ask to stay at Jubilee a free woman, but Master's like a hound with a scent. Any chance she had of getting those free papers is already gone.

Chapter 55

Henry

On Sunday morning, I wait by the river behind Jubilee Plantation for Mister Johnson to finish sermonizing so Sarah can come see me. I spend the morning sitting and pacing and growing impatient.

From the bank, I pick up five flat stones and skip them over the slow-moving river. Each makes three skips before sinking into the water. I dig a stick into the mud by the bank, listening over the cry of the thrush and sparrow for the sound of her coming.

She calls my name and I turn to the sight of her rushing toward me. I drop the stick and, arms open, face smiling, I scoop her close to me. She gets more beautiful every time I see her. When I dip my head down to kiss her, she rakes her fingers through my hair. The feel of her makes everything speed up and slow down all at once. She's in my blood, making me alive and she's in my head making me want to be alive.

I pull out the wooden door hidden in the bushes and settle Sarah on top of it. I wade into the water and float her across. At the other side, she takes my hand and follows me down the path.

In our clearing, I've already left two blankets and a wrapped bundle of cornbread and smoked fish. She doesn't want to eat, but asks me to hold her. I feel in her touch that something's happened and when she crawls on to my lap and curls up against me, I'm terrified.

"Tell me what's happened," I say.

"Henry," she says into my neck.

My name on her lips is a precious thing, alive with possibility.

I wait for her to speak, but she stays silent. I stroke her back for encouragement and she takes my hand and lays it low on her stomach.

"Did someone hurt you?" I ask. I probe her belly gently with my fingers.

She pulls a long, slow breath in and then pushes it out again. "No one hurt me," she says.

I tip her chin up so that I can see into her face. "Did someone say something to you? Threaten you?"

She takes my hand and puts it back on her belly. She tries twice to say something. Then she looks down to my hand on her stomach and her hand holding it there. "Your baby's in there," she says.

She says it like an apology, so it takes a second for her words to be clear in my mind. And then, less than a second for the shock to turn to joy. "My child?" I say. "You're carrying my child?"

I can barely kiss her for smiling. I lay her back in the grass and rub my lips across her belly. Softly. So softly. My little one is growing in there. I'm going to be a father. My beautiful Sarah is going to have my child. I lay my head beside her belly.

"Hello, in there," I whisper. "I'm your da."

"You ain't mad?"

I pick my head up and kiss her from her belly, up her chest, to her lips, a smile stretching my mouth so wide I feel it in my cheeks.

"I'm so happy," I say. "You're giving me a child. We're going to be a family." I can't stop touching her. Mother of my child.

I desire her more than ever. Everything I feel is deeper and stronger. Before she had my heart. Now she is my heart.

When I lay with her, I cannot get close enough or deep enough and when she shouts out my name I'm overwhelmed, crying like a child as I shudder my release.

A breeze licks at the sweat on my back, cooling me as the sun bakes my skin. Somewhere in the wildflower field a bullfrog croaks. I trail my fingers up and down her body and end by circling her belly.

"I thought you'd be upset."

"Never," I say. "I'm counting on you giving me lots more little ones. I want six, or seven. Maybe eight." I prop myself up on my elbow to look into her face. "Do you think it's a boy or a girl?"

"I don't know," she says.

"It doesn't matter," I say. "We'll have plenty of each by the time we're done."

I kiss her then, but she doesn't respond. Instead, she looks away and curls on to her side, pulling her knees up. It comes to me, only now, that she might not be happy about this at all.

"Sarah? Don't you want to have my child?"

She looks up into my face hovering over hers. I can see the distress in her features and I'm sorry I've asked the question because now I don't want to hear the answer.

"I'm scared," she says.

I kiss her forehead and take her hands. "There never was a mother who wasn't scared for her child," I say.

Tears that have formed in her eyes leak out and into her hairline. I coax her back around to me with strokes and caresses, but it doesn't calm her. She clings to me and cries.

I don't understand the depth of her fear, until she says, "I don't want him to have our baby."

The realization hits me like a cold slap. It's followed hard on by revulsion and horror. According to the law, the child follows the condition of the mother. A slave owned by a master. I push down the panic rising up and grab Sarah close to me, wrapping myself around her. I will not let it happen.

"He'll never own our baby," I say, making another promise I've no earthly idea how to keep.

Holding my wife tucked up in my arms, with my child nestled inside of her, I know that America is a lie. Because where's the liberty and the freedom and the rights and the justice, when the law says Matthew Johnson owns my child after already owning my wife? What kind of Constitution for the people allows a thing like that? A country can claim that wrong is right, but that'll never erase the sin of it.

I'm taking my family out of Jubilee. My child will not be that man's slave.

Chapter 56

Sarah

The water buckets slosh at my sides, wetting my skirt, as I carry them from the well pump out by the kitchen house back inside. When I pass through the carry-through and head up the stairs into the main house, I go slow and careful though my arms are tired. I can't be spilling water on Master's floor.

In Missus's room, I pour the buckets into the bathtub that's starting to fill up good. When I go back to the well, I think I see someone creeping behind the tree line. Straightaway I think it must be Henry. When I get my buckets full, I set them down and, looking round to make sure no one's watching, I go down into the trees. I don't see him. When I call, I don't get an answer. Pushing deeper into the woods, I search through the shrubs, behind trees. When I'm ready to call myself good and crazy and turn back, I see a man crouched in a ditch, holding long, wide fern leaves over himself to keep from being seen. He's wearing the slave rags of a field hand and his right foot and ankle are torn and bloody. His eyes lock on me, but then dart around everywhere like he's looking to see who all I brought with me.

"Where'd you come from?" I ask.

He don't answer, and I reckon I don't need to know.

"You break that?" I ask, pointing at his ankle.

He shakes his head. "Dogs got me."

I step in close to get a look at his leg. I can't see the bite clear through all the blood. I rip a clinging vine off a nearby oak and strip the leaves and wrap it tight around the man's leg above the bite. I work fast so I can get back before someone notices I'm gone.

"Thank you," he says as I tie his leg up.

He shouldn't walk on it for a day or two, but you can't expect that from a man who's running. "Good luck," I say, standing. I turn to go, meaning to leave him in the ditch. I've barely taken a step when he calls to me.

"Hide me," he says.

I feel a tingling fear just from him asking.

"Not long. Just a few days, till my leg heals."

I mean to say no. I can't risk all that for a stranger. But on his face I see the desperate determination I've been seeing on my own face these last weeks. Maple calls it being sour, but it's long past sour. It's being ripe.

"Come on," I say.

I help him to his feet and lead him, leaning heavy on my arm, to my cabin. I know Bessie won't be there. Master's got her with him on his talking tour to show everybody the slave who asked "please don't set me free." Red won't hardly look at her since it happened, even though she's up there next to him on that buggy day after day. I told him she was just asking to be with her family, but he don't care how it happened. He says if someone's giving out freedom you got to grab it for all of us, and don't let no one or nothing turn you round. He says there's bigger things to think of than where you get stuck in the ground. Master's touring just proves his point.

In my cabin, there's Bessie's table and chairs, her bed and my pallet, and a fireplace against the wall.

"Get under the bed," I tell him.

It's a poor hiding place, but it's the only one in the room, unless I stick him up the chimney.

I go back out to the well where my buckets sit waiting on me and pump some water to clean my hands with. My heart is racing, thinking about what I've done, and I stop to just breathe, trying to steady myself. With Annie and Willa up cleaning out the Big House, nobody's around who would have seen. Except maybe Maple if she took that moment to step outside.

I pick up the buckets and head to the kitchen house where Maple's muttering to herself over a pot of stew. She's moved the buckets I left on the fire to the side. I dip my finger in and find them lukewarm.

"You moved these buckets?"

"I don't want your buckets in my way when I'm trying to—"

I cut her off. I'm spitting angry but my words come out calm. I say, "If you don't let this water get hot, I will throw your stew on this floor." I mean it too. Right at this second, I would fight her to the death over those buckets.

Maple pulls up shocked, but for once keeps her tongue.

I step in front of her and make her see me. "Or maybe I'll just use the chili like Bessie," I say. I know I got that look, that desperate determination, and she reads it right. I will do what I say. That and more.

She sucks her teeth and blows out her lips, but then she moves the buckets over to the fire.

I walk out of the kitchen house shaking.

Up in Missus's room, I lay out her soaps and scrubbing brushes. She's spread an evening gown out on the bed to change into when she's finished.

"Sarah," she says, coming into the room, and I jump near out of my skin.

"What on earth is the matter with you?" she asks. "You're acting like a spooked cat."

I lay my shaking hands against my belly and breathe deep trying to get my nerves in control. "I'm fine, ma'am. Just a little tired, I guess." I cross over to where she's laid her clothes. "That's a right pretty dress, ma'am."

She smiles. "After three days of roving the countryside, I wanted to greet your master home in style."

"Then I best go back for the hot buckets," I say, ducking quick out of the room. I need to be away from her before she figures out I'm hiding something and wants to know what.

Maple ignores me when I step into the kitchen, but the water's on the cookstove, boiling hot. I lug each bucket, one by one, up to the copper bath. When I'm done, I stick my hand in to test the water.

Missus calls my name sharply, and I jump.

"Well, you're about to leap right out of your skin," she laughs. "Help me with this tie," she says.

I loosen the bow knotted at her back.

"I know what's going on with you," she says.

My heart flails like a fish fighting the hook. She couldn't have seen me. She's never anywhere but the front rooms.

"I do believe that blacksmith has turned your head right around. I mean, imagine being in your position and hearing a white man speak to you about love and marriage. That's the most disgraceful part. I'm sure you had no earthly idea how wicked it all was. And now you're all unsettled. Don't you worry, Sarah. I know just how to settle you."

"I'm fine Missus," I say, stepping away from her. "You need anything else before I go?"

She sits on her lounge chair and pats the corner for me to join her. I perch on the end with one half of my bottom.

"There's nothing wrong with wanting to marry and have a husband and some children," she says. "And I know just the right one for you. I haven't forgotten that you were fond of Red before all this happened. I remember he gave you that headscarf you used to wear."

I pinch my mouth closed and look at the floor.

"Oh, Sarah. I understand," Missus sighs. "Scripture says no one was made to be alone. I'll talk to your master," she says and turns me out of her room to take her bath.

I stand at the other side of her closed door, listening to the bathwater slosh as she washes. It's a good while before I can get my feet to move.

By the time Master comes home with Bessie and Red, I've near about bitten my nails off. I tell Bessie a story about squirrels digging at Ben's grave and, just like I thought, she goes straight out there without even looking in the cabin. Then I go find Red.

"I need your help."

He's in the stable, brushing down the horses in strong, steady strokes. He's in a foul mood from riding around Virginia showing people that well-kept slaves don't want to be free.

"Not today," he says.

"I got a runaway to hide," I tell him.

The brush slips out of his hand. He pulls me into the stall beside the horse, eyes flashing. "You don't go announcing something like that."

"I want to know where you put the man you helped."

"The one you wouldn't help me hide?" he says, picking the brush back up.

"Yes," I say. "I should have helped back then."

He taps the brush against his leg.

"And you should help me now," I tell him.

He runs his hand over his face. "It won't work this time. I put him in the cotton shed, but it's picking season now. That new overseer'll be in there every day."

He goes back to brushing the horse, but he's calmer and thoughtful.

"How about down in the carry-through?" he says. "Ain't nobody going to look there."

"Until he makes a noise and Master comes down with his shotgun."

I follow Red into the coach house where the buggy sits waiting to be cleaned. He starts by washing the dirt down with a rag and some water.

I haven't been back in here since that last night with Henry in the hayloft when we thought I was going free. I climb the ladder and sit where we used to lay. There's nothing left of him up here. It's all just hay now.

Below me, Master walks in to talk to Red and I freeze. I don't even want to know what he'd think to find me up here. He tells Red he wants the buggy ready after breakfast tomorrow to take Bessie to the Pickering plantation.

"Yes, sir," Red says, scrubbing harder with his rag. Master don't seem to hear how much anger is wrapped up in it.

When he leaves without seeing me up in the loft, I know where I can hide the runaway.

I wait for dark to settle, glad Bessie's still up at Ben's grave. I get Red to look out for me, and, when he says the way is clear, I sneak the runaway, Finny, to the coach house and climb up after him. Red's got a little water and a little cornbread up there already waiting for him and Finny pounces on it. I clean his wound and smear yarrow paste over it and wrap it up. When I'm nearly done Red climbs up to the loft. The runaway looks to me and I nod that it's all right.

"This here's Red," I say.

Red looks him up and down, taking in his bare feet and torn clothes, and lets his eyes linger on a rope mark around Finny's neck I hadn't noticed myself. "Where're you headed?" Red asks.

Finny shrugs and just says, "North."

"How you plan on getting there?" Red asks.

"Walking," he says.

I see the anger rising up in Red. He grabs Finny by his ragged shirt and hisses in his ear. "Sarah and me's risking our necks to help you. Now, I ain't sitting here, pulling your story out bone by bone. You get to talking, or you get the hell out."

It don't take but a minute for the runaway to see he's got no choice. He tells us he means to follow the river to where it bends and then strike out toward the blue mountains. He says before the mountains get started there's a town. The second house you come to is green with a white door, and that house will take in runaways, and helps them move on.

Red and me, we can't talk for staring and gaping. I'm tingling from head to toe. This is the underground railroad. This is the way out.

I move in closer to Finny and say clear in his face, "I'm coming with you."

He shakes his head. "No, you ain't," he says in a whisper sharp as spurs.

"Yes, she is," says Red, like he's the new master laying down the law.

We both turn to look at him.

"And I'm coming too."

Chapter 57

Maple

Miss Martha leads me around the lawn at the front of the house, pointing at patches of grass. She wants flowers.

Mrs. Gantly, Mrs. Ridgemore and Mrs. Welleby've all planted flowerbeds, and she means to out-plant all of them. Miss Martha don't know the first thing about flowers, but she's got a notion to heap every blooming thing known to mankind in her front yard. It's gonna be the ugliest garden in Virginia.

Master's pleased as a cat with cream, acting like she got the best idea since the cowboys took to chasing off the Indians. I reckon he's just glad she's got herself busy with something.

She walks through the grass with her wide-brim hat to keep the sun off her face. "Jasmine and daffodils," she says, pointing. "And here we'll have violets and sunflowers and geraniums."

"All up next to each other like that?"

"Of course. I want a riot of color."

I nod my head, but when she calls out she wants a row of magnolias next to her daisies, I got to pinch my arm to keep from laughing. "You want a row of trees?" I say.

"That's a flower. The magnolia flower."

"But it grows from a tree."

Miss Martha gets a face like a wet sock stretched wrong from wringing out, but she won't admit she don't know what she's talking about. "I'll explain it to you another time, Maple. It's too hot to stand here discussing it."

She marches up to the house and stands in the shade of the front porch. "Land sakes," she says. "It's heating up and humid to boot." She unties her hat and holds it out to me, standing down in the grass. I climb the steps and take it.

From over the paddock hill, in the direction of the fields, a white man comes walking toward the house. In his workman clothes with his broad hat and the whip at his belt, he could almost be Master Mulch. Miss Martha prattles on about bluebells and petunias as he plods closer.

"Afternoon, ma'am," he says when he reaches the bottom of the porch. He touches his hat and bobs his head to her. Then he turns to me and does the same. "Ma'am," he says.

My nerves go tight. It ain't never good when a white man finds out he's been bowing and ma'am-ing to a slave. Hurts his pride, and a man with hurt pride can turn, quick as lightning, into the lashing-out kind. Especially if he's already got a whip on his belt.

"Such fine manners." Miss Martha shoots me a look full of mischief. "You must be our new overseer, Mister Laramie. My husband mentioned he hired you. Won't you join the two of us ladies in the shade?" She winks at me and I shake my head at her.

Mister Laramie climbs on to the porch and then, remembering, takes his hat off. "Pardon me, ladies," he says, removing it.

Miss Martha giggles like she's playing a game. "We do hope you'll be comfortable here with us." She turns to me and pokes my side with her elbow. "Don't we?" She acts like she don't know how this could turn on me. I can't have him thinking I played him for a fool.

"Well, thank you, ma'am." He bobs his head to her again. "Both of you." He bobs to me.

I give her a hard, nudging look to tell her to quit it and set him straight, but she flashes me one of her rascally grins. This man and me's her entertainment.

"Begging your ladies' pardons," he says, "but I was looking for Mister Johnson."

I say, "I think Master's in his study, sir. I'll let him know you're out here looking for him."

The *Master* hangs hard and stiff in the air as surprise washes over his face.

I turn to my sister, whose sour face pouts like I took her toys. "Unless you need me for anything else right now, Miss Martha."

"No, Maple. I do not." She snatches her hat back and fixes it on her head.

When she was little, I could stop her sass with a look. But then she grew.

"I think we'll have roses," she says. "Lots and lots of roses." She tilts her nose up and marches down the steps to her patchy grass.

Chapter 58

Henry

I leave early in the morning, walking up from Liberty Valley, through the woods and along the brush at the river's edge. When I reach the spot behind Jubilee Plantation, Sarah's waiting for me by the water, but Red's there with her. I get an uneasy lurch in my gut seeing them with their heads leaned in close. Then he puts his hand on her shoulder.

I call her name and when she hears me and turns, I see everything I need to. Her pinched face, her furrowed brow and her tight lips all smooth when she lays eyes on me. When I reach her, I hold her close and, with Red watching, kiss her right on the mouth. I want him to see it, and to know that she's mine no matter what anybody thinks about it, and that he should keep his distance.

She starts to pull away, but I lock my arms around her. "Wait," I say. "I need to hang on to you for just one more minute."

She leans back into me and it's her who's kissing me then. I have to hold myself back from pawing at her in front of Red. He's seen what I needed him to see. Now I just want him gone so we can be alone.

"You going to tell him, or you going to make me watch this all day long?" Red's stepped away from the two of us and stands with his arms crossed.

I slip my arm around her waist and pull her to my side. "Have you got something to say to me, Red?"

It's Sarah who speaks, tugging at my shirt. Her eyes are wide and dancing. "There's a runaway come through. Red and I got him hid up top of the coach house where you bunked."

I know what she's going to say, and my whole world comes into sharp focus waiting for her to say it.

"Me and Red's going to run with him when he goes. He knows about a place where folks'll hide us and help us move on."

"Do you trust him?" I ask.

"He's running too," says Red. "If we get caught, so do he."

"We're leaving tomorrow night," Sarah says. "We waited so I could tell you where to meet us."

Red cocks his head. "You said his dog bite needed to heal."

"I . . ." She looks between Red and me. "It did need healing."

Red blows out a long breath. "But maybe not as long as you let us think. Woman, if you let your fancy man mess this up, I swear." He lets the threat sit half-baked.

Sarah quickly tells me about a green house with a white door on the road into a town called Culpeper. She doesn't know who lives there, or even how to get to Culpeper exactly. The plan is dangerous, maybe even reckless, but I see in the set of her jaw that she means to run tomorrow. No matter what.

"I'm coming with you," I tell her.

"No, you ain't," Red says, and I want to punch him where he stands.

He says, "It's gonna be bad enough trying to sneak around with the three of us. Adding you makes it harder. More chance to catch our scent. More chance to find our tracks. You coming ain't helping."

I clench my teeth and tuck her under my chin. "You'll be safer running with me," I say. "If there's trouble along the way you can hide while I sort it out."

"You think your white skin is going to save you from everything? They catch you, they'll say you's either a slave stealer or a nigger lover. Probably hang you and take your shoes 'cause you ain't worth no eight hundred dollars to no one."

"You can meet me there, Henry. At the green house. That's the safest way."

"I'll watch out for her," Red says. "I promise."

I shake my head. "You can promise what you will, but I'm going with Sarah and that's an end to it."

Red runs his hand along the back of his neck. "Then be here tomorrow night. We go when they sleep."

He nods Sarah a farewell and heads up the path back to the plantation.

Her face is a mixture of terror and elation, and I think it must surely be mirrored on mine.

I place my hand on her stomach, over the babe growing in her belly. "The three of us are going to be together," I say. "You're going to be free and we're going to go west."

She smiles at me and it's like the sun, so bright it'll melt your heart.

In the morning, I'll quit my new job at Liberty Valley and send a telegraph to Ennis telling him we're ready, and to meet us in Maryland in a week, at the start of the Cumberland trail. And in the evening, I'll be with Sarah on the road to freedom and future.

Chapter 59

Sarah

I barely close my eyes all night and, when I wake, I'm so nervous I'm jumping at my own shadow. Bessie's up at first light to sit by Ben's grave. That's all she wants to do, ever since Master took to dragging her away to show people how much she loves being a slave. She's hardly seen Samson and Clover and the children since this mess started.

The cellar off to the sides of the carry-through is the coolest place we got at Jubilee, so that's where we keep the extra food we buy in town before we get ready to use it. It's where I fetch the eggs for Maple in the mornings, but today my timing's on double slow. Everywhere I go, it's like I'm saying goodbye. By the time I get the eggs to Maple, she's already got the ham sizzling in the pan. She says she's in a hurry and doesn't have time for my dawdling, but she's sure got time to scold me for being slow. I tell her I got to get in to Master Thomas and check on him, but really I need to check on Finny. I get halfway across the lawn when Red meets me coming from the coach house.

"I just checked on him," he says. "We can't both be going in there all the time."

He's right, so I reach into my skirt and pull out a folded leaf wrapped around a thick paste.

"I made up more of that poultice for his leg," I say. I hand it to him, telling him to get Finny to wrap it fresh. I also tell him I made up two sacks of food that I hid in the cellar, and one of us needs to sneak them out before tonight.

Looking up to the house, I see Master standing at his upstairs window watching us. I startle and gasp. When Red looks up to see him too, he grabs my arm.

"He don't know what we're talking about. If he asks, you tell him you was getting me to go help Bessie."

"Help her do what?" My heart's beating faster than a hummingbird's wing.

"I don't know." He looks around like he's searching for an idea and steps closer, dipping his mouth to my ear. "Say you asked me to carry her chair out into the shade for her."

"But then you got to do it," I say. Panic pinches my voice.

He takes my other arm and squeezes both of them hard, giving me a little shake. "You got to calm down right now."

I nod, drawing a deep breath.

"I'll put the chair out. That's all you need to say about it."

When he lets me go, I scurry down through the carry-through and up the stairs into the house. I dash up to Master Thomas's room, quick as I can. He ain't even thinking about getting dressed. I hurry him along and get him downstairs for breakfast and head out to the kitchen house for the breakfast platters. Willa takes in the biscuits and butter, and I bring the ham and eggs, with Annie following behind with the coffee.

When I serve up the eggs, I'm starting to calm down again from Master catching Red and me, when he says, "Sarah, I've noticed you getting pretty friendly with Red."

I don't know if that's good or bad in his books so I keep my mouth shut.

"In fact, I noticed you two together just this morning."

"Yes, sir," I say, 'cause I know he seen us and I got my story ready to go.

"We've discussed it," he says, nodding at Missus. "I agree it's time you were matched, and I approve of you and Red. I think he's a good choice for you. I don't know why I didn't think of it sooner."

The look on my face must give away what I think about that.

He says, "Now, don't look so worried. I've seen Red watching you. In fact, I wouldn't be surprised if he's been working up to asking me himself."

At first, I can't talk for wanting to scream I won't do it, but then I remember it don't matter. We're running today. Can't nobody match me up when I'm gone.

I get my tongue working again and say, "Yes, Master." And because I'm leaving and I don't want him looking at me twice today, and because I'll never have to say it again, I say, "Thank you, Master."

He smiles. "You and Red'll be the next Bessie and Ben around here."

"Yes, sir." I set down the egg platter and dish out the ham. Master and Missus both watch me, smiling like they're God's own angels.

"Red don't mind?" I ask, knowing full well they never said a word to him about it.

"Now, don't you worry about Red," Master says. "He's got eyes in his head, don't he? He'll like the idea just fine."

I don't hear Missus come in while I'm making the bed in Master Thomas's room.

"Oh, Sarah. There you are," she says from behind me. She knows I always make up his room after breakfast, but she likes pretending she don't keep track of us every hour of every day. "I want you to pack some things for Thomas. We're all going to Richmond for a few days."

"Yes, ma'am." I don't let myself act excited, but I sure am. If they're all gone, running is going to be a lot easier. I could be at the safe house before they know I'm missing.

I get out a trunk to pack Master Thomas's clothes and some toys for the next few days and carry it down to the front porch.

When Red sees me and comes up to take it from me, he's got a face like it's the end of the world. He don't say a word as he settles Master Thomas's case on to the roof of the carriage alongside Master's one twice the size. I reckon he looks like that because his nerves are getting to him about tonight.

I step up close to him and whisper, "They's leaving."

He gives me a look like I'm the biggest fool he ever saw. "I know."

I peek inside the carriage where he's got the three pillows for sitting on already on the seats. Up front, Red don't get no pillows. As soon as I think it, I could smack myself. If they're riding out to Richmond, then Red's going to be the one driving them. He won't be running with us tonight. I glance over at him tying the case down. The muscles in his jaw work back and forth. I don't know what to say to him. Ain't no words to make it better.

Up at the Big House Maple comes out with two cases from Missus. She's not hardly out the door before she's hollering at Red to come help. When he marches up there you can see the sadness in his steps.

"What's wrong with you?" Maple huffs. "You gonna get two whole days in the city with nothing to do."

I want to smack her quiet.

Master steps out and circles the coach where Red's tying up the trunks. Then he looks around and frowns at me.

"Where's Bessie?"

"I guess she's out by Ben's grave," I say.

"Well, go get her," he says, flipping open his pocket watch like Bessie's making him late. Missus ain't even finished packing her last case.

"Yes, sir," I mumble and scuttle away.

I run, but not because I want to get her for him quicker. I feel like there's a swarm of bees in my whole body trying to get out and if I don't run I'm going to split apart with their pushing out at me.

"Good girl," I hear him call after me, and I just run and run.

Bessie sits crouched next to Ben's grave like I knew she would be. She's talking to him and stroking the grass that's sprung up out of the mound of dirt covering him. I reach her, panting for air. The rasping of my in-and-out breaths fills my ears.

When I can get the words out, I tell her Master wants her to come on so they can take her with them to Richmond.

She lays her hand flat on top of Ben. "I'm tired," she says to the grave.

"You got to go," I say.

She shakes her head. "He's gonna keep dragging me out till I fall over."

I crouch beside her and sling my arm over her shoulder.

"This ain't the kind of staying I meant," she says.

"At least you'll lie next to Ben like you wanted," I say.

"Lord knows I'm ready."

I get up and help her to stand. She's shaky on her feet and I take her arm to steady her. I been thinking so much about Henry and me, I barely thought about Bessie, but I see what I been missing. Her skin sags off her bird bones, her eyes sink into her face, and her hair's fallen out in two bald patches. It takes her a spell before she can walk with me and she has to go slow, leaning on me the whole way.

When I get her to the wagon, Master, Missus and Master Thomas are nowhere around. Maple's gone off too, and it's just Red there stroking the horses while he waits. The disappointment in his face is a terrible thing to see. I slip my hand in his and squeeze. I hope he can forgive me for leaving without him.

"There you are," I hear the Missus exclaim behind me, and I slip my hand away. She shoos Master Thomas along in front of her and he don't seem happy about it.

He mopes and drags his feet. "But I don't want to go. Why do I have to? I could stay here and Sarah could look after me."

I look away from him. I don't want to tear up seeing him go, but I don't want him to stay and make me have to leave him.

"Matthew, would you talk to your son."

Master comes stomping out looking pleased with himself. He calls Thomas to him and the boy bolts up the porch steps to his father.

"Let me tell you something, Thomas. This whole plantation," and he sweeps his arm around in an arc, "is going to be yours one day. But there are Yankees up north who want to take away our very way of life and destroy the plantations across the South. We have to stop them and that's why we're going to Richmond. I know you can't understand it all now, but one day soon it's going to be your job to keep this for your children and your children's children. In a way, Thomas, we're going on this trip to protect your future."

With his daddy's full attention on him, Master Thomas quiets down and takes his daddy's hand. He walks down to the carriage and climbs in without a fuss. Missus goes to follow him inside, but pauses just before she does.

"You should sit next to Red," she says to me. "Bessie won't mind being on the edge."

I can't find my tongue as she climbs in and then the Master after her.

"I'm supposed to come with you?" I finally ask, stricken.

"Of course," she says, peeking out the window. "I told you this morning, we're all going. You have to look after Thomas."

From being dead set against going a little while ago, Master Thomas is calm and peaceful sitting next to his daddy.

"If he don't want to go," I try, "I could stay here and watch Master Thomas."

"Don't get him started again," Master says in a tone that means he don't want to hear no backtalk. Then he knocks on the frame of the carriage. "We're ready, Red," he calls out. And to me he says, "Sarah, get on your seat."

Bessie's slumped next to Red on the bench seat. She shifts over to make room for me. I'm in a panic. I look around wildly for a way out. Red reaches down to help me climb up between them. All the pain and anger I feel is pouring out of his eyes. Neither one of us is running tonight, and no way Finny's gonna wait around till we get back. I tuck my hands under my thighs and grip so hard I'm making welts. Tears blur my vision and soak my cheeks. When Red clicks his tongue and flicks the reins, the horses trot, pulling us away from Jubilee.

Chapter 60

Henry

I wait in the woods from before sunset, watching the shadows spread long, until well after darkness settles thick and true. I sit and stand and pace and wait some more. When I can't take it another minute, I sneak to Sarah and Bessie's cabin under the cloak of black and find it empty. Then I make my way to Red's cabin. It's empty too. I rake my fingers through my hair and pace his floor, worrying. They were supposed to wait for darkness. I don't know if they changed the plan because they saw a chance to go and took it, but my gut is twisting in knots thinking of Sarah out there without me.

I know she's headed to Culpeper, to the green house at the start of town, so I creep back to the woods and make my way to the road. I can travel faster out in the open than she can slinking through the forest, so I figure if I head for the safe house I might get there first. I can make sure it's really safe before she arrives. I tell myself all this to calm my nerves and stay positive, but ten steps down the road I have to stop and lean against a tree and breathe. Anything could happen to her on the run.

I get to Culpeper the next day and find the green house easy enough. A moonfaced man opens the white door. He's shaved his beard to right up under his chin so that his face looks like it's poking out from a wreath of black hair. The man looks me up and down and takes a peek over my shoulder. He doesn't speak a word. Just raises his eyebrows at me to explain myself.

"Afternoon," I say. "I'm looking for a woman who would have come here with two men."

It takes him a while to respond to that, but he finally comes up with, "I live here alone."

"I don't suppose I care who you're living with," I tell him. "I want to know if you've seen the woman."

"Why have thou come to me?" he asks.

It's a strange way of talking, for sure, and it hits me then that he's a Quaker. A sect famous for being against slavery. I guess he doesn't rightly know if he can trust me.

I check over my shoulder to make sure no one's sneaking up on us, paranoid, and of course the road is clear. "They were told they'd be safe here. Second house coming into Culpeper. Green with a white door. They escaped on Monday," I tell him. "A woman with two men."

The Quaker stands like a goddamn mute, taking in my clothes. Or maybe he's looking for a gun in my breeches.

"I'm a friend," I tell him.

He says nothing to that so I push on. "She stands yea tall," I stretch my hand out level with my chin. "She's got a slight frame, but she's stronger than she looks. She has a wide face with a narrow chin and round eyes and soft lips and a scar over her left eyebrow no bigger than an ant. She's got a crooked tooth on the bottom. Right here," I point in my own mouth. "And she's got a hint of a dimple on her left cheek when she smiles."

He looks me in the eye and then steps aside to let me in. Pulling out a chair at a rough planked table, he sits and nods at a second chair for me to join him.

"You love this woman," he says. "God help thee."

I feel myself reddening. I hadn't meant to be so transparent.

"Many abolitionists who'd risk life and limb to help people out of bondage would take a dim view to the idea of the two of you."

I know it's true. I could still deny it, but instead I say, "But not you?"

"But not me," he says.

"I'm taking her west," I tell him.

He looks at me gravely, like a chastising father. "West?" he says. "Not north?"

"West," I say. Out where things are less formed. Less settled. More possible. "There's a business opportunity I'm joining in Independence, where all the pioneers leave from."

He strokes his beard thinking about that a moment and then says, "Independence might not be far enough."

I discover his name is Aaron Newman and that he's a widower—his wife and child dying together in childbirth. His story makes me even more anxious for Sarah. I learn that he works with a network of free blacks here in Culpeper, and other Quakers just north in Loudoun County, helping to move slaves north to freedom. Conducting slaves is risky, dangerous work that needs patience and planning, he tells me, but when there are only a few more hours of daylight, I can't sit around waiting any more. I go off to search, striking out toward the river, the way they'd come, keeping the Blue Ridge Mountains at my back.

I've only just left Culpeper when I come upon a posse of men. Two have rifles slung over their shoulders. The rest have pistols at their hips. All five are on horseback.

"Has there been trouble around here?" I ask one of the rifle holders.

He stares at me with cold eyes and says nothing.

"I'd like to be warned if I ought to be carrying a gun."

The second rifleman spins his horse around and trots in front of the others. "There's a runaway coming up this way. We got some men flushing him out with dogs. You should move on so you don't get hurt in the scuffle."

"Just the one runaway?"

"That's the word we got. Why? You know of some more? You see something in town? We heard someone around here's been helping them."

I keep myself still and make sure to hold his eyes. "Just seems like a lot of men and firepower to catch one person."

He shrugs. "He's got a fat bounty on his head."

"So, it's a man that you're after?"

"That's a lot of questions for someone passing through," one of the pistol men says. "He might be a bounty hunter himself, Earl."

Earl looks me up and down and dismisses me with a spit of tobacco. "He's no bounty hunter," he says. "What he might be is the nigger-lover who's been hiding runaways." He steps his horse in front of me as his friends pull their horses in a line behind him.

"I've not been hiding anyone," I say. "I'm passing through."

I close the gap between me and Earl's horse and stroke her neck. The horse nudges her nose on to my shoulder. I scratch between her ears and she lowers her head.

Earl yanks her away. "Then keep on passing and get away from my horse."

"Suit yourselves," I say backing away from them.

I walk at a good clip until I'm out of sight, and then I dash into the woods and break into a run. I scan left and right as I go. They're not after Sarah, but they might catch her by accident. Twice my feet get tangled in the underbrush, making me fall. I softly call her name every hundred yards or so, and get back the trill of the warbler and the wren.

In the distance, I hear dogs barking.

"Sarah!" I scream. I sprint toward the noise, which gets louder and closer every second.

Bursting up over a ridge, a man charges toward me. He sees me and swerves toward the edge of the woods where the men wait with guns.

"Not that way," I shout waving my arms, but he ignores me, or can't hear me. Maybe he thinks I'm one of them.

Behind him three dogs come howling and charging over the ridge. I don't see Sarah or Red, and I'm afraid they've already been caught and that's why they're hunting just the one man. I run after him with no idea how I can help. He bursts out of the woods to shouts and gunfire. When I get close enough, I spy through the trees the posse of five men. They're off their horses in a huddled, frenzied heap. I hear the thud of fists and boots on flesh. I hide myself, pressed against the trunk of a pine, as the shouts of three more men trailing behind the dogs echo through the woods. When the other three reach them, the posse of five back away, revealing the bloodied and bludgeoned body of a dark-skinned man. The eight of them flip him over on to his stomach and stretch out his legs. He doesn't struggle. I'm not sure if he's conscious.

"Your running days are over, boy," the rifled man, Earl, says.

He takes out an ax and with four swings, hacks off the man's toes. His scream is something to freeze you up and melt you down.

Earl wipes his blade in the grass and spits a wad of tobacco chew.

Bile rises in my throat. I turn away, headed back toward Jubilee. I can't spare a moment to grieve for this man. I have to find Sarah.

Chapter 61

Sarah

It's evening by the time we get back to the plantation, but there's no break from the heat we been suffering under all day. The back of my dress is soaked through with sweat from just sitting up between Red and Bessie. The front of my dress is covered with road dust, and the baby's been having me feeling sick for miles.

When Red pulls the carriage up in front of the Big House, I'm relieved to be done with all that jangling and jostling, but I'm so anxious I'm about to split in two. Red helps me down and I stand there trying to think of what next. Finny will have gotten to the green house by now. And Henry will know I'm still stuck here. I'm hoping Finny knows to tell him that I didn't get cold feet, I just didn't have no choice. Or else I hope that Henry knows it on his own. When he comes back here looking for me, we can run together.

"He'll make you a good match," Master says, and I jump, pushed out of my thoughts. He's looking at Red unloading the cases, thinking it's him who's got me forgetting myself.

Master has him set the cases by the front door and calls me and Red on to the porch to stand with him in the shade.

"I've decided," Master announces, "that Sarah will move into your cabin, Red."

I glance at Red, who just looks straight on at the floor.

"I considered moving you to hers, I know it's a little bigger, more space for children, but Bessie hangs on it because of Ben and I'm inclined to be gracious toward her."

I curl my fingers by my sides and bite my lip. I hate him.

"Yes, sir," Red says. When I don't speak, he adds, "We thank you, sir."

"Well, now, that's all right," he says, hands gripping on his lapels, chest puffed like an old rooster.

He struts inside the house, and Red and I look at each other before he leads the horses off to the coach house.

Bone tired, I drag a case of clothes inside and run into Maple, up from the carry-through with a jug of lemonade and three glasses. Seeing me coming in through the front door, she stops and gives me a look full of hateful meanness, then she marches into the sitting room.

I hear her voice sing out bright as sunshine. "So glad to see you all back. I made your favorite, Miss Martha, to welcome you home."

The way she goes on, you could see how a body might be fooled into thinking she wasn't a hateful shrew.

I hear her pouring the lemonade, saying, "You must be plum worn out from keeping that Sarah in line. I just saw her coming in the front door with her uppity self, bold as you please. That trip to Richmond's gone straight to her head."

"She's just a touch distracted," I hear Master say, from where I stand at the bottom of the stairs with the case hefted over my shoulder. "It's a big night for her and Red."

I climb the stairs and unpack the cases and, when I get that done, I slip out to my cabin. Laying on my pallet, I curl into a ball. I should be free right now and with Henry.

It's late when Bessie drags herself in. Already the cicadas' sharp chirp is up and going. I don't have the energy to greet her, let alone see how she's doing.

She stands over me and says, "You got to come with me."

I don't move. I want her to go and leave me be. Whatever it is they want up at the Big House, I just can't.

"Get up, now."

I close my eyes and pretend like she's not there. In my head, I put myself in the wildflower field with Henry, butterflies landing right on his shoulder.

"He's here," she says. "Up at Ben's grave, worried about you."

I sit up and look at her. She nods and I jump up and dash out. At Ben's grave, Henry's pacing the line of trees. Almost right in the open. I run to him and drag him into the woods.

"I couldn't make it out," I say, words spilling out before we're even out of sight. "They took me to Richmond. I couldn't—"

"Thank God," he says. He leans us against the back of a tree and nuzzles the side of my head. He kisses my ear, my cheek, my forehead. "Thank you, holy Jesus." He rubs his hand over my back and pats at my arms. "You're all right," he says, patting me some more.

"I'm fine. I just couldn't run. I wanted to, but I couldn't."

He folds me into his arms and doesn't say anything for a long time. "I waited from before sunset," he finally says. "You were gone. You never made it to the green house. I didn't know what to think."

"Let's leave tonight," I say. "You've been there. You know the way. We could go right now. They won't miss me till morning."

Henry shakes his head and I push him from me with both hands. "I have to leave this place. I can't stay here no more."

Then he tells me about Finny and my bones go soft.

"Those slave catchers knew someone's been hiding runaways," he says.

I slide down to the ground and clutch my legs up into me.

He sits beside me and wraps his arm around my shoulder. "We'll find another way, Sarah. I promise."

Chapter 62

Maple

It's too early in the morning to rise so I lie awake on my bed, thinking of roses. I don't want them in her crazy garden reminding me of my daughter every minute of every day. Keeping me wondering what he's doing to her and when and how often till I'm out of my mind.

I breathe in deep, and warm humid air fills my nose. Under me, there's a damp patch of body-shaped sweat. I spread my arms and legs like a star to try to get cool.

Dragging myself out of bed, I take up a bucket, and go to the well pump. I splash my face and arms with cool well water and let it drip down my back.

Cupping my hand, I slurp in a long drink. When I look up, I spy Sarah picking her way through the trees and darting into Bessie's cabin.

Looks like she had a big night all right, but not with Red like Master thinks. I suck my teeth and shake my head. Here she's got a chance to live decent with Red, and instead she goes sneaking around with that white blacksmith. Some people got the bed-wench baked into them.

It should be Sarah at Belle Grove Plantation. Not Rose.

After I fix the breakfast, I take myself out to Miss Martha's flower garden, to get today's planting done before the afternoon heat hits. She don't want the magnolias. Says they're too messy, when what she really means is the flowers grow from a tree, like I said. The rest of her garden's gonna be exactly as bad as she described it.

I got Annie out here digging with me. She's putting in a row of petunias, and I'm right next to her with the roses. When I plant each one, I fish a bottle of vinegar out of my pocket and pour some into the roots. Annie sees straight off what I'm doing, 'cause she's got the sharp eyes of a thief.

"You fixing to give them all your special water?" she asks.

I shake my head. "Just the roses."

She goes back to planting and I go back to watering.

Behind us, the front door bangs open and Mister Laramie, the new overseer, comes barrelling out with Master hot on his heels.

"If you walk out on me, with my fields full of cotton, I'll see to it you don't ever work as an overseer again."

"That's fine with me, Mister Johnson. My overseeing days are done."

He keeps on walking and Master keeps on following, right down the front porch steps.

"You're a fool if you think you're going to march off to California and stumble into a field of gold. People don't get rich by doing nothing for it."

"No, sir. I mean to dig for it." His heels crunch on the driveway and his arms swing in step with his stride.

"Don't you think hundreds of men have had the same idea? Do you think the gold's just waiting for you?"

"That's why I've got to leave now. Get there while the getting's good."

"But I've got cotton that needs picking. Just wait a few weeks until after the harvest."

"I don't mean to leave you high and dry, sir, but you got your fortune. This is my chance to go make mine."

When that overseer marches off, Master kicks at Miss Martha's petunias. He's madder than a spitting cat.

"You all right, Master? Can I get you something?"

"No, Maple. No, you can't. Not unless you can get me a new overseer. Can you do that, Maple? A new overseer before I lose my harvest?"

I ain't never seen him panicked and I'm lapping up the show. This, I want to say, is what it's like to feel helpless against a thing. I got no pity. I been feeling it for too long, and it's about time he has his turn. Watching him fall apart in front of me because of a cotton crop just makes me want to twist the knife.

"I reckon you could hire that blacksmith, since he's still poking around here anyway."

Annie looks up at me sharp. Guess she knows too.

"What are you talking about? He left weeks ago."

I shrug. "Sarah's been sneaking out to him. I reckon she got him hid somewhere close by."

"She wouldn't dare."

"No, Master," Annie says from where she crouches in the dirt, "she wouldn't dare, like you say. And now she got Red anyhow. What she want with that blacksmith?"

I'm gonna smack her upside the head when I get her alone. "She ain't staying in Red's cabin like you told her," I say. "She's with that blacksmith."

"Have you seen him?" Master asks. "Here?"

"I seen her coming back from him just this morning."

"But you ain't seen him?" Annie says. "Maple, you gonna get her whipped for a hunch that ain't even true."

"I don't need to see him to know where she's been." I glare at Annie to shut her trap. "You can see for yourself, Master. She ain't sleeping with Red like you told her to."

"I seen her with Red," Annie says, ignoring my glare. "I seen her with him plenty. And, like you say, Master, that blacksmith went weeks ago. He's gonna be long gone."

"Yes. You're right, Annie. And Sarah and Red were both very grateful for the pairing," Master says. "I'm sure you misunderstood whatever you think you saw, Maple. But you were right to bring it to my attention just the same."

He looks down at the beginnings of Miss Martha's garden, the roses already wilting and the petunias with their heads kicked off. "Well, this is coming along nicely. It needs a bit of work, but it's going to be splendid."

Chapter 63

Henry

At twelve minutes past ten o'clock, I take the railway to Washington to let Ennis know we won't be in Cumberland, and because what I have to ask him needs to be done face-to-face. It also has to be done quickly. I have a new plan to get Sarah out, but it's full of holes and has a hundred different ways it could fail. Without Ennis Flanagan it can't work at all.

Waiting for him at the Golden Eagle Tavern, I pull out the strip of cloth from Sarah's dress that she used for my hand and that we tied as our binding cloth, rubbing it like a worry stone. I twirl it around my fingers and order another drink. I'm on my third whiskey when Ennis shows up, my nerves clenched tighter than a fist.

He storms into the room frowning, his mouth skew under his bushy beard. "What the hell's the matter with you? I told you to be ready to go and you disappear for weeks. And then suddenly you're ready. And then you're not again. The West won't wait for us, you daft bastard. Now, do I need to look for a new blacksmith or are you going to do what you said you would?"

"I need your help," I say.

He sinks on to the barstool beside me and rubs his forehead. "You look like shite," he says. He takes the drink in front of me and tips it back. "So tell me, why am I meeting you here when I should be meeting you in Cumberland?"

With my fingernails, I trace the veins of the rough wooden planks running along the bar, finding my words.

"It's that girl of yours, am I right? Her father found out what the two of you were up to."

"Ennis, listen," I say.

"Christ, Henry. Give it up. You'll find a nice frontier girl in Independence."

"You don't understand. I can't leave her." I dig at the wood around a nail hammered bent into the bar.

"Yes, you can, because if her father won't have it, it's finished. You don't get the girl." He points to the rickety wooden staircase at the side of the tavern that leads to a few rented rooms. A woman in a garish dress and with messy hair climbs slowly down, looking over the men at the bar. "You should let someone take your mind off of her," Ennis says. He tips his hat to the bar whore.

I grab his arm so he'll stop his jabbering and hat tipping and listen. "I have a plan to get Sarah," I say, "but I need your help."

Ennis scratches the back of his head and looks to the ceiling. "Jesus, but she must be something special if she's worth all this to you."

My nerves slip into my leg, making it shudder, so I stand. "Will you help me or not?"

"Fine. I will. But after this we go. With or without her. And your plan better not involve her da getting the law on us."

I lean in close to Ennis and lower my voice. "I have the money to buy her, legal, but the bastard who owns her won't sell her to me. I need you to pose as a buyer. And I need to find a reason that you want Sarah, and no one else."

"Jesus, Mary and Joseph. You're talking about a slave? All this waiting, risking my fortune for a bloody slave."

The way he's talking hardens me. I don't like hearing him call her a slave. It's what she is, but it's not who she is, and the word grates in my ears. "I'm taking her with me."

"No, you're goddamn not, you daft bastard. If you bring her out there, we're dead in the water." His blue eyes darken to storm clouds.

"She can help us. She's a hard worker and she knows how to—"

"I already told you. There's a man out there, Hiram Young. We need to take his business."

Right there I know I've missed something important. "You said he's a cheat and a scoundrel. We'll take his business sure enough."

"I never said he was. In fact, I doubt he is. Hiram Young's a Negro, Henry. They'll come to us because you and me are white men, and if you bring your slave girl everything goes to shite."

I'm angry in a way that I can't explain to Ennis. I can't explain it to myself, except to say that it's like he's not just doing this to Mister Hiram Young. He's doing it to Sarah. He's doing it to my child.

"That's your plan?" I say. "Stealing business from a man because he's not white?"

"A minute ago, you were happy for us to take his customers."

"A minute ago, he was a scoundrel." It's an ugly thing to see a man who's had his own neck ground in the dirt trample on another the first chance he gets. "Did hungering in Ireland teach you nothing about treating people right?" I ask.

He turns red as a beetroot. That's his conscience talking. But to me he says, "It taught me to never starve again, that's what. I thought you learned the same lesson. Wasn't that the point of changing your name, O'Toole?"

"I changed it because I wanted work, is all. I wanted a fair shot. Same as any man deserves."

He leans in close and points his finger in my face. "I told you I mean to make my fortune," he says. "I can't do it if you're out there with a Negro woman. Hiram Young can't help his skin, that's what folks'll say, but Henry Taylor's made a choice."

The whole adventure is souring in my mouth.

"They won't hire you, Henry. In fact, Missouri's a slave state, now that I think on it. What you're wanting to do is illegal. You'll end up in jail. Or worse."

"Then we'll go further west. Into the territories."

"You'll not wreck this for me as well as yourself. I'm telling you right now, she's not coming with us. Now, you forget all about her," he says, as if that were an option, like throwing water on a cook fire.

"I can't," I say.

"You can't even get her from the man that's owning her, you bloody eejit. You said so yourself."

A pulsing pain starts up at the base of my neck and I rub at it with both hands. "Aye," I say. "That's why I need you to help me."

"You're a loyal bastard and it does you credit, it does, but your loyalty should be to me as your partner. And to your own kind. Not to some other man's slave."

"She's my wife." I pound the bar and earn a glare from the barkeep.

"Holy God in Heaven. She's not your wife."

I don't care to tell him about the ceremony we had that made it so, witnessed by God himself and a host of his butterflies. "In a manner of speaking," I say.

"I'm telling you as a friend, this is madness. I know you've got a mighty fondness for her, but it will never work. You won't get hired anywhere with a Negro woman at your side."

He knocks his drink back and stands. "I'll not help you ruin your life, and I'll not let you ruin mine. Just ditch the girl, Henry. Come west with me and make your fortune. Be ready to leave tomorrow or I'm leaving without you."

Chapter 64

Sarah

All day, Red never asks where I was last night, which is fine by me. When night settles over the plantation, I wait for the Big House to go to sleep. Then I creep to Bessie's cabin, soft as a cat. I stretch out on my pallet, still pushed up against the far wall.

I think Bessie's asleep, until she says, "When're you gonna go to Red?"

I turn to the wall.

"Last night out there with your blacksmith. Tonight back here with me. How you think this is gonna end?"

I flatten my hands across my belly. "Good night, Bessie."

"You got to go to Red's," she says.

"Henry's coming for me," I tell her. For us.

In the morning, I lie on my pallet listening to someone draw water at the well. I'm so tired, my arms and legs weigh down like logs. I hear fast footsteps and then Red comes bursting through the door.

"Get up, both of y'all," he hisses. "Quick, before he sees."

Even if I hadn't understood his words, the tone of his voice would be enough. I jump up. Fear is like a bolt of lightning that will get a body moving every time.

"Master's coming, Master's coming," he says, pushing my pallet under Bessie's bed. He pulls Bessie upright and when she wobbles, I rush over to keep her standing. That's when Master walks in the door.

"There you are," Master says, and I don't dare look at him in the face.

"Morning, Master," I say, and prod Bessie to say the same. Since she started her happy-to-be-a-slave tours, all she do is sleep, drag herself up to Ben's grave, and stay away from Master.

"See, here she is, Master. In here helping Bessie like I say. Every morning and evening."

"Well, that's good. That's good. I didn't think of how pulling Sarah out would affect you, Bessie, but I'm glad you're being looked after."

"Yes, sir," I say when she don't say nothing to that.

"You two settling in all right?"

"Yes, sir," me and Red both say.

"Good. Good." He purses his mouth looking at us. "I was thinking we should have a celebration to mark your union. What do you think of that?"

"No, Master." I shake my head and both he and Red look at me like I done lost my mind, but I don't want to celebrate me and Red. Not with Henry's baby in my belly and me waiting every day on a way out of here. "I mean, you don't need to put yourself out on account of us. Ain't that right, Red?"

Red don't say nothing to help and Master plows on, "Nonsense. It'll be good for the whole plantation. I'll let you all cut off an hour early tonight and I'll send down a ham and some of Old Willie's hooch."

"Thank you, Master. We both thank you for this kindness," Red says, swinging his arm around my shoulder and squeezing to warn me from saying anything else.

Master waves Red's thanks away. "You're two of my best slaves. It feels right to celebrate the two of you together. It'll be good for the plantation. You'll be our new Bessie and Ben."

He slaps Red on the shoulder and leans in close. "She looks exhausted, Red. You should ease up on her a bit. Let her get some sleep or you'll wear her right out." Red and I keep our mouths closed as he slaps him a second time on the shoulder and saunters out.

After he leaves, Red turns to me, nostrils flaring. "From now on, you sleep with me."

"He won't likely come back to check," I say, but Red's too shaken to listen to "likely."

"Could be your blacksmith gets you out of here, but until then we do like he says. I ain't lying for you no more. And I ain't getting no stripes 'cause of your blacksmith."

Chapter 65

Henry

When Ennis leaves, I order another whiskey. I hate that there's a truth in what he says. I can't get Sarah out. And, if I could, where would we go? A white man with a Negro wife who I can't even marry under the law. We'd be walking through life with both hands tied behind our backs. Like I'm Henry O'Toole again, but worse, because even if no one would hire me for being Irish, at least they couldn't arrest me for it. Did I give up my father's name for nothing?

Every time I come to see her at Jubilee, I put her in jeopardy. I can't protect her. I'd make it worse to try. And if God was feeling in a prayer-answering mood and let us flounce off that plantation together, what then? Do I want folks chasing her from town to town at the wrong end of a pitchfork just because she's stuck by my side?

There's a thought that I've been shoving into the back corners of my mind that slips out, demanding to be considered. It's that maybe she's better off with me walking away. Maybe it's better for both of us.

I throw back the shot of whiskey and it burns something fierce going down. The Americans can't make it like the Irish, but I wave for another.

I watch the clear brown liquid rise in my glass as the barkeep fills it. It seems somehow right that it's this bad. It ought to be bad. Good whiskey would be too much like a celebration.

I stare into my glass, at the chestnut brown of it. Clear and bright like Sarah's eyes. The tavern whore comes sidling up next to me at the bar.

"Your friend said you could use some company." She lays her hand on my thigh.

I tip the whiskey back and hold out my glass for another.

"He said you need to get your mind off someone."

"She's got the prettiest eyes you ever saw," I say.

"Come on with me," she says. "I'll make you forget all about her eyes."

My brain is fogging, and my tongue feels heavy in my mouth. She takes my hand and leads me up the stairs to a cramped and dingy room filled with a large bed. It smells of unwashed bodies and mold. It's not a place I would ever want to bring Sarah, but, as foul as it is, they'd never let us in here as man and wife.

I sit heavily on the bed and pull off my shoes. Ennis is right. I have to give her up. There's no future in a forbidden match. We've not got a chance, I tell myself, but just thinking the words makes my chest squeeze in tight with pain, collapsing to where I can barely breathe. I fumble at my shirt trying to open the buttons for some air, but my fingers are numb, tingling sticks that won't obey. My heart races beyond what's safe and, as I break out into a sweat, I know I'm going to die in this stinking tavern room because I turned my back on the woman I was made to be with. This is God's punishment, plain and true.

I grab at my chest as I slide off the bed and, in this moment, dying on the floor, I don't regret my lack of fortune. I regret not having more time with Sarah. Not having her here to say goodbye to. Not meeting our child. I yearn for the life we could have had together.

The whore crouches down in front of me.

"Hey. You all right?"

I can't answer. My mouth is too busy sucking in air that my lungs don't seem to know what to do with.

She tears my shirt open, her features twisted in fright, and I close my eyes. I don't want her face to be the last thing I see. Holding still on the floor, my heartbeat begins to slow. Soon after, my breathing comes easier. I open my eyes and see the whore sitting in front of me, confused. I clench and stretch my fingers while they get their feeling back.

"Something wrong with you?" she asks.

"I thought I was dying."

She wipes a gray kerchief along my face, taking the sweat. She smiles uneasily at me, showing tobacco-yellowed teeth. "You going to be okay for this?"

I'm dizzy and don't move when she strokes my chest under my open shirt. She smells of cheap perfume and whiskey and sweat. She dips her hands to my breeches and I grab her wrist.

"Stop," I say. "I need to leave."

"Come on now, honey, you sit back and enjoy yourself. When I'm through with you you're going to think you died and went to heaven."

She unhooks her bodice revealing large white breasts with pink nipples. They look wrong. She straddles my legs and I push her off, rougher than I mean to. She lays sprawled on the floor as I drag myself up, clinging to the bed against the dizziness.

"What in Sam Hill's the matter with you?"

"I'm sorry." I grab my shoes and shove my feet inside.

"You've got problems, mister."

She's right, sure enough, but I'm going to fix them. I head downstairs and straight out of the tavern. The cool air of the evening tastes sweet and clear after the foul tavern room. There's a calmness that comes with being decided. I feel heavy in my knowing, like a rock that doesn't care about the wind or the rain because it's stuck solid and it's not shifting. Sarah and me belong together. The rest of the world will have to step aside and make room for that fact.

Ennis made it clear he won't help me get her free, so I have to find someone who will. As frightening as the realization is, the best chance I have is trusting a man I barely know. I strike off with a strong hope and a stronger prayer, headed for Aaron Newman in Culpeper, the Quaker in the green house with the white door.

Chapter 66

Sarah

Every slave on the plantation's down here whooping it up like it's Christmas. The ham and hooch from Master's got everybody fired up. A handful of the field men sing some old songs, slapping their thighs and stomping their feet, and Red's dancing with about every gal here. He's trying to show me that he could have his pick, and I reckon it's true. Long as it ain't me.

I sit on a stump, staring into the trees, praying tonight'll be the night Henry comes back. I rest my hand on my belly and stroke over the baby with my thumb till I catch myself doing it and pull my hand away before someone sees.

Maple comes up to me, sucking her teeth. "What you doing way over here, letting your man dance with any young thing he sets eyes on?"

I keep my face pointed to the woods, so she leans right in front of me.

"You still hoping for that blacksmith, ain't you? Running around here thinking you're better than the rest of us 'cause you let some white man plow your field for a while." She puckers her face and shakes her head. "How long you think Red's going to put up with your mess?"

"Go away, Maple. I got nothing to say to you."

"You better go dance with your man before he moves on to someone else." She grabs my arms and yanks me to my feet, dragging me toward the circle.

"He ain't my man," I spit. I slap at her arms and twist free from her grip.

The neighing of a horse makes us both whip around and look. Master is on a large gray stallion, walking toward us, watching us. We straighten up and dip our heads.

When he's right up in front of us, he says, "What's this about?"

Neither one of us says a thing.

"Maple, I won't have you spoiling this evening for Sarah. She and Red are celebrating."

Maple casts a look of pure hate to me and then picks up her head. "She ain't celebrating, Master. She ain't dancing with Red 'cause she's sulking after that blacksmith."

Master looks at me and then over to Red who's stopped dancing but still holds on to Willa in the middle of the circle. He lets her go and digs his hands into his pockets, looking away.

"That damn blacksmith." Master yanks his horse's reins and pulls him round, so the pair of them are standing right over me. "You listen to me, Sarah, and you listen good. I paired you with Red, and that was a kindness. If you keep pining for that devil, you'll get the punishment you deserve. Now get over there and dance with your man."

I hug my arms around myself and walk over to Red.

"Dance!" Master shouts.

And we hop. Stomping around to no music, waving our hands in the air like fools. Jim starts to clap out a rhythm for us and a few others join in.

"Hold her like she's yours, Red."

He wraps his arms around me and pulls me close. I set my hands on his shoulders. He presses me tight up against him, and I feel sick and dizzy, tripping over my own feet.

Master watches us from atop his horse. There ain't nothing to do but keep hold on to Red and wait till Master's seen enough.

When he has, he says, "Take her up to your cabin, Red. Make her yours."

Every slave master expects the women he owns to have babies. There's no cheaper way to make money. I even heard of breeding farms where that's all you do. Master putting me with Red was him deciding it's my breeding time.

I feel the eyes on my back as we walk to Red's cabin. My heart's thumping like a jackrabbit. I stand outside his door whimpering and he shushes me and pulls me in.

Red goes over to the bed and sits down, rubbing his palms to his thighs. I press my back up against the wall.

"I ain't never going to force you," he says.

I sink down to the floor and pull my knees up to my chest.

"But one of these days you're going to come to me on your own." He looks at me then, and I know what he's saying. He means Henry won't never get me out of here, and Red and me together is how it's going to be 'cause that's how Master wants it.

"Best get some sleep," he says, and scoots back on the mattress to the far edge, leaving room for me.

I lie on the floor, making a pillow with my arms, listening to him breathe.

Chapter 67

Maple

Scurrying after Master, I'm short-breathed as I run to catch up with his trotting horse.

"That's what I been trying to tell you, Master. She ain't never gonna settle here."

"Red will set her straight," he says. "And if not Red, then their child."

"Master, you could trade her for Rose," I pant, trying to keep up. "Master Jeremiah's sure to take a grown woman ready for breeding for a girl just out of childhood."

"No!" he thunders, pulling up the reins, stopping his horse to glare down at me.

Any fool would know to leave it be, but I keep on. I have this one last chance. "And Rose won't give you trouble. She'll work hard and be obedient and—"

"Enough!" he shouts. "I'm not going to beg my father-in-law for a bad bargain. Sarah will stay and do as she's told."

He pulses with anger, but I tremble with rage.

I open my mouth to speak again and think, this is how Momma got sent to the fields. And then I think, if I can save Rose it will be worth it. "Master, you know what Nathaniel Keeler's doing to her," I say. "She ain't but a girl."

He grips his crop and I expect him to strike me. Instead, he sits back in his saddle, the polished leather creaking under his shifting weight. "I do not own Rose," he says in a quiet voice strung through with tension. "There's nothing I can do for her." He kicks his heels into his horse's flank, flicks his crop against her rump and trots on.

Left behind on the hillside, I collapse to the ground. I can't get her out. I can't save her. Master Nathaniel could be with her right now. I want to burn the whole world down.

There's two ways to keep a child when you're held a slave. You can hold her precious, right close to your heart, pouring all your love into her because you know you could lose her any day. Or you can hold her loose, not loving too deep or caring too much or getting too close, knowing that you could lose her any day. Two sides of the same fear.

When Freddy couldn't stop that devil from coming after her night after night, and couldn't stand to hear her screams and see her pain, seems he learned to love the second way. He held her loose and ran. A surviving choice.

I feel the blades of grass poking into me as I dig my fingernails into the dirt. I can't protect her. I can't help her. All I can try to do is love her loose.

Chapter 68

Henry

Aaron Newman, the widowed Quaker in the green house, is a cunning man for being so Godly. It takes some convincing to get him to leave his farm to help me, but once he's decided, he comes up with a scheme that I think will work. Even shaves his Quaker beard for it. He agrees to be at Jubilee in two days' time, but I can't keep myself from worrying. I'm trusting in a stranger, but I'm out of options. And I'm running out of time.

I set out before dawn walking to Jubilee. I mean to get there by late afternoon, before the Quaker shows up in the evening, to tell Sarah what we've got brewing. When I'm close, I cut through the woods to be sure not to run into Matthew Johnson. That would be about the surest way to ruin the plan.

I'm light on my feet as I scramble through the trees growing close and thick, approaching the plantation from the forest behind it. Ahead is the wildflower clearing and then the river and then Jubilee Plantation. The sun beats at me, burning me, though I've had all summer to toughen up to it. I keep pulling my shirt off for the heat, and back on for the burn. I'm thinking about how nice it will be to dip into the river as I walk into the wildflower clearing.

A figure steps into the field from the other side and my first hope is that it's Sarah, but immediately it's clear it's not.

It's a stocky white man with a broad-brimmed hat. He takes another step in, and there's no mistaking him. Mulch. The overseer sees me too and his face pulls into a sneer. I feel the hatred bubbling up in me as my nostrils flair.

"Taylor," he says.

"What're you doing here?" I spit.

"I've just been over at Jubilee. Thought I'd take this here shortcut back to town and look at here who I find."

My muscles tense. "You've no business around there," I tell him.

"Turns out I do," he says. "Johnson wants to hire me back. Imagine that."

I come a few steps closer, balling my fists.

"He says he was hasty to fire me."

"Nobody'd be fool enough to take you back once they're shot of you," I say.

"He found out I was telling the truth about you, so he figures you were lying about me," he says.

My blood surges through me as my breath goes deep and heavy.

From his pocket he takes a piece of iron with four finger loops and slips his right hand into it.

"He told me you wanted to shack up with that slave."

My jaw tightens as I circle toward him, and he rounds the clearing toward me.

"You're dumber than you look, Taylor. You don't know which piece of ass is for keeping and which is for seeding. Next thing you'll be proposing to a tavern whore."

My teeth grind as I search the ground for a rock or stick.

"Now, don't you worry, blacksmith. When I'm back in my old job, I'll make sure she don't miss you at all."

He thrusts his pelvis miming the act, and I picture him on top of her, holding her down in that stable. I fly at him and he's expecting me. He catches me hard in the ribs with his iron rings. I stagger back, fuming.

"My right hand wasn't the same after you, so I got a little help for it." He holds it up for me to see.

"Figures you'd need something like that to fight. Your dainty soft fists can't handle a punch?"

"Come tomorrow, I'm gonna pick up where I left off. Same job, same cabin, and what else was I doing? Oh, yeah." He palms his groin. "Showing your slave gal how a real man does it."

He wants me to lose my head and, goddamnit, it's working. I'm shaking and I can't think straight. "If you ever touch her. If you go near her," I shout.

He comes at me with his iron fist and I throw myself against him. We both fall to the ground, and I scramble away from him.

"I bet she's a squealer," he says. "I can't wait to find out if she's a squealer."

There's a palm-sized rock a few paces off and I grab it and face him just as he's coming at me with those damn iron knuckles. I take a strong blow to my ribs, but I smash the rock to the side of his head, catching him unawares and sending him reeling. Blood flows from a gash on his hairline and he swipes at it with his arm. I hurt where he hit me and I want to curl into a ball, but I straighten up, wincing and clutching at my side.

"I'm gonna have your whore every goddamned night."

I lunge at him, howling like a wounded beast, raining wild blows with that rock. He smashes his iron fist into my jaw, my ear, my neck, but I don't stop. He will not touch her. Not ever again. He shoves me and I stagger backward, but when he comes for me again, I'm ready for him. He lunges at me and instead of dodging or hitting, I pull him toward me, tipping him off balance. I twist as we fall, landing on top of him, pinning him under me. With the rock, I bash at his face again and again. Beneath me, he squirms and bucks, but I right myself each time he shifts. I hear the crack of his nose breaking.

I raise the rock again, but a wet rattle when he breathes stops me cold. It sounds like the dying man in New York whose clothes I still wear. I hover with the rock, knowing that if I keep striking him, I'll kill him. I imagine the terrible gush of blood from the traveling blacksmith's head coming out of Mulch's. I want to smash his skull in. I want to. But the doing it. I hover, confused.

My hesitation is all he needs. He swings up his hand, which now clutches a knife he must have fished out of his trousers somewhere. It slices through my arm. He knocks me off him and turns the blade to slash again. I bash at his knife hand with my rock, knocking it from his grip, and dive after it. He throws himself on top of me, pounding and kicking. Blood gushes from my arm, seeping into the grass. The knife lies under my belly, and I know I ought to try to fish it out from under me and use it on him, but my arms are like lead. If I pull it from its hiding place and he overpowers me and takes the knife, he could use it to finish me off. My vision blurs and I know my best chance is to stay where I am, hiding the knife but taking the blows until my vision darkens and I finally black out.

Chapter 69

Sarah

Maple sucks at her teeth and rolls her eyes when Red pokes his head into the kitchen house to say there's going to be one more for supper.

"We already made most of the meal," she tells him, huffing. "Who they got coming at the last minute like this? They need to stop inviting any old body who gets it in his head to come wandering up the driveway."

I step outside 'cause I can see she's fixing to ramp up her meanness. Just outside the kitchen house, my foot lands on a toad that took a wrong turn somewhere. I yelp and hop off it.

Red checks to see what's what and gives me a look that says just what he thinks of me getting scared by a toad. He grabs it by its hind leg and bashes it twice on the doorframe and throws it in the grass. Then he turns back to Maple. "Reckon you best get working," he says. "Or you can tell Master you won't feed his fancy guest."

When he goes, he don't even look at me. I got nothing against Red, but he's sure building up to have some bitter feelings about me.

When we've bulked up the supper, Maple sends me to set the table. I hurry along to the carry-through and up the back stairs where I almost crash into a round-faced stranger poking his head down the stairs that seem clear ain't for no visitor.

"Sorry, sir," I say, pulling back before I run clean into him. I sure don't see what business he's got down in the carry-through, but I drop my eyes and wait for him to get on out the way.

"Are you Sarah?" he asks, barely above a whisper.

I don't like that he knows my name. "Yes, sir," I say, keeping my eyes on my toes.

"Are you the only Sarah here?"

That don't seem like a safe question to answer, so I hold my tongue.

"Are you?" he says it sharp and urgent in that way that says trouble'll come unless I answer.

"Yes, sir." I glance up to see him nod and I'm sure it means something's about to happen if I want it to or not.

"Can you cook?" he asks with his voice hushed.

I tell him, "Yes, sir, but Maple's the cook here," hoping to get him on to her.

He nods and goes along to Master's study and I breathe out slowly, my stomach twisting into knots.

At dinner I learn that Master's visitor is a timber man from Tennessee. He got his eye on me most of the night, stroking his chin like he got an imaginary beard, making me jitterbug nervous. There's something not right about him. He don't smile all night, but he sure do eat.

"Mister and Missus Johnson," he says, when he's had his fill, which is three helpings of everything. "Your kind hospitality has got me realizing how much I miss a good home-cooked meal."

"I'm sure the excitement of your adventures out west makes up for the lost comforts from back east," Missus says.

"Not at all, madam. There is nothing so warming as a good meal on a cold night. But the frontier is a rough place for a woman and a logger's camp is no place at all. Though thanks to your hospitality, I do believe I've found my solution." He nods to his empty plate. "Your Negress is an enchanting cook."

"She is," says Missus, "but she cooks for us, here. I don't know how that helps you in Tennessee."

"Indeed. But there are other slaves who cook. This girl here," he nods at me standing against the wall, "tells me she also cooks."

My eyes go wide and I lift them from the floor, settling them on the timber man. He's staring right back at me and the hair on the back of my neck prickles. I drop my eyes.

"It would be a tremendous comfort if I had a house girl to cook and clean for me."

"I don't doubt it, sir. Frankly, I don't know how you manage without," says Master.

"I feel certain that Providence has led me to you today to lighten a heavy burden. I would like to request to purchase this girl here, and take her with me to Tennessee."

"Well, gracious," says Missus. "That certainly is quite a request."

"There's a slave auction in Fredericksburg in a few weeks. You might find someone suitable there," Master says.

"With all respect, sir, there's no guarantee I'll find a house slave at auction who cooks. And, in any case, I can't wait. I'm prepared to pay you fair market price plus a little extra for the trouble."

"I don't usually like to sell off my slaves once they come on to my land. I like for them to think of it as home. It makes for better workers and a better yield if you let them be rooted to the place."

The man nods, considering. "I see your point. And how long has she been with you?" he asks, tipping his head toward me.

"Nearly a year."

"Pardon my saying so, but that's hardly time to settle in. It's more like passing through. What about these two? Have they been here any shorter?"

"Oh, no," Missus says. "Willa was born here, and Annie came here as a little pickaninny, about three years old."

He nods. "Then this one," he says pointing to me, "seems indeed the best choice. I want to be fair about the price and your trouble. For my part, I sure am tired of eating baked beans."

Master and Missus both laugh at that.

"I must say, I have heard about the poor diet of the Western settler," she says.

"Well, whatever you've heard I can assure you the truth is much worse."

They all laugh again and I start to worrying that they just might sell me to Tennessee.

"I'd like to help you," Master says, "but I've just paired her off with a loyal and likely buck. I'd hate to do that and then sell her away."

The man's eyes flash to me and I read the disturbed surprise in his face. "Paired her off? How long ago was this?"

"Saturday," Master says.

"Well, really, it was last week," Missus says, "but we moved them in together on Saturday."

The timber man takes a moment to recover his surprise. "At the risk of sounding impertinent, I wonder how strong a bond may have formed in a few days. Might he not be equally happy with someone else?"

Missus sets her napkin down and straightens her spine. "We wouldn't pair them and then take her away, sir. That seems uncommonly cruel."

"The Lord giveth and the Lord taketh away, madam. And as I say, sir, I'm prepared to compensate you appropriately. Do consider how much the inconvenience may be worth to you."

Chapter 70

Henry

When I come to, my face is throbbing, it hurts to move, and I can't feel my arm, but at least there's no sign of Mulch. The fog in my head keeps me from concentrating, but I know I have to do something about the knife gash. At the edge of the clearing, I see the plant Sarah used on my cut hand that first day in the thunderstorm. I crawl to it, chew the leaves like she did, and spit it on to my wound. I tie my arm tight with the strip of her dress that served as our binding cloth. The effort is immense and, when I'm done, I pass out in the grass.

The cicadas' evening song wakes me, their harsh clicking and rattling passing into my dreams and jarring me into consciousness. Everything hurts, but I jolt upright with fear and urgency. I've lost the day. Aaron Newman will already be at the plantation.

I have to get to Jubilee. If what Mulch says is true, we've run out of time. Sarah has to get away, tonight.

I moan as I rise, drowning out the croaking of a bullfrog. I sway on my feet, slowly shuffling to the edge of the clearing and lean against a rough-barked tree, catching my breath.

With faltering steps, I make my way along the path to the river. I fall, striking my knees badly. I pick myself up and keep going.

When I reach the river, the cool water is a balm to my sun-burnt skin and pummeled body. I submerge myself, savoring the relief, but swimming across is a painful task. When I get to the other side, I have to rest on the riverbank before I can go on.

It's late by the time I make it to the plantation. Under the cover of the dark and the trees, I limp into Sarah's cabin. Bessie starts as I enter. She's sitting at a spinning wheel, feeling the fibers twine against her fingers. The turning of the wheel makes a whirr, the only noise in the room.

"Who's that?" she calls when I step inside.

"It's Henry," I say.

The wheel stops. "You won't let up till you get that girl killed."

It's a knife to my heart. "Has something happened?"

She sighs and purses her lips into a deep frown. "You got to get out of here and let that child be. Master done put her with Red now. Things'll get worse for her if you two don't stop."

Blood rushes through my ears making her words sound dull. My heart splutters.

I stoop in front of her, my face level with hers. "I'm taking her with me. Tonight. I'm getting her free."

She reaches out and pats my face. "You're about as big a fool as she is."

"Can you get a message to her? Can you warn her that I have a man helping me? Tell her not to be afraid. Tell her I'm here."

Bessie shakes her head. "I can't go stomping into the dining room, when they got a guest in there all the way from Tennessee. You got to forget about all this. Ain't no point to keep fighting."

I straighten up, my temper flaring. "How can you say that?"

She starts her spinning wheel back up, feeding the cotton into the wheel. "Some things just ain't gonna be."

"Well, they have to be," I say. "That's why you fight for them."

She feels the line of thread and then pulls more cotton from a sack at her feet. Spinning.

"But you wouldn't know about that," I spit out. "You've spent so long groveling behind your masters, being grateful for every scrap they give you, that you don't know how to want for yourself." Her complacency is making me cruel. I know she's just a crumpled widow who's got all the hope crushed out of her, but I'm angry and I'm frightened for Sarah and I don't stop. "Anyone else who'd been handed their freedom would be long gone," I say. "But you handed yours back."

Her wheel slows and then speeds back up. "I didn't give it back," she says.

"Well, whatever you did, you didn't take it, did you? So, pardon me if we don't give up on the opinion of someone who can't understand caring enough to do something about it."

Chapter 71

Sarah

Master wants whiskey in the parlor for him and his guest, and Missus wants sherry, so Annie brings both bottles in for the three of them.

I bring Master Thomas upstairs and refill his wash pitcher with water, but then I leave him to undress and get himself to bed like he's been doing since Henry shamed him into it.

When I get downstairs, I hear Master in his study and the Tennessee man and Missus in the parlor. I don't waste a second.

I knock, and before he gets an answer out I slip inside the study.

Master stands at his bookshelf, running his finger along the spines, searching for something particular. He glances at me and gets right back to looking.

"What is it, Sarah?"

"You going to sell me out to Tennessee, Master?"

He stops his searching and looks at me with eyes cold as the moon. "Do you wish to stay here?"

"Yes, sir."

"I really should sell you to Tennessee, as ungrateful as you've been."

"I'm sorry, Master. I'll be better. But please don't sell me out there."

I need to stay put for when Henry comes. He'll never find me in Tennessee, in all that wilderness. There's a quiet voice in my head that says I'll wait forever waiting on Henry, but he said he's coming back to get me free and I choose, against my nature, to trust and believe.

"I have given you everything you need to be happy and content here and instead you're sullen and sulking."

"No, sir. I appreciate everything. I won't never sulk again," I say.

"Maybe I should sell you on to get rid of a bad apple before it festers." He turns his back to me and runs his finger across the books, lifting one and thumbing through its pages.

"Master," I say, and I'm about to tell him that I'm with child and I'm worth more to keep than sell until the baby comes, but I can't do it. I can't betray our child, and I won't say that it's his, because it ain't. Instead, I get down on my knees and clasp my hands. "Please, Master, sir. Don't let that man take me away. I'll be good. I'll do everything just like you want me to. Please."

And please let Henry come quickly, I think. I can't stand to stay here much longer. I can't keep bowing and scraping and smiling in front of this man who I hate.

On my knees, begging like a dog, I think that if I wasn't waiting for Henry, it would be better for me to go to Tennessee. Away from Red, away from the overseer who I hear is coming back, away from Master who thinks he can tell me what to feel.

I wonder what kind of master the Tennessee man would be. There's all kinds. Some are vicious and cruel and serving them is like a musket to your head. And some are so gentle and kind that it takes a while for you to remember they got you trapped against your free will, like an animal in a cage for their pleasure. And it takes another stretch of time for you to see that they've been eating away at you like a crow, peck, peck, pecking at your flesh, taking years to do the work, till you don't remember how it was to be whole. I don't reckon I ever knew. Until Henry showed me. I won't go to Tennessee, or anywhere else. I'm waiting right here for Henry.

Master frowns at me on the floor and slams his book closed. "I don't want any more trouble out of you."

"No, sir." I shake my head.

"Then I'll decline the offer, but I expect you to be a mate to Red. And I don't want to hear another word about that devil who turned your head and tainted your salvation."

"Yes, Master. Thank you, Master." The words curl up on my tongue and it feels like another chunk of flesh is being pecked from my body.

Chapter 72

Henry

I leave Bessie and go straight to the Big House, ducking and skimming along the walled garden before dashing in through the doorway of the carry-through. I slip into one of the attached cellar rooms and hide myself behind a sack of beans. When I hear steps, I peek out, but it's Maple, so I duck back and wait. My legs cramp, crouched in the corner. The next time footsteps come down the back stairs, I know it's Sarah without looking. I hear it in the lightness and the rhythm of her step. The pad, pad of her feet has her mark on it, as clear as hearing her voice or catching her scent. It's a pleasurable thought that I've found another thing to know about her.

I stand up and step out from behind the bean sack. When she sees me, she nearly drops the tray of glasses she's carrying. I rush over to her and stay the glasses, but she sets the tray right on the floor in the middle of the carry-through, knocking over three glasses in her rush, and flings her arms around my neck. God, I love this woman. I wrap my arms around her and lift her off her feet. She's kissing me before I set her back down. I can't believe I even thought about giving her up.

She takes my hand and leads me deeper into the cellar, past the bean sack and bolts of cloth and a broken spinning wheel, stopping at the furthest corner beside an old baby cot.

"I knew you'd come," she says, eyes shining. She runs her fingers over the bruising and swelling on my face. "Who hurt you?"

I slip one hand behind her neck and plant the other on her hip. Touching her heals something in me. I dip my head down to her shoulder and breathe in the smell of her. "I ran into Ralph Mulch," I say. "Excepting for that, I would have been here earlier."

She holds my face in her hands and, pulling me to her, brushes her lips over every battered inch of it. Feather soft. Like a dream. She takes off my shirt and runs her fingers over my cuts and bruises. My skin sings. As much as I ache when I move, I want her badly.

"He got your ribs," she says. "Let's wrap you up."

Slipping back through the cellar to the bolts of cloth, she takes a fine shimmering blue and wraps it snug, round and round my ribs, tucking the end underneath. It eases the pressure.

She unties her dress strip from my arm and sees the knife cut and the chewed leaves.

"Yarrow?"

I nod, and she reties it firmer.

"I'll make you something for the pain later."

"I already feel a good sight better," I say. And I do.

She lays her hands on the skin of my waist, just under the blue bandage. I'm almost embarrassed at how I respond to her touch.

"I'm glad you're back," she says.

I run my hands up her arms. "I made a plan, and I got us some help," I say. "The Quaker from the green house."

She nods her head, her eyes dancing. "You think we can run?"

"Not running," I say. "He's going to buy you legal, so we'll not be looking over our shoulder, hiding from the law."

"You trust this man?"

I know what she's thinking. If Aaron Newman decides to double-cross us and keep her as his slave, bought with the money I gave him to buy her freedom, there'd not be a thing in the world we could do about it. I don't trust anyone enough for that.

"He's already signed change of ownership papers back in Culpeper, so the minute he buys you, ownership'll pass to me. And the first thing we'll do is go down to the courthouse and get your free papers."

She lets out a long, shaky breath, letting that all sink in. "How many days till he comes?"

"He's already here. I'd have warned you earlier if it weren't for Mulch."

She shakes her head, worry drawing up her eyebrows. "Master's got a timber man from Tennessee up there with him."

"I know," I say. "That's the Quaker."

Her mouth falls open. She backs up against the cellar wall clutching herself like she's the one with the busted ribs. "I thought he was going to take me to Tennessee."

"It's all right," I say. "He's on our side."

She shakes her head as her face crumples. "I didn't know," she says. "I was afraid you'd come back and I'd be gone. I begged Master to let me stay, and he agreed."

It's like the air's been sucked out of me. My face throbs where Mulch hit me with his iron knuckles. Goddamn Mulch. Goddamn everything. I circle my arms around her pulling her close as my insides knot up. My chest burns when I think of her asking to stay so she can wait for me.

"I'm sorry," she says, and my heart is breaking that she'd be apologizing to me.

She hangs her head, withdrawing into herself, and I graze my cheek across her hair and tuck her under my chin. There's a ball forming in my throat, and I swallow once, twice, three times before I can speak.

"Don't worry," I say. "We'll find another way."

She looks up at me and the devastation in her eyes could stop your heart. She lays her hand against my swollen cheek and I nuzzle into her palm. The feel of her skin against mine is a kind of balm.

When she kisses me, the longing and need surge through me, and I press into her, broken ribs and all. I am on fire.

"You're hurt," she says, but she's got one hand on my backside, pulling me closer.

"I love you," I say.

I lift her skirts and she fumbles at my breeches. When I enter her, she wraps her leg around my hip and pushes into me as I push into her. I'm lost in her, and there's only one clear thought outside of the two of us, and that is that I will never give her up.

Chapter 73

Maple

I go down through the carry-through and some lazy good-for-nothing has left a tray of glasses on the floor. I suck at my teeth and shake my head. I could have walked right into it.

When I stoop down for the tray, I think I hear an animal from deep in the cellar. I creep back there, careful not to startle it, to see what trap I'm gonna need to lay out. When I get far enough back and my eyes adjust to the dark, I see them. The blacksmith is pressed up close against Sarah. He reaches for her and she pulls him closer. He hikes up her skirt and she throws her leg around him. The two of them move together, rubbing into each other. Like animals.

My stomach churns and my dinner yams climb into in my throat. I rush out gasping at air that's too humid and hot to be fresh. My head goes light and my eyes prick and darken. And I'm back there in that room, in front of the fireplace.

I feel the floorboards against my back and the ripping, ramming feeling between my legs. And his hand on my mouth when he says, "Look at me."

I see Rose, trapped under Master Nathaniel, pinned to the floorboards, and then held against the wall like Sarah, with him thrusting into her. And I see her pull at him like Sarah pulled at her white man to keep him ramming into her. And I throw up my yams into the grass.

My eyes water as I gasp. My head swims. I breathe in air that's thick as cream and blink away the pinprick feeling in my eyes. I make my way to the kitchen house where, on the grass a few feet away, the toad that Red smashed against the doorframe lies dead.

An idea is forming in my mind, warm and settling, like fresh baked bread. I gather up Sarah's herb bundles from the kitchen house and from where she had them stacked in a corner of Bessie's cabin. I'm prepared to strike the blind woman out of my way, but I don't need to. She isn't there. On my way back to the Big House, I scoop up the dead toad.

In the carry-through, the tray of glasses still sits abandoned. I pick it up and carry everything up to Miss Martha.

Chapter 74

Sarah

I check that the way is clear and watch Henry scurry out the carry-through and across the yard to Bessie's cabin to wait for me until I can get done here.

It's not until I'm back upstairs in the house that I remember the tray of glasses I left in the carry-through that weren't there when me and Henry came out of the cellar.

"Maple was looking for you," Willa says, coming downstairs with an armful of sheets. "She wanted you to change the bedding in the guest room for that Tennessee man staying tonight."

"He's staying the night?"

"Course he's staying. Ain't his fault folks told him he'd find a blacksmith here to shoe his horse but he don't. Master ain't gonna turn him out." She hefts the sheets on her hip. "But you'd have known that if you was here to do the bed like Maple wanted."

I start up the stairs, hoping to catch the timber man alone.

"I already done it now," Willa shouts after me.

"Is that you, Sarah?" Missus calls from her sitting room.

"She here, Missus," Willa answers for me. "You best get in there, she been looking for you too, lazy." She sneers at me, pleased for the tongue lashing I'm sure to be getting after escaping extra work that she got stuck doing.

In her sitting room, Missus stands plucking at her clothes.

She folds her arms across her belly when she sees me. Hovering beside her, Maple never looked more like her sister. They both scowl the same hateful scowl with their matching foreheads wrinkled in distress. Their small eyes are hard as flint. In her hands, Maple holds the tray I left in the carry-through.

"We were looking for you," Missus says. "You disappeared after dinner when you should have been helping Maple."

I start off looking at her, but my eyes dip down to the tray of glasses. I feel my heart leap into my throat.

"I know what you were up to, Sarah," Missus says. "Did you think I wouldn't find out?"

A chill goes up my back like ice fingers, and I know whatever's coming won't be good.

"I…I…" There's nothing to say. I look to Maple.

"Yes, Maple told me all about it. To think I let such a godless creature into my house."

My insides are quivering.

"You watch her, Maple, while I get your Master."

As soon as she's out of the room, I hiss at Maple, "What did you tell her?"

Maple draws her close-set eyes closer. "I can't stand to look at you no more."

"You know what they'll do to me," I say.

She shakes her head. "I don't want you punished," she says. "I want you gone."

A second later, Master comes stomping in, frowning, with Missus scurrying up behind him.

"Now, please tell me what's so important that you had to pull me away from our guest and leave him sitting in there on his own?"

"It's Sarah," Missus says. "Maple discovered the truth of it tonight."

I close my eyes. My body's already tensing up for the punishment of my life.

"She's been suspecting it for a while, but now she's caught her in the act, out by the kitchen garden, under the full moon," Missus says.

My eyes snap open. That ain't right.

"What's this about?" Master says, more annoyed than concerned. "What do you accuse her of?"

"I hate to say it, Master, but there can't be no other truth to what I seen." Maple pauses till she's sure she's got every lick of attention in the room. "That creature right there, standing right in front of you now, is a bona fide witch."

I can't tell if my hearing's going crazy or her mouth is.

Master laughs. "This is preposterous," he says. He smiles down at Missus. "My dear, don't let the superstitions of simple minds trouble you. Come." He holds out his hand to her. "We must not neglect our guest."

Missus seems unsure, but gives him her hand, just as obedient as any of us.

Maple don't waste a second. She digs into her pocket and pulls out the toad that Red smashed dead against the kitchen house doorway. "I found this in a pot."

Missus yelps like I did when I stepped on it and felt it squirm underfoot. She shields her eyes with one hand and, pulling away from Master, reaches for a chair with the other. She sits, fanning herself with her flat hand, more for show than for air.

"Put that disgusting thing away," Master says to Maple. "Have you lost your senses, bringing that in here?"

"Sarah's making witch potions," she says. She drops the dead toad on the tray of glasses. Then, from her aprons, she pulls out my dried Joe-pye weed, squawroot, boneset and ragwort, and she waves them over her head. "She been gathering to make a brew."

"Lord almighty preserve us. Matthew, what have we let into our home?"

Master looks confused. Not rightly believing, but not sure otherwise either.

"That's for healing," I say. "For helping."

"Witch's work is the Devil's work," Maple says. "Ain't no wonder she been turning white men's eyes. The overseer and the blacksmith both. She probably brewed it up like she was fixing to brew something up tonight. You just a stronger kind of Christian, Master, that she didn't get you too."

Missus jumps right on that idea. "There was that man at the auction, too. Remember, Matthew? The one she bewitched till he bid more than he could pay. She's been hexing people all this time."

I got trouble enough breathing, so there ain't no way I can speak. I shake my head, and shake it, and shake it.

Master takes the dried plants from Maple. He rubs his fingers over them, like he's got to feel them to believe they's real. They crush in his hands and he throws them at me. The dried weed pieces are too light to travel far, and fall in front of my feet, like I got some spell to keep them off me.

I get down on the floor on my knees and pick up the ragwort, a cluster of golden flowers and heart-shaped leaves. "This is good for a woman's monthly pains and for childbirth pains, and for broken bone pains too, sometimes." I raise it up to him to see it's just a simple plant.

Maple sucks her teeth.

I hold up the bushy clutch of tiny pink flowers from the Joe-pye weed. "You boil this for tea to ease a fever." I scrabble around on the floor for another healing herb to explain.

"I seen her use her weeds and potions on Master Thomas, too," Maple says.

I shake my head. I have, but God help me if they believe I have.

"Our son," gasps Missus. "Matthew, our son."

"No, Master. I never hurt him," I say from where I kneel on the ground.

"If that ain't the forked tongue of the Devil, just like you preached us about," Maple says.

"Get Thomas," he says to Maple. "Wake him up and bring him down here."

Maple sets her tray down against the wall and hurries out of the room.

"I never hurt no one," I say. "I use these things to heal people."

"Such devilry in my own house," Missus says, wringing her hands. "We weren't even supposed to have her. Remember, Matthew? She should have gone to that other man, but the Devil brought her here."

Master crosses to his wife and reaches down to where she sits and takes her hand. "Don't be afraid, my dear. The Lord protects his own."

Maple comes in with Master Thomas and says, "Go on and tell your momma and your daddy what you told me."

When she says that, I know it's over. They gonna hang me. Or burn me.

"When I got sick," he says, "Sarah put yams and pine needles on my chest and then I got better."

Maple nods at him like he's supposed to say something more, and then he remembers and says it.

"Like magic."

She smiles. "And the drink?"

"The tea?" he asks. "It tasted awful, but it made me better."

I lower my head, shaking. I'm surely dying tonight. There's never been much living to my life, but I don't want it over.

"Are you sick, Sarah? I can pick some plants for you, like you showed me."

He ain't helping. He means to, I know, but he's doing the opposite of helping. He walks toward me, but his daddy grabs him back.

"Stay away from her," Master barks. "Don't let her touch you."

Thomas looks at me, worried.

"Take him back to bed," Master says to Maple. His voice cuts like a blade.

As Maple takes the boy's hand and leads him out, he asks, "Has Sarah got the catching sickness? Is she gonna get better?"

Missus is fanning her hand again. "What do we do with her, Matthew? What do we do?"

He paces, ignoring her and me.

"A witch in our home," she says. "And we didn't even know it. What will they say about us? And I lent her to Edith Welleby. Do you think we'll have to tell her?"

"Keep your voice down," Master says. "Somebody will hear you."

The only somebody in the house is Henry's Quaker. I see my chance and I take it. I hop up and dash down the hall to the parlor where the Quaker waits on a settee.

"They think I'm a witch," I blurt. "They're gonna kill me if you don't buy me. Ask them again."

Master storms into the room, furious and embarrassed, looking like he'd like to cut me down where I stand. The Quaker rises, taking on the posture of a gentleman.

"Have I heard this correctly? Do you keep a witch as your servant?" the Quaker asks with the sternness of Jesus on Judgment Day.

That surely stumbles Master for what to say. He croaks out some choking noises until he finds his voice. "Of course not, sir. At least, not intentionally. That is to say, you must not think that we condone this. I assure you, sir, I would not have devilry on my plantation. We are staunchly Christian here."

Missus rushes in with Maple coming up behind her.

"I do hope, sir," says Missus, "that you will not judge us based on this frightful scene."

The Quaker looks from Missus to Master and then to me. "It's hard to know what to think," he says. "But I suppose we cannot control the trials our Lord sends us."

My heart's about to beat out of my chest.

"Indeed, we cannot," Missus says, with a relieved sigh. "May we trust in your discretion to keep this between ourselves?"

She crosses the room, sits in a chair and arranges her skirts about her, the picture of Southern charm.

He watches her, thinking, and I watch him, praying.

"I have great sympathy for what is transpiring here this evening," he says. "In fact, I am prepared to offer a solution to your problems."

Master's head whips round to him. "Can one be found?"

The Quaker reaches up and strokes his imaginary beard. "I believe God uses men for His purposes."

Master nods his agreement. "The truth of that has long been settled in my mind."

Henry's Quaker rounds to me and places his hand on my shoulder. "And I believe God placed me here, in this moment, to intervene on his behalf."

Please, God, is all I can think. Please, God, please, God.

"To do what, exactly?" Missus asks.

"To relieve you, this very night, of this slave."

Master and Missus look at each other and I get needle pricks to the back of my neck.

"The Lord moves in mysterious ways," the Quaker says when no one speaks.

"Does that mean you're gonna take her?" Maple asks from just inside the room.

"Leave us, Maple," Master says. "And not a word to anyone."

"Yes, sir," she says, practically singing. Ain't no way she can keep this kind of news to herself.

She leaves the room and Master closes the door behind her. "I appreciate your offer, sir, but why would you take her, knowing what she is?"

"I have experience with ones such as this," he says. "You will agree, sir, that she does not belong here with your wife and son. I know just what to do with her, and it will be right and pleasing in the eyes of God."

Missus goes pale and sits back in the chair. "Will you kill her? Can we allow that, Matthew?"

"There's hope for every soul, madam," the Quaker says. "I mean to deliver her for God. Sell her to me, legal and proper, and I will take this burden from you. May God's will be done."

Missus and Master lock eyes on each other. She nods to him and he nods to the Quaker.

"Then let us draw up the papers," the Quaker says. "And I trust, sir, that you will consider the extenuating circumstances in setting the price."

Chapter 75

Henry

I slip out of the carry-through and slink my way back to Sarah's cabin. Bessie's gone. Up by Ben's grave, more than likely, and I'm glad to have it so. I close the door and lay on her bed. She'd howl if she caught me, but my ribs are sore and painful, so I take the chance.

I've had barely a minute to think about everything that's been happening, but now I do. Mulch is coming back. And Aaron Newman hasn't been able to buy Sarah free either. And it won't be long before Matthew Johnson sees what she's carrying. It'd be a reckless thing running off with no plan, but staying feels more reckless, knowing what's coming.

There are too many slave catchers around Aaron Newman's place. Escaping that way is too dangerous. But maybe he could find somewhere else for us to run to. Maybe he could help us get out to a free state. Ohio, or Pennsylvania.

We could fix it so she looks like she's my slave, and I'm transporting her, fair and legal. I could get a cart and she could sit in the back. Except he'd be sure to take out notices saying to look out for a Negro woman looking like her, traveling with a white man looking like me.

Even if we make it up north, they could find us out and snatch us up. The Fugitive Slave Act sees to it that no runaway can be safe in the whole of the United States. Which maybe leaves the territories. Out west, past Independence, taking the Oregon Trail, or maybe not. Plowing through the wilderness into Indian country to scratch out a life between the bears and the wolves, where illegal doesn't have quite the same meaning.

"Red!" I hear Matthew Johnson calling from the house. "Red!" He sounds agitated.

I tense as feet pound past the cabin door. Red's voice carries back to me as he hurries on. "You call me, Master?"

I keep listening into the quiet, but when there's nothing else to hear, my mind goes back to Sarah. The main thing is, we're getting out of here. I close my eyes and see her. Soon I will lay down with her every night and wake up with her every morning. We'll find some land and stake a claim and we'll plant and harvest and raise a family. No richer man ever lived than that.

I hear fast feet running outside. Light feet, like a woman's. Like Sarah's. I sit up with a mind to going out to have a look when she comes bursting through the door.

"We did it," she says. She's breathless.

My brain stutters. "Do you mean?" I don't dare hope. I know the plan has failed. But she's beaming. "Are you saying?"

She nods. "And we have Maple to thank. Cruel, hard-hearted, bitter Maple."

I don't know what she means by thanking Maple, but I know what she's saying. I jump up like I never even heard of broken ribs. I grab her and twirl her and feel nothing but joy.

Sarah is free. Or as good as. A wave of elation and relief hits me. With the transfer of ownership papers, she became mine as soon as Matthew Johnson sold her to the Quaker. Now we can go to the courthouse for her free papers.

We collect her few things from under her pallet. The bracelet I made her that she stopped wearing for fear of Johnson seeing it, and the pressed flowers of her wedding bouquet.

"They'll be crumpled on the road," I say.

"I won't leave them in this place," she says. She folds them into the pocket of her skirt. "I wish I'd gotten my green headscarf back from Annie."

"Leave it," I say. "We'll get you a new one. We'll get you a hundred new ones."

We go to the coach house, her walking normally and me skirting behind the trees in case Johnson's come out to bid her farewell. He hasn't. Red's in there hitching up the coach and Aaron Newman's helping him do it. I can tell from the tightness of the Quaker's shoulders that he's eager to leave. And I see from the stiffness of Red's movements that he's upset.

He has his back to us and, when he finishes, he steps away from the horse and dips his head. Sarah walks up to him while I hang back in the shadows by the door.

"Take care of yourself, Red," she says.

He reaches over and hugs her.

"It ain't right," I hear him say. "You ain't no witch."

"It's all right, Red."

"I killed that toad."

"I'm gonna be just fine."

"What's he talking about?" I say.

Red whips around to see me standing there, shock and confusion playing across his face. He looks from Sarah to me and back again.

"I ain't going to Tennessee," Sarah says.

The Quaker comes around and shakes Red's hand. "Aaron Newman," he says.

Red looks at him like he's just sprouted two heads.

"This here's the man from the green house Finny talked about," says Sarah.

Red's jaw drops and he stands still with shock before reanimating and pumping Aaron Newman's hand with enthusiasm. "The man helping slaves?"

"The very same."

"Will you take me in if I get to you?" he asks, not wasting a second, still pumping the Quaker's hand.

"It would be my pleasure. But take a lesson from what happened to thy friend. There are still many slave catchers near my home. But, when the weather turns cold and the nights are longer than the days, they will head for their hearths. That will be the time to run."

Red's face is a riot of emotion.

Aaron Newman clasps his shoulder. "Take comfort, friend. There are many who wish to see thee free."

I offer Red my hand. We've never been friends, but I wish him well. I wish him free.

"Be careful out there," he says.

I'm sorry to leave him behind. I'm sorry to leave all of them behind, but I take Sarah's hand, and we climb on to the buggy.

Aaron Newman has me crouch in the back under a blanket so as not to provoke Johnson, should he be looking out of the window at our departure. I'm cramped and hot under the covering, but I barely notice it. I feel giddy with excitement. Sarah reaches back and touches my shoulder through the blanket.

I feel the buggy move and hear the change in sound of the horse hooves as we pull out of the coach house and on to the grass. And then the crunch of the wheel and the sharp clop of the hooves as we drive from the grass to the driveway. We pick up speed, breaking into a trot, and then slow down again to a walk, and then a slow walk, and then we stop. My heart is in my throat. I picture Johnson blocking our path with a shot gun having somehow figured out he'd been tricked and threatening to revoke the sale.

When the seconds drag on and no one speaks, I peek out, spying through a crack under the blanket.

Beneath the wooden archway entrance to the plantation, below the painted sign that says *Jubilee*, Bessie hangs at the end of a rope. Matthew Johnson's favorite happy slave.

Her face is bloated, and her eyes are popped open wider in death than they ever were when she lived. Around her neck, her spun cotton is braided into a noose.

"Should we cut her down?" Aaron Newman asks.

"No," Sarah says. "Let him find her."

The Quaker clicks his tongue and flicks the reigns. The horses go jittery and he has to coax them into a slow walk, easing us beside Bessie's body. Their hooves clop against the stones and the carriage wheels squeak as we pass her. The cicadas screech in the background. In a few more steps we're off the plantation. Aaron Newman urges his horses into a trot and then a canter. They willingly oblige, all of us eager to get far away as fast as we can. As Jubilee recedes into the distance, I climb over the seat, taking my place beside Sarah. With her gaze trained on the open road before us, and her eyes wet with tears, she reaches for my hand and weaves our fingers together.

March 1850

Chapter 76

Sarah

My fingers cramped from clutching Henry's hand, squeezing with joy but also with guilt and grief and fear. Riding away was like a dream, but the whole way I kept wondering how the next day was gonna be for Red and the others. And how long Bessie'd hang there. And every few miles I'd look over my shoulder for someone coming to snatch me back. All my life, freedom had been too much to hope for. That night, leaving Jubilee, it was too big to feel all at once. Even now sometimes it hardly seems real.

We got to the Quaker's place in the middle of the night, and by the time the wagon stopped, my heart was racing. His green house was about the size of the overseer's cabin, but there was a friendliness to it, ringed with flowers and smelling of strawberries.

"I can make up a bed with blankets in front of the fire," the Quaker said. "Or I can offer the hayloft above the barn."

Henry looked at me and I looked at him. We read the answer in each other's eyes. We wanted that night for ourselves, even if it meant lying above the cows and the pigs.

"The hayloft," we both said, and I smiled for the first time since leaving Jubilee.

When we lay down in the straw, Henry was still Henry and I was still me, but everything was different. The weight that had been holding us was lifted, and when we came together, it was like flying to the stars.

In the morning, Henry left to get my free papers. I wanted to come with him, but it would've looked strange and we didn't want to go raising eyebrows.

I was a bundle of nerves the whole time he was gone, thinking on one thing after another that could go wrong.

Hours passed before he got back. When he did, he lay the thick, sturdy paper in my hands. All those loops and dashes on it made me a free woman. I ran my hand over the smooth cream surface and a relief washed over me so strong it numbed me. I clutched the paper to my chest, weeping over marks I couldn't even read.

We stayed with the Quaker for the next two weeks, trying to get news about Isaac and Momma. Seems Momma got sold after Isaac and me, but there weren't no word on where either one of them went to. Being free with no way to get to them tastes bitter, but finding them was always gonna be like catching smoke.

From Aaron Newman, we learned that I couldn't stay in Virginia. They made a law that if a freed slave doesn't leave the state inside of a year, she can be arrested and dragged back into slavery, so we headed over the state line into Maryland.

On the first night we struck off on our own, we stopped at an inn and Henry ordered a room for himself while I waited outside. Then he came out to fetch me. We knew they'd never let me in as a free woman, and as his wife they'd have had the law on both of us, so when they stopped him asking what in tarnation he was doing, we had a different story ready to go.

"I'm bringing my slave to my quarters," he said, haughty as a rich planter. "What does it look like I'm doing?"

"We got a hayloft for the slaves, sir."

Henry stilled, collecting his nerves. "That's very kind, but I'll be needing her ministrations tonight."

The clerk let us go without another word. When we got in the room, Henry's jaw was clenching.

"You all right?" I asked.

"They'll let you in here as my whore but not as my wife. They're pigs, perfumed over and draped in fine clothes."

"Just 'cause you play-acting like them, don't mean you is like them."

He barely ate that night, which is something for Henry, 'cause he don't never turn down food.

At another inn, a customer complained about letting bed-warmers stay in the rooms, but he was overruled by the customs of the South. When we traveled on to the next place, another customer offered Henry money to have me warm his bed for the night instead of Henry's own. And all the while Henry had to treat me like a slave, and I had to call him Master.

We'd planned to keep up the disguise and settle down somewhere with no one knowing the truth, but that weren't for us. Henry hated the man he had to pretend to be. And I hated that I had my freedom, with my papers tucked inside my pocket, and I still had to call myself slave.

"And the children," Henry said. "Do we pretend they're slaves as well?"

It wasn't how I pictured freedom.

In Maryland, we got clear away from white folks. We went to the tucked-off, leftover parts where blacks go to live. There were people of every color, from as dark as Jim to as light as Maple. Me and Henry reckoned we could just blend right in. We let them believe Henry was like Maple, coming from a long line of slave mommas and slave-owner daddies, washed whiter and whiter, till all his color just about faded out. If anyone knew different, they didn't say so. Leastways not to us.

The first thing Henry did was build us a house. The good bargain Aaron Newman made on the sale of Matthew Johnson's *witch* meant we had nearly a thousand dollars to get started with. Henry bought wood and tools and got to building soon as we found our spot. Not three days in, Pete Freedman came by, a high-yellow man with small ears and a big heart. When he saw Henry trying to build the house by himself, he walked over and picked up a plank of wood.

"You want this over here?" he asked, and then he just started hammering it into place.

The next day he brought seven more men with him. Soon enough, he and Henry got to where they're like brothers.

Our house has two rooms downstairs and a loft above to sleep. The bigger room is for us to live in, and the small room is a kind of shop. I gather up just about every plant I know and dry them and put them in jars on the shelves. It don't take long for people to know they can come and tell me what ails them and, chances are, I've got something to soothe it.

I seem to get a new customer every day in my little shop. Today, it's Mister Duke come in to ask for something for his wife's cough.

"It gets her into a fit and don't let up till she's doubled over with it."

"She got a fever, Mister Duke?"

"No, Missus Taylor. Just the cough."

Here, everybody's got a last name and we use it. Folks either take their old master's name, so lost family can find them again, or they make one up to suit them. It strengthens your soul to be called Mister or Missus Somebody when you been Hep or Old Carrie your whole life. Or sometimes "hey boy" or "you there."

I take down my jars and mix up a pouch for Missus Duke.

"Here you go, Mister Duke," I say. "One pinch in boiling water. Give it to her all through the day for the rest of the week."

He gives me a basket of eggs and a loaf of bread for payment.

I smell the bread, baked fresh today, and go out to Henry who's in his lean-to workshop built up along the side of the house. His leather apron and tools hang on the wall, and in the middle is his forge and anvil.

Henry's in there with Pete Freedman, who picked his name to match his new place in life. Freedman. The two of them have their heads huddled together over their secret project.

"Got fresh bread," I say. "You two hungry?"

"Should we show her?" Henry says, grinning.

"I guess it's ready. Don't know what else you want to do with it."

Henry has me cover my eyes and, he leads me over to his project. "All right then, Sarah. Open them up."

The two of them have made a cot for the baby. They've rounded the feet into rockers, and on the soft pine of the headboard they've carved Irish hills and Virginia mountains.

"You two made this?" I say, running my hand along the wood. "It's the prettiest cot I ever saw. We got everything we need now."

I hold my belly, large and round, and Henry slides his hands down over mine. "Yes," he says. "I believe we do."

Acknowledgments

So many people have contributed, in large and small ways, to bringing this book into the world. I'd like to thank Gillian Anton, Heather Critchlow, Eugenia Hall, and Chris May for their invaluable feedback throughout the writing process, and for helping me shape this story into a better version of itself. A huge thanks to the eternally generous Adrienne Dines for Ireland lessons and resources, critical feedback and a well-timed introduction. Thanks to Kelly Gerrard, Linda Jorgenson, David Wolfe and the entire AWS writer's group for their supportive critique. Thanks to Brenda Shelton for her tireless appetite to beta read and unwavering support. Thanks to George King and Janine Desvaux, early readers and encouragers.

I am extremely grateful to the entire team at Myriad Editions for the enthusiasm and support they have shown me. I'd like to thank Candida Lacey, whose editorial insights have made this a better novel, Vicki Heath Silk for her patience and for catching my many blunders. Thanks also to Louisa Pritchard, Emma Dowson, Corinne Pearlman, and Lauren Burlinson for their efforts in guiding this book into as many hands as possible. Thanks to Leah Jacobs-Gordon for the beautiful cover design. And a special thank-you to Anna Burtt, who loved the book from the beginning and whose support put me on the path to publication.

The historical resources I have leaned on have been many and varied, but I would particularly like to acknowledge the historic preservation work at James Madison's Montpelier and their efforts to honor the lives of the enslaved community.

I owe an enormous debt of gratitude to my relative Barbara Cross, for not letting the old stories die, and an even bigger debt of gratitude to my great-great-grandparents, Suzie and Henry Taylor, whose story fascinated me enough to write this book.

Finally, I'd like to thank my entire family for their constant love, encouragement, support and patience. Viola, Mara and Daniel Huf, thanks for always cheering me on. And the biggest thank-you to my husband, Peter Huf, for so *viel mehr als ich hier erzählen möchte*.

Reading Group Guide

Author's Note

Up until the summer of 2020, a slave auction block sat on a street corner in downtown Fredericksburg, Virginia. I've passed it many times over many years, and when I decided to write this book inspired by my enslaved great-great-grandmother and Irish immigrant great-great-grandfather, I knew I would incorporate that auction block. For years it stood as a quiet reminder of a horrible past but also a reminder that the long fingers of history stretch right up to the here and now.

Today that slave auction block is housed in the Fredericksburg Area Museum, not all that far from the plantation on which I modeled Jubilee—former president James Madison's Montpelier in Orange County, Virginia. If you visit Montpelier, you'll see Jubilee's walled garden, the "Big House" with its wide, columned porch, the "carry-through" cellar passageway, and the view of the Blue Ridge Mountains in the distance. Thanks to recent historic preservation efforts, you can also see re-created slave cabins and the artifacts discovered in archaeological digs of the former slave quarters. Walking the grounds of Montpelier, the plantation of the "Father of the Constitution," it's hard not to be acutely aware of the divide between the aspirational "more perfect union" that Madison wrote about and the reality that existed.

As an African American woman married to a white

European man, I felt a strong connection to my great-great-grandparents' plight and a huge admiration for two people who had every reason to give up on each other but did not. Their lives are a testament to the fact that the world is full of people quietly doing extraordinary things all the time. Their story gives me hope, because if they could overcome the incredible obstacles of their time and move past the seemingly insurmountable racial divide, then we, in our more enlightened age today, must surely be able to do the same.

Although I don't know exactly where my great-great-grandparents met, I do know what became of them. They eventually settled in a "colored" neighborhood in Florida and, despite Henry being a white man, integrated themselves into that community. He worked as a blacksmith, they built a home, and she bore eight children, including my great-grandmother.

Looking back, it's fascinating to see how the past shapes our present. Without their decision to choose love in a world mired in extreme prejudice, I wouldn't be here and would not have written this book that honors them.

Discussion Questions

1. The title, *A More Perfect Union*, is taken from the first line of the US Constitution, "We the people, in order to form a more perfect union." How do you think the title refers to Sarah and Henry's situation? How does it refer to the country at large?

2. Both Henry and the overseer are attracted to Sarah when they see her, but Henry sees her humanity while the overseer sees her as an object. How has Henry's Irish background contributed to the way he sees Sarah and the other enslaved people at Jubilee? How has his background blinded him to her full reality as a slave?

3. The book is told through Sarah's, Henry's, and Maple's points of view. Were you able to see Maple as a sympathetic character? What do you think including Maple's point of view adds to the story?

4. When Sarah and Henry meet, Sarah is much more hesitant about allowing their relationship to blossom.

If Henry had initially understood the extent of the difficulties they would face in the way that Sarah did, do you think he would have pursued the relationship?

5. Initially, Henry feels justified in making the chains and feels Sarah's response is an overreaction. He comes to understand that, although his involvement in the institution of slavery by making chains is very small, he is complicit. Simply loving Sarah does not change his mind. What does?

6. In some ways, Matthew Johnson and Henry are similar characters. Both consider themselves to be good, decent men, though both have engaged in questionable actions for the sake of economic gain. Matthew Johnson enslaved people for profit; Henry helped destroy a widow's home, stole clothes from a dying man, and fled New York with the murdered blacksmith's forge and horses. Yet they are also very different. How would you compare the morality of the two characters?

7. What role does religion play in excusing slavery in this story? What role does religion play in opposing it? How does Matthew Johnson use religion to object to Sarah and Henry's relationship? How does that compare to Father Michael teaching Henry that "Jesus was always flapping on about loving people"?

8. Sarah explains to Henry about the emotional conflict caused by growing attached to a child you helped raise and knowing that this same child will eventually own you

as property and have dominion over your life (Chapter 36). To what extent do you see this conflict played out in Bessie and in Maple? To what extent do Miss Martha and Master also have a conflicted relationship to the enslaved women who raised them?

9. Miss Martha intervenes against punishment for Maple (Chapter 5) and Sarah (Chapter 49) but does not help save Rose from her situation (Chapter 52). What does this say about the nature and limits of her power and the risks she is willing to take?

10. What does Henry mean when he says "America is a lie" (Chapter 55)? Would he make that same assertion today?

11. Ennis intends to make his fortune by using Hiram Young's race against him and taking his white customers. Henry condemns the plan. Do you think Henry would have joined the scheme if it had been put to him while he was still working as a blacksmith in New York?

   (Historical note of interest: Hiram Young was a real person. A former slave, he became wealthy making wagons in Independence, Missouri, in the 1850s.)

12. Sarah and Henry's relationship is highly unusual for the time. Others in the enslaved community at Jubilee assume it is a transactional relationship (sex for trinkets or favors) and condemn Sarah for it. Why might they think this and what changes their minds?

13. When Maple betrays Sarah at the end of the novel, do you think her actions show a vindictive spitefulness or is what she does an act of self-preservation?

14. Matthew Johnson claims that it is morally acceptable to own slaves as long as they are treated in accordance with his own standards of decency. On several occasions, he talks about his slaves being happy. Do you think that Bessie's actions at the end of the book will force him to question his beliefs?

15. Throughout the story, Sarah and Henry face obstacle after obstacle to be together. Did you expect them to ultimately succeed? Or did you think that the struggles they faced would prove too great? Did you think they were well-suited?

A Q&A with the Author

What inspired you to write the story of your great-great-grandparents?

Their story is so unusual and so unexpected. It's a great testament to having the courage to follow your heart no matter where it takes you and no matter how strong the naysayers. When I think of my great-great-grandparents, I'm in awe of how much they must have loved each other, choosing to be together even though it meant facing enormous obstacles. It felt like a story that needed to be told.

Did you always know about your great-great-grandparents' story? Was this family history or was this something you discovered more recently?

I didn't grow up knowing their story. I was an adult and married when I was told this part of my family history, and it really resonated with me because I myself am in an interracial marriage. Even in our modern, enlightened society my husband and I have experienced moments of disapproval, so when I think back to their situation in the middle of the nineteenth century, where being together was such a monumental thing, I'm full of admiration that they were able to persevere.

Did you do much research for the book?

So, so much! I read firsthand accounts of the famine. I spent many hours combing through slave narratives. I visited a former plantation and revisited a former slave auction block. I read political arguments and laws of the time. The laws a society passes say so much about that society and who and what they value.

Incredibly, I was also able to listen to digitally remastered audio recordings of former slaves. Available through the Library of Congress, you can hear people who were once enslaved speak about their experiences with slavery before the Civil War. It's fascinating to hear their voices, the stories they tell, the details they include, and the way they talk about what their lives were like. We think of slavery as long-ago history, but being able to listen to people who actually experienced it made it feel so much more immediate.

Were you a fan of this kind of historical fiction before you wrote this book?

I am a fan of historical fiction. But for me, the marriage of a fictional narrative with my family history has been a unique experience. Through countless hours of research, I got a feeling for the historical time and the lives of the people, but that abstract history became personal when I considered that it was the world my great-great-grandparents lived in. And then I had the pleasure of weaving this tale and imagining their lives, which made me feel connected to them in a profound way.

Why did you create Maple as a character in the book?

In the first instance, it is a love story, but Maple serves as a kind of counterbalance because, as inspiring as the love story may be, it wasn't really the norm of the time that an enslaved woman and a white Irish man would fall for each other. A very different narrative would have been much more common, so I created the character of Maple to show that other experience.

What were your biggest challenges when writing the book?

Knowing where to start, where to finish, and the events that should happen in between. I realize that sounds like everything but it's not. For instance, knowing how characters would respond to a given challenge wasn't nearly as hard for me as deciding on the challenge.

Is there anything that didn't make the final edit of the book that you wish you could have included?

There is so much more research that went into the book than you see on the page. It would have been nice to be able to include more of it, but it wouldn't have been right for the story.

What do you hope that readers will take away from reading this story?

We are living at a time when racial tensions are at the highest they have been in decades. It can make us start to think that human beings are just this way. I hope that a story like *A More Perfect Union* can help to remind us that this isn't true and that individuals have always found a way to see past the things that divide us, even during far greater periods of strife than what we're dealing with now. I hope that knowing that the novel is inspired by a real love story will encourage people to remember that we can come together in love.

Have you always wanted to be a writer?

Yes. The practicality of earning a living or raising a family means, for most of us, that writing is something you have to scratch out time to do. I'm fortunate that lately I've been at a place in my life where I can devote more time and energy to it, but it took quite a while to get here.

What is your creative process?

First comes the idea of the story, and then I like to flesh it out before I jump in and really get writing. I've done it the other way around before, where you get a story idea or find a character and just start writing, seeing where the story leads you, but I've found that my story thread gets a bit tangled that way. I like to know where I'm going and then have creative freedom in how to get there.

What are you working on now?

My next book, which is also historical fiction. It spans from the bombing of Pearl Harbor and the US entry into World War II until the postwar years and the prosperity promises of the GI Bill. The story follows the lives of a brother and sister who experience this period from opposite sides of the color line when the brother passes as a white man upon enlisting, which is something that actually happened in my family.

Do you have any advice for fellow writers and what helps you to focus?

One thing I do is give myself permission to be less productive every now and again. Some days I'll be ticking along just fine, and other days I need more breaks. Tea breaks, dog walking breaks, reading breaks, even yoga breaks. Taking time off when I need to helps me to be more focused when I go back to my desk. I think the main thing is to be kind to yourself, but always get back to the desk.

Who are your biggest writing influences?

That's a really difficult question to answer. I think everything I read feeds me in some way. Maya Angelou was the first Black female writer I read, and her work made a big impression on me. I remember reading Orwell and really realizing for the first time that telling a story is only the beginning of what a novel can do. Toni Morrison was the first writer for whom I went total fangirl, traveling to the city to hear her speak and then standing outside the venue to watch on a video monitor because the hall was too small to accommodate everyone who had turned up.

More recently I have been expanding my reading with Colson Whitehead, Tayari Jones, and Sebastian Barry. But I've also been influenced by poets like Walt Whitman and Emily Dickenson and playwrights like August Wilson.

Even the books I read as a young child, books like the Chronicles of Narnia and *A Wrinkle in Time*, had a huge impact, making the unknown feel like an exciting adventure.

What are your go-to book recommendations?

The book I've probably recommended the most is *The God of Small Things* by Arundhati Roy. The books I've recommended most recently include *Days Without End* by Sebastian Barry, *The Nickel Boys* by Colson Whitehead, *The Long Song* by Andrea Levy, *Such a Fun Age* by Kiley Reid, *Where the Crawdads Sing* by Delia Owens, and *The Dutch House* by Ann Patchett.

What five celebrities—alive or dead—would make up your ideal dinner party and why?

I couldn't possibly resist a chance to invite past authors who blazed a trail. The list is long, but if it has to be five, then perhaps Toni Morrison, Zora Neale Hurston, Maya Angelou, Alice Walker, and Octavia Butler.

VISIT **GCPClubCar.com** to sign up for the **GCP Club Car** newsletter, featuring exclusive promotions, info on other **Club Car** titles, and more.

About the Author

TAMMYE HUF is a former teacher and now works as a translator and copywriter. Her short stories have been published in various magazines, including *Diverse Voices Quarterly* and *The Penmen Review*. She was runner-up in the 2018 *London Magazine* Short Story Prize. Originally from the United States, she moved first to Germany and then to the UK with her husband and three children.